# THE GAMBLER'S NEPHEW

## A NOVEL

T0166468

### JACK MATTHEWS

## ALSO BY JACK MATTHEWS

BITTER KNOWLEDGE

AN ALMANAC FOR TWILIGHT

HANGER STOUT, AWAKE!

BEYOND THE BRIDGE

THE TALE OF ASA BEAN

THE CHARISMA CAMPAIGNS

PICTURES OF THE JOURNEY BACK

COLLECTING RARE BOOKS FOR PLEASURE AND PROFIT

TALES OF THE OHIO LAND

DUBIOUS PERSUASIONS

SASSAFRAS

CRAZY WOMEN

BOOKING IN THE HEARTLAND

GHOSTLY POPULATIONS

MEMOIRS OF A BOOKMAN

DIRTY TRICKS

ON THE SHORE OF THE BEAUTIFUL SHORE

AN INTERVIEW WITH THE SPHINX

STORYHOOD AS WE KNOW IT AND OTHER STORIES

BOOKING PLEASURES

READING MATTER

SCHOPENHAUER'S WILL

# THE GAMBLER'S
# NEPHEW

Etruscan Press
Wilkes University
84 West South Street
Wilkes-Barre, PA 18766

 WILKES UNIVERSITY

www.etruscanpress.org

Printed in the United States of America

Library of Congress Cataloging-in-Publication Data
Matthews, Jack.
 Gambler's nephew : a novel / Jack Matthews. – 1st ed.
     p. cm.
 ISBN 978-0-9819687-7-3 (pbk,)
 1. Ohio–History–1787-1865–Fiction. I. Title.
 PS3563.A85G36 2011
 813'.54–dc22
                          2011014080

First Edition

Design by Michael Ress

Produced and printed by The Sheridan Press, an environmentally responsible print
and publishing services provider.

# THE GAMBLER'S NEPHEW

## A NOVEL

etruscan press

## JACK MATTHEWS

## ON THE VIRTUES OF HANGING

There is a wisdom found in this:
To find the curse within a kiss—
And kiss within a curse, of course;
It's hard to know which one is worse.
Some angels have their share of sin;
Some devils show some good within.
And yet, you know as well as I
That some mad dogs deserve to die.

—J. H. Macomber

People never turn out the way you expect. But then, hardly anything else does, either.

—Loftus Gandy

It is sheer horror to all concerned—sheriff, halbertmen, chaplain, spectators, Jack Ketch and culprit; but out of all this, and towering behind the vulgar and hideous accessories of the scaffold, gleams the majesty of implacable law.

—Alexander Smith

It's never a gambler's son who follows his trade; it's usually a nephew.

—Ned Fairwinkle

To Barbara: Married to me for more than sixty years, and you're still my girl.

# Book One

# THE GHOSTS OF OPPRESSION

Years ago, way back in the 1850s, there was a wealthy merchant in the little Ohio River town of Brackenport by name of Nehemiah Dawes who got to brooding over slavery and grave robbing so much that his mind became unbalanced. Hardly any of the townsfolk understood these passions of his, not so much because of what he believed as how hard he worked at it. Even those who sympathized with his views and agreed with him that the abolition of slavery was all right and grave robbing was all wrong; even those people figured there had to be a limit to how much you should let such principles interfere with your peace of mind. Not to mention that of your neighbors.

But whatever that limit was, it was a boundary Nehemiah had crossed over long ago, staking out a claim in the darkness beyond, where lunacy and mulishness dwell. He was a gangly man, and a Presbyterian. He had the black, deep-set eyes of a raccoon, a large shiny hooked nose, and a thin-lipped mouth all sewed and puckered up in an expression of bilious disapproval. He was eloquent, in his way, but it was the sort of eloquence that tended to make you uncomfortable and cast your thoughts upon escape.

Outside business affairs, his conversation was pretty much confined to the two great evils of slavery and grave robbing. If you asked Nehemiah Dawes the price of top hats or boots or when the Valley Belle or Shawnee Maid was scheduled to come steaming into town, he might tell you, or he might not, according to his mood. But no matter what subject you brought up, he'd eventually find a way to start complaining about how medical students in Cincinnati went around at

3

night digging up corpses. Or it would be the Fugitive Slave Act that fired his wrath, which he claimed was the wickedest statute ever devised by man, copperhead snake, or infernal demon from the deepest cellars of hell.

Nehemiah wasn't the kind who'd be content with just *telling* you his thoughts; he'd come upon you all of a sudden and yell them in your face, even if you tried to turn away. But he was quick for a man his age, and could move so fast it was hard to get out from in front of him. He'd holler things like: "Why do you need to carve up a cadaver, Sir, to know what's inside a *body*?"

If nobody had an answer to a rhetorical question like that, he'd take a skip and a hop and yell: "Why should Ohioans have to add fuel to the evil and conflagration of slavery? By whose authority are we to return those poor escaped blackamoors to their debauched and corrupt masters? What allegiance do we owe those Lords of the Lash in the Kanawha Valley? Why, Sir, those satraps of hell sit on their verandas and sip mint juleps and laugh at honest Ohioans who milk their own cows and grow their own corn and feed their own chickens, instead of leaving it all to African slaves, the way *they* do, Sir, whipping and starving the poor critters and putting them out into the fields to labor like brute beasts and die like fruit flies and skeeters!"

Nehemiah's rhetorical excesses served their purpose, in a way, but like most orators, he was not constrained by facts. Nobody ever bothered to point out that he was confusing the planters along the Kanawha with the big plantation owners in the deep South, with maybe some exceptions out west in Kentucky. No Kanawha planter was ever seen to hold a mint julep in his hand; most of them wouldn't have known a julep from a gin fizz. Wealthy or not, they tended to be ignorant of the great world beyond the boundaries of their land and some of them probably hadn't even *heard* of a mint julep, let alone partaken of one in the spirit of genteel insouciance—although they were as well-acquainted with brandies and whiskies as you'd expect of a gentleman of property and means.

But old Nehemiah was riding a different breed of horse, and once he got on the subject of the Kanawha slave owners, there was no stopping him. He'd growl and spit like bacon in a skillet. He couldn't get it out of his craw how those damned rich and profligate planters lived in decadent ease and paid their murderous thugs to come fetch the poor escaped slaves trying to reach freedom by way of Ohio into Canada. "Why," he'd yell in a seizure of indignation, "they even put *bounties* on their heads, like they're nothing more than wolves or Indians!"

Of course they wanted them brought back alive. One time on the *Ben Franklin*, a sternwheeler bound for Cincinnati, a Kanawha planter was heard to ask rhetorically, "A live nigger ain't much, but what good is a dead one?" His attitude was no doubt representative of a considerable majority on board the Franklin, but there seemed to be a kind of poetic justice in the fact that this planter left over four hundred dollars on the gaming table that night.

Of course, knowing the slave owners, it's hardly surprising that bounty hunters were instructed to shoot their quarry if they couldn't get them back across the river. It was their opinion that as worthless as a dead nigger is, he's a sight better than a live one who's escaped to Canada and lives up there across the border like some fat African king, grinning and showing his teeth and dancing a jig and a galop and mocking his old masters.

"If those godforsaken planters ain't the wickedest and most cussed scoundrels who ever set foot on God's earth," Nehemiah would cry, losing control of his grammar along with his temper, "they come prodigious and infernal *close!*"

"Amen," folks would answer, half in agreement and half in desperation to escape the heat of the old merchant's fanaticism and the awesome range of his rhetoric.

Not to mention his breath, which tended to be foul because of bad teeth and a diseased gall bladder.

## SAM KILLIBREW'S SHED

Some years before, back in the late 1840s, a local carpenter named Sam Killibrew had built a shed for Nehemiah, and he'd had such a damnable time collecting what he was owed, he never got over it. Sam was a good, hard hater, steady and determined, gifted with a flair for resentment and wrath, so people reckoned maybe he was the one who was behind the story that Nehemiah couldn't even depart from his fanatical raving on the cold January night when his dear wife, Elizabeth, died—a time when the thoughts of most decent God-fearing men would have been on the Four Last Things, not to mention who was going to preside over the cooking and cleaning now that his poor dear companion was dead and gone forever.

By the time of this dire event, Nehemiah's brother was living with them, and you might suppose his presence could have lessened a widower's grief, but you would be wrong, because you didn't know Nehemiah's brother. His name was Isaac, and he was as short and stout as Nehemiah was long and lean, and he didn't care a fig for grave robbers or slave owners, either one. He didn't care a fig for much of anything, in fact, except maybe rye whiskey, fancy fiddle music, and other creature comforts, along with having a general good time.

No, that's not entirely true . . . those things weren't all he cared for—he also liked a good argument. One time when Nehemiah was exasperated by one of Isaac's profane comments, he called him a "freethinker," which was strong language for Nehemiah, about the worst thing he could think of to call somebody, let alone his own brother. Calling somebody a freethinker was his version of blowing a boiler and cussing up enough of a fiery streak to shake the heavens and singe the nearby grass and leaves.

But Isaac grabbed the word the way a terrier grabs a rat. "Of *course* I'm a freethinker," he said. "The way I figure it, if you're not a *free* thinker, why you're not a thinker at *all*! How else can you *think* if you can't do it *free and unfettered*?"

"That's a freethinker's argument, all right," Nehemiah told him. "And I've heard them all."

"Not from me, you ain't!" Isaac growled.

"The same profane argument remains the same, no matter whose mouth it fouls."

"And the same pig-headed bigotry is the same, no matter how rich and famous the damned fanatical fool is who utters it!"

And so it went, back and forth. Both of them were mighty talkers, and they muttered and growled at each other for half an hour, ending up with no clear result of the issue, the way it is with most arguments.

Back around 1850, Isaac had succumbed to gold rush fever and taken off for California, where it was rumored he'd panned enough gold to buy the whole town of Brackenport, with a circus thrown in. Only, the night before he was planning to depart for San Francisco with his bag of gold dust, he was accused of killing a man who'd been shot in the back of the head the morning after he'd won six hundred dollars at poker. Since the corpse had empty pockets and Isaac Dawes had been the big loser of the night, he was a natural suspect.

Folks believed this in spite of the fact that Isaac had gotten so wealthy that six hundred dollars was hardly any more than a hiccup to him. Still, as everybody knows, riches change your perspective. When you're poor, you think you'd be satisfied with just a little more, but once you get a little more, the plot changes, and before long you're as greedy as a hog standing knee-deep in slop.

So instead of climbing on a stage coach the next morning, it looked like Isaac was going to be handcuffed and made to stand up in a witness box and be questioned. He knew that the fact he'd gotten drunk over the gaming table—which helped explain why he'd lost so much money—and had staggered a spectacularly crooked path to his bunk wouldn't have left a particularly good impression on the minds of his accusers. He figured they figured he was guilty, convicted, and only a few steps away from the hangman's noose.

Nope, Isaac didn't find being accused of murder an encouraging prospect. Isaac had seen the boots of many a corpse dangling shoulder-high in the noonday sun, and he had witnessed many a quick and perfunctory trial that had led to the dangling. Neither crowds nor juries liked to see a man go free in those days; they liked to hear a feller speak his last words, especially when he broke down and cried and spoke of his mother; then they liked to see him hanged, by God! It was such lugubrious thoughts as these that led Isaac to break out of jail that night and hightail it, leaving all of his gold behind except for what he could stuff in his pockets—but even that was enough to make him wealthy by the standards of some.

On the way back east to New York State, where he'd left his home and family, Isaac got into a scuffle somewhere in Kansas, and was shot in the groin by a phrenologist named Stillingfleet. Nobody knows the whole story, but by the time Isaac finally recovered and found his way back home, he learned that his poor dear wife had died of a fever and her brother had taken in their children to raise as his very own, since he and his wife were childless. Isaac was going to protest and claim his rights to his progeny, but he himself took ill with a fever at the last minute and for several days lingered on the brink of Eternity.

But he recovered. And by that time he had to face the realization that his children were strangers to him. So with a great show of self-sacrifice, he relinquished all legal rights to them. He was a pretty good actor, but his tears and choked voice didn't fool anybody. Folks could tell that deep down inside he was mighty relieved to be rid of his children. It showed. He'd reached one of those moments of truth that most of us have to face now and then, and concluded that he was more interested in faro and three-card Monte than in raising his children.

So it was right about then that Isaac decided he should find some way to become about two rods richer than just plain solvent. This naturally made him think of his brother, Nehemiah, who had gotten bit by the religion bug way back when they were boys together. Right from the start, Isaac had been as immune to religion as a snake to a sprained ankle, but now he was glad that Nehemiah had come down with it, and he would have said a prayer of thanks if it hadn't been for his immunity to divine inspiration.

So without even writing ahead, Isaac traveled to Pittsburgh and got a steamboat down the Ohio River to Brackenport. He showed up one dark night unannounced and identified himself to his dear brother and then told his story—that he was now a widower whose very own children had been stolen right out from under him, and he asked for a place to spend the night. He said he had seen the darkness of his ways, and had reformed. He said he was helpless and bereft, and thanked

God that he had a brother stuffed with righteousness to take him in and give him a place to rest.

Brothers have ways of understanding one another, so Nehemiah didn't believe much of Isaac's story, although he conceded that part of it might have a whiff of truth to it. Not only that, he didn't like what he saw, for Isaac was a rough-looking character, with dirty linen, a mashed-in face and a big dent in his top hat, as if he'd just escaped with his life from some vulgar fracas or other. One eye was half-closed in a permanent wink, and his mouth was twisted to the side like that of a man who has just tasted something awful. His skin was as brown as the hide of an Indian, and when he removed his top hat, you could see that he was bald in front.

He was a hard specimen, all right; but even so, Nehemiah could not for a moment forget his own standing in the community. He had his reputation to think of. He reckoned that folks would just automatically assume that such a good Christian would take his own brother in, when said brother was so shaken, battered, and needy; so with a sigh, that's what he figured he had to do. Especially when it looked like Isaac's stay would be only temporary. But he sure didn't like the looks of him, and never had, as a matter of fact. Still, what's a day or two in the span of a human life? Or a week or two? Or maybe even a month?

But that's not the way it turned out at all. Right away Isaac got himself comfortable and settled in, and six months later, Nehemiah was spending long hours neglecting his business, trying to figure out some way to scoop his brother out of the house and set him on his own two feet, headed outward in some direction with little prospect of ever showing up in Brackenport again. He stayed awake at night brooding over the matter, and in the midst of dictating a letter, he would often pause and think of this ruffian he'd been forced to acknowledge as his own brother.

A whole year passed. Isaac tried his best to be lazy and shiftless and make extra work for everybody in sight. He gambled and drank and blasphemed, and seemed to go out of his way to proclaim how indifferent he was to slavery and grave digging. He liked to say that niggers were no better than pigs and donkeys, only not half as bright, which made Nehemiah mutter and raise his eyes to the Almighty to witness his suffering. And as for grave robbing, Isaac liked to say he'd have taken it up himself if there'd been more money in it. People said that never were two brothers farther apart in their ways and temperament than these two men. Nehemiah prayed that his brother would leave forever, or die of the delirium tremens, or maybe get shot or drowned or carried off by a fever.

But Isaac was not the sort to pay any attention to a mere brother, and he kept to the uneven tenor of his ways. He wasn't any more sensitive to the feelings of others than a hog can respond to fiddle music. Nehemiah wracked his brains, trying to remember, but he couldn't recall that Isaac had been quite this bad as a child. It was true that Isaac was the brother he favored least. Noah, Ulysses, and Fred were all harder workers and had shown far less tendency toward cussedness, but still, he couldn't remember that Isaac had been such a problem back in the old days when they were all pups.

As for Isaac, he was as content as a cat in a butter churn. He liked everything about Brackenport. He liked being the blood relative of one of the town's wealthiest, most important, and respected citizens. He liked living in a rich man's house with a score of rooms, a fancy porch topped with curlicues and arabesques and other such fancy work, and either eight or nine gables—he wasn't exactly sure of the number, because every time he started to count them, he either lost count or lost interest. He liked being waited on by the two servant girls, Lizzie and Prue, and he liked eating the big meals cooked by an old woman named Agatha Tremblow. All three women worked like galley slaves and never once opened their mouths in anything you could interpret as a complaint. He liked being free to roam, and he did a lot of it. He was gone so much during the day that it made everybody curious, especially when Isaac gave devious answers. Sometimes he'd say he was looking for land to buy, which didn't seem very convincing when you tried to picture him as a landowner. Other times he said he was one of those who needed to commune with God's nature, but that didn't wash, either, when you realized that he didn't seem to have any more religion than a rabbit.

Often he would come back with mud on his boots, muttering and cussing and sending black looks in every direction. This was mysterious, too, because for all his faults, Isaac was usually amiable enough. Having a bad nature was not his problem; his problem was irresponsibility, immorality, and selfishness, along with a tendency to gamble, cheat, lie, and get drunk. So what did he do on those long excursions of his? Usually he was seen along the river someplace, but that was hardly surprising, because what else would you expect of somebody living in a river town like Brackenport, even when that body was Isaac Dawes?

In spite of his mysterious wanderings, Isaac didn't try to disguise the fact that he was comfortable in Nehemiah's home. He liked just about everything about it, and who could blame him? It was a two-story Federal house of white-washed bricks, with a large grassy yard, a white paling fence, and a brick walk extending from gate to door. It had a porch with fluted columns and Doric capitals, a huge brass knocker on the front door and two twelve-pound brass cannons facing the street. Inside, Nehemiah's house was just as handsome, with six-inch stained pine boards for flooring, mahogany tables and cushioned chairs, fancy ingrain carpets from Pittsburgh, oil portraits on the walls and bookcases filled with leather-bound volumes of books on hydraulics and legends, law and gardening, religion and poetry. Oil lamps with green and yellow shades stood on the tables, lighting the rooms. And on the painted mantels there were colorful baskets filled with wax fruit. Whatever room Isaac found himself in, he would look around and realize that this was a house he had always been destined to live in, and he by-God intended to make the most of it.

By the time his poor sister-in-law, Nehemiah's wife, Elizabeth, died, Isaac had been living there like a parasite on his brother for almost three years. Her death caused Isaac to pause, take stock, and think. That woman had been a marvel of industry. She had knitted and spun, and she had sung in the church choir, where Isaac admitted to enjoying her voice, whenever he bothered to attend services. And when it was pie-baking time, Elizabeth would run old Mrs. Tremblow out of the kitchen and bake the best pies a man could ever hope to taste this side of Glory.

The ground was frozen so hard at the time Elizabeth died that they couldn't dig a grave to drop her in, so after they'd packed her corpse in an expensive coffin made of polished wild cherry inlaid with pale butternut, and after Reverend Willis preached his funeral sermon and everybody said their prayers, they carried the coffin back to Nehemiah's house and put it in the shed that Sam Killibrew had built, where it froze as hard as a statue and was preserved until the spring thaw. Then they took her out and buried her like a Christian in the graveyard plot Nehemiah had selected for her personally, some twenty feet above the surface flood line. Maybe fifteen. Everybody agreed that Elizabeth Dawes had been a good woman, though left-handed and with a strabismus that made you uneasy when you talked to her, wondering which eye to look at. Her maiden name had been Kittle.

There were some who speculated that Nehemiah was the cause of his poor wife's death. They claimed she might not have been able to stand listening to his ranting and raving any longer. They claimed that it would have been only natural for her to choose death over listening to one more of her husband's diatribes against grave robbers or the Kanawha slaveholders. Yes, Nehemiah Dawes was a man who seemed to have only two strings to his bow, and you could see how those strings might outwear the patience of any dutiful wife. Not to mention her peace of mind and will to live.

Others, however, claimed that it was Isaac who had hastened the poor woman on her trek to the grave. The difficulty of having a houseguest like Isaac Dawes was not lost upon such folks. He was a physical as well as spiritual burden. For one thing, he had a loud voice, and it was hard to avoid hearing his views on certain topics. In this, he was like his brother, only they disapproved of different things, the way it usually is with brothers.

Still others said that such matters hardly mattered. They argued that the poor woman died of childbed fever in giving birth to their ninth child, who also died, although not before it was christened Florence Anne. Nehemiah was fifty-two years old at the time, and his wife, Elizabeth, was forty-six. She was a proud housekeeper and famed for her skill in baking peach and apple pies, as has perhaps been mentioned. She had a soft contralto voice and sang in the church choir and was especially good at needlepoint.

Both of them were active in the local Bible study and underground railroad societies, helping escaped slaves make their way up north in Ohio to Athens, then on up the Hocking Valley to points farther north, clear on up to Toledo and Detroit and by steamboat across Lake St. Clair into Canada. They'd hide the poor negroes in false bottoms built into the wagons, so those Virginia bounty hunters, relying on the letter of the law, couldn't find them and drag them back across the river; or they'd just take them by farm wagon or horseback at night from one station to the next of the Underground Railroad, on their flight to freedom and glory.

Many were their devices for frustrating the detectives hired by those slave owners south of the Ohio, not to mention a certain class of townsfolk who had copperhead tendencies and showed more sympathy for those damned Virginia scoundrels than for the Abolitionist cause. Long afterwards, folks liked to say that Nehemiah and his cohorts were fighting the Civil War years before the firing at Fort Sumter, not to mention those godawful bloody slaughters at Shiloh, Gettysburg, and Antietam.

Isaac looked upon his brother's eleemosynary doings with an indulgent though judicious eye. He liked to say that there was nothing wrong with charitable acts, for those who felt a need to indulge themselves in such sentiments. He liked to say that others, however, were content to mind their own business and let the world wag on. It was clear to everybody that Isaac considered the latter class the wiser and more privileged, and thought of himself as prominent among their number.

One of Nehemiah's sons became a cattle rancher in Wyoming, and another became a local dentist and married a girl named Juanita Paffenbarger. One of his daughters married a banker in Chillicothe, joined the local Congregational church in defiance of her daddy, and lived to be ninety-two years old. Her name was Miranda, and by the age of twelve she'd learned to speak and write French like a native, without ever once setting foot on foreign soil. They say she learned it from Charlotte DeLong, a girlhood friend whose family had moved upriver from Gallipolis. Or maybe Charlotte's last name was Martin. I forget. Also her first name, which might have been Josephine.

# CROSSWIND

Early one hot afternoon the summer after his wife died, Nehemiah Dawes was standing before his big office window overlooking the broad and peaceful bend in the Ohio River at Brackenport. His mind was occupied with business matters, although he was fighting sleepiness from eating a substantial noontime dinner of pork chops, fried chicken, succotash, candied yams, stewed beets, green onions in vinegar, and hot buttered cornbread muffins. Not to mention three cups of coffee. He stood there with a toothpick in his mouth, rolling it back and forth without touching it directly, because his hands were in his pockets. He was thinking about a shipment of barrel staves that he'd sold downriver to a cooperage firm in Portsmouth, payment for which was now two months overdue.

Then suddenly he saw something out on the broad sweep of the river that stopped the toothpick dead in its tracks and made him take his hands out of his pockets. He knew right away what he was looking at. Two Kanawha men, snug as turtles under an umbrella, were in a boat approaching the deepest part of the channel, headed for the Virginia shore. One of the men was pulling slowly at the oars, while the other was sitting in the prow with a rifle across his lap. At the stern was a third man, a light-complexioned negro slave sitting with his wrists held so closely together that it was obvious he was manacled.

Right then, Nehemiah decided he had been patient too long and it was time to act. The boat was near enough that he reckoned he might be able to pick one of the bounty hunters off, or maybe send both of them plummeting to hell, where they belonged, and good riddance. So he hollered out to his book-keeper, a man named Biddle, to load his polished and fancy Kentucky halfstock rifle with a good, heavy charge, and be double-tarnation quick about it.

Biddle was used to his master's sudden and loud demands, and he had learned to be swift and efficient in his movements, even though you might think he was seldom in a condition to be that way, being as devout an imbiber of strong drink as Nehemiah was a Presbyterian. Nevertheless, Biddle could move pretty fast, and by the time the oarsman had pulled another six or seven strokes, and the rowboat had hardly gotten any farther away than the far side of mid-channel, the rifle was loaded and ready.

"Biddle," Nehemiah said through clenched teeth as he took the rifle from him, "we've got two of the damned scoundrels in range, and by Jehosophat, we're going to make one of them pay the price of his wickedness!"

Saying this, Nehemiah raised his rifle, sighted just above the chest of the oarsman to allow for about a six-inch drop in the trajectory of the ball, took a deep breath and held it, then squeezed the trigger.

At the sound of the report, the oarsman stopped in mid-stroke, and for the merest instant seemed to look directly at Nehemiah's window, which was no doubt blowing smoke from the discharged rifle. But then he let the oars swing free in their oarlocks, and reached out with both hands to the captured slave at the stern, who was slowly easing over sideways, as if he had a sudden notion he wanted to listen to the sound of the current. But the oarsman couldn't reach him in time, and the poor slave twisted sideways and splashed into the water on his back, holding up his manacled hands like a man wanting folks to see that he was handcuffed and couldn't swim, or maybe figuring he was praying right up to the end.

"You hit the wrong one!" Biddle said.

For a moment, Nehemiah was so flabbergasted he couldn't say a word. He stared at the boat as it lurched stroke by stroke out of range, the man at the oars now pulling mightily while the other fellow sitting in the prow yelled and shook his fist at Nehemiah's window. Thinking back on it later, Nehemiah wondered why the villain hadn't lifted his rifle and sent a rifle ball flying into the window, even if he couldn't see him . . . in which case the two of them could have traded some lively fire. But whatever his reason, he didn't, and that was that.

"You hit the wrong one," Biddle repeated.

"There must be a crosswind out there that carried my ball to the right."

"I don't see a sign of any crosswind."

"You wouldn't know a crosswind if it rode up on a horse," Nehemiah growled. "Yep, there was a crosswind, all right. There had to be."

"Maybe so. But you sure hit the wrong one, anyway."

"Confound you, Biddle, do you have to keep on saying that?"

Biddle thought it over, and was almost imprudent enough to nod yes, but decided against it. He was a thick little fellow and had a big head with dark brown hair and a curl that he cultivated with macassar oil so that it would cling to his forehead as stiff as a hawk's talon, or maybe a semicolon, because there was a bald spot separating it from the majority of the hair on top. He also had a red face, with eyes inflamed and swollen from drink, along with a pursy little mouth and fat cheeks.

Now, as usual, he had an awful time keeping his mouth shut, and said, "All I know is, you sure missed him."

"Shut up, Biddle!" Nehemiah muttered. "And what if I did, Sir? Better to be dead than live as a slave, is my philosophy."

"Maybe *your* philosophy," Biddle pointed out, "but I wonder if it was *his*."

"Watch your insolent tongue, Sir!" Nehemiah growled at him, and Biddle looked down at his boots and twisted his mouth to the side in a crooked grimace with the effort of holding his words in, which was always a hard task for him, considering how hard it was to tolerate working for such a hard man. Also considering the sort of fellow Biddle was, being a pretty advanced tosspot, especially for a clerk who had to mind his Ps and Qs, not to mention all the numbers and get them in the right order.

With that rowboat pulling mightily for the Virginia shore, and hardly before Biddle could have had a chance to say anything else, even if he'd had a mind to, Nehemiah dropped his rifle and rushed out of the room. Then he ran down the staircase and quick as a rabbit out onto the steamboat dock, waving his arms and calling for help and yelling that there was an escaped slave in the river, and somebody ought to go out and save him.

"It'll be too late for that," Biddle called out from the window. But he didn't call it out very loud, so nobody heard him.

Eventually, two loafers sitting on the ramp managed to stand up and bang a couple of oars together and stumble into a rowboat, swinging the oars around a lot, after which they finally managed to hit the water with all four of them and then flail their way out into the river to search for the body.

21

Watching them floundering like that, Nehemiah suddenly realized that they must have been drunk and hungover. They were all the human assistance available, however, and about all you could expect from the loafers in a river town, so he just stood and watched them splash their way out toward the channel, leaving a wake as white as chalk and as crooked as a snake behind them.

By the time they got there, the body had long since disappeared. Sunk for good and headed for Cincinnati. The corpse wasn't found until two days later, when it snagged on a trot line staked on the Ohio shore, ten or fifteen miles downstream. Hearing about it, Nehemiah told everybody he hoped the poor slave's spirit would rejoice, knowing that his bodily remains had reached free territory, even though his soul hadn't been along to share in the glory.

"Some kind of freedom," Biddle muttered, although he didn't say it loud enough to be heard.

Then Nehemiah had an idea, so he ordered Biddle to go and bring the corpse back to town for a Christian burial. Which he did, and everybody was surprised to see how pale the poor escaped slave's skin was, and how fine his features were, almost like a white man's. Nobody had said he was a quadroon, but just a slave, so people naturally assumed that his skin would be black, or a dark gray, at least, instead of being as pale as a muskmelon and lighter than the skin of half the farmers along the river. While the body was still lying there on the wagon, some ignoramus took red paint and printed, "The Croppe Kanawha Plantiers Raize!" on a board and stuck it in the burlap the corpse was wrapped in. Some people figured it might have been Biddle who was behind the sign, or maybe even Nehemiah himself, though neither one could have managed to misspell three words out of five, even if he'd tried. Still, you couldn't tell for sure, because if one of them had done it, he might have *figured* that's the way folks would figure, and that would be a good way to hide his tracks and rest as safe as a babe pulling contentedly at its mother's breast.

Somebody else suggested that it might have been Isaac, who liked to show up wherever there was a crowd, only he was also too good a speller, so their speculations took off in another direction until they finally piddled out when a fellow named Rutherford said, "What difference does it make who did that sign, anyhow?" which left a lot of people scratching their heads, because it didn't make any difference at all.

Biddle brought more than the dead slave's corpse back into town. He brought back a rumor that a sack with a small fortune in gold and silver coins had been found in an oilskin wallet the slave had been carrying. Some folks believed it, and some didn't. Drowned corpses in the river were common, but most of them didn't carry money. A man named Elijah Boggs was the one who'd snagged the slave's body on his trot line, and he said he was willing to swear on two Bibles that there was nothing to the rumor. It was his brother, Bill, who claimed otherwise, and made a considerable point of it, until Boggs got him aside and talked to him earnestly and in private, whereupon Bill shut his mouth as hard as a snapping turtle and wouldn't say another word to anybody.

Most people hearing the story pretty much reckoned that there was a lot of money, all right, and Elijah had pocketed it, but when Elijah got wind of what people were saying, he did something clever—he quieted them by an argument so ingenious that it was hard to believe he had invented it. Still, as everybody knows, it sometimes takes a crisis like holding on to some ill-gained money to bring out the best in a man.

Here was Elijah's argument: "Since the only way a nigger like that could get money is by stealing it, why then, the only kind and fair assumption is *that he didn't have no money at all!*" Then he asked folks if they thought it was right and decent to malign the memory of a poor dead African by accusing him of theft when such a charge could not be proved and the poor critter was not around to defend himself.

That argument shut everybody up right away, even if they weren't abolitionist. And Elijah strutted around just a little prouder than he'd been before, not to mention more self-righteous, and richer by what everybody reckoned must have been three or four hundred dollars. Or—who knows?—maybe even a thousand. Since there was no way of telling, people reckoned they might as well be generous and make it a goodly amount.

But of course there was another dimension to the question of how a slave's corpse could have so much money on it. Wouldn't the bounty hunters have relieved him of it? Folks asked this question all up and down the river, until a Gallipolis lawyer named Colfax explained it. He said that in his experience the bounty hunters liked to wait until they got their victims back across the river into Virginia before they appropriated whatever possessions they had on their person. He said this was their general way of doing it so that there was no chance of being intercepted by an Abolitionist mob and having them charge the rascals with theft along with kidnapping.

A few minutes after Biddle had returned to Brackenport with the slave's corpse, Nehemiah started to get excited, and then he became inspired. He climbed up onto the wagon and held his arms out like an orator and people gathered around, and right then and there, Nehemiah made a public announcement that he would give his very own personal burial plot, signed and paid-for, to the poor escaped slave's body, so he could be buried there in the proudest and most exalted spot in the whole graveyard.

Everybody knew what a considerable honor that was, because several years earlier, Nehemiah had bought the best plot, which was right at the top of a hill overlooking a bend in the Ohio River, up near where it looks toward Long Bottom. It was a grand place he'd chosen for himself; and in anticipation of his demise, Nehemiah had hired a Welsh stonecutter from Oak Hill to carve a tombstone for him. Now he liked to paint word pictures of how it would look, standing there in lonely majesty above the waters of commerce flowing past like time itself, while his tombstone rose above the murky flood, as lofty, pure, and still as Eternity. Safe in the lap of the Lord, which in this case, was God's earth.

But now, he said, he was going to do the Lord's work and relinquish that exalted spot to the black man he'd shot and killed by mistake because of a sturdy crosswind that had carried his ball to the side. Everyone was impressed when they heard the news, even though nobody recalled that there'd been any wind to speak of on that afternoon. But as we all learn, sooner or later, the Past is always vulnerable to such adjustments.

Nehemiah was mightily pleased by their reaction. He told them that he would now happily resign himself to being buried in a far humbler place, about fifty yards away, not too far from where he'd buried his dear wife. Only about twenty-five feet above the floodline. Maybe thirty. Isaac pointed out that for all his wealth, his brother hadn't bought *him* a grave plot yet; but he said he was glad, anyway, for he rejoiced in his brother's high-mindedness, even when it stopped somewhere short of his very own brother, blood of his own blood. Still, he rejoiced, and kept on rejoicing until people started to walk away from him, after which he stopped.

A couple of days later, news from across the Virginia shore about the escaped slave reached Brackenport. The slave's name was Hosea, and he'd belonged to a planter named Lysander Crenshaw, who was said to be a man of great wealth, not to mention being an eccentric and scholarly attorney. He was also said to be descended from a long line of Episcopalians and owned a whole village of slaves, acres of corn and tobacco, along with great herds of cattle and fine horses. They said his crops were such that in harvest time, he kept two steamboats busy hauling his corn and tobacco to the markets in Pittsburgh and Cincinnati. Much of that was only talk, of course; even so, where there's smoke, there's fire, as the saying goes—which isn't a bad saying, even though sometimes you can't tell smoke from fog.

It was also said that there were extensive peach orchards on the Crenshaw plantation, used to supply peaches for the brandy made in his own distillery. They said he needed practically a whole orchard just to keep himself in liquor, because he was not only a slave owner, but a sot, gambler, and infidel cynic. They said he could read Latin and Greek, but was a freethinker who never bothered to attend church services, being the sort of skeptic who is hateful in the eyes of God, and scornful of his ancestors and their love for the Church of England—though some folks reckoned that if you had to be unfaithful to a Christian faith, the Episcopalian branch was a good place to start.

They said Lysander Crenshaw was an ill-favored brute— short, ugly, and gruff, with a wild thatch of red hair and skin that was cracked and wrinkled, not to mention a smashed nose and a damaged, half-closed eye from an old injury. Everybody talked about his great physical strength, and said his grip was so strong he could lift an anvil just by grabbing it by its nose with his right hand—something he'd learned that the novelist, Sir Walter Scott, had done, so he reckoned he could do it, too; and by God he tried it one time and accomplished the feat.

It was Lysander Crenshaw's monstrous strength, along with a violent temper, that gave him a fearful reputation, and people all up and down the Kanawha tended to walk around him whenever he was standing in the way.

## A VILLAIN IN A VEST

Hosea was buried the next day, and Nehemiah Dawes and Isaac and a few of his clerks and almost a hundred local Abolitionists attended the service. It was a fine and sunny day, smiled upon by Heaven, as the Reverend Furman Willis said. Right after the coffin had been lowered into the grave by ropes supplied by Nehemiah himself, Biddle came up to the old merchant and said he'd just heard a story that Hosea had not escaped alone, as everybody thought. No, there'd been another slave who'd escaped with him, by the name of Darius, only he'd gotten away from the bounty hunters, and was now said to be on his way to Canada.

"May Darius reach his destination!" Nehemiah intoned. "Who escorted him?"

"Joe Hitchcock."

"Well, Sir, he should be safe, then."

"I just talked to Joe this morning."

"Oh?" Nehemiah looked around. "Why didn't he come to the service?"

"He said he had too much work to do."

"He allowed *his* work to interfere with the *Lord's* work?"

"Well, that's what he told me," Biddle said.

"Sir, I must say I'm disappointed in him."

"Joe told me something else, too." Biddle rubbed his hands together.

Nehemiah raised his eyebrows. "And what might that be, Biddle?"

"He told me where the two of them were headed when those bounty hunters flushed them from their cover."

"And where was that? Athens?"

"That's where they were headed, eventually. But at the time, they were on their way to *your* house. They'd heard it was one of the sanctuaries, and they wanted to spend the night there before heading north."

Nehemiah frowned and solemnly shook his head. "But the good Lord said that such was not to be."

"Joe said it was kind of strange that poor Hosea was coming to your house for safety that night, and here you were the one who killed him the next day."

"That's hardly the way to put it," Nehemiah muttered severely, glaring at his clerk through his eyebrows. "The moment they caught that poor fellow, his life was as good as over, and you know it!"

"I don't know about that. Those slave owners want to protect their property so they try to keep them alive."

"Confound it, Sir, enough is enough!"

"I'm just reporting what Joe told me," Biddle pointed out. "It wasn't *me* that said it."

"Maybe not," Nehemiah said through gritted teeth, "but you show too great a willingness to repeat it, and I am confoundedly tired of your insolence! Do you hear me?"

Biddle did hear him and was surprised. And it was right at that moment that he knew his tongue had gotten away from him and that for some reason beyond his understanding he had sassed his employer one time too many. Seeing the glare in Nehemiah's eyes made him fully aware of the fact.

Nehemiah shook his head and intoned, "As of this moment, Sir, you may consider your employment with me terminated. Do you grasp my meaning, Sir?"

Humbly, Biddle muttered that he did. Then he went off and got even drunker, whereupon he ceased to be humble and in fact got mighty indignant and rhetorical and talked to various people about the wrongs done to him by the high and mighty Nehemiah Dawes, a villain in a fancy vest if there ever was one who walked upon God's green earth. No matter how much the old tyrant preached to others about the evils of grave robbing and slavery.

One of the places where Biddle spoke of this was the Major Enslow Tavern, and one of the people who heard him was Isaac Dawes, who was himself a trifle afloat on grog, but sober enough to understand what Biddle said. And to remember every word.

## NEHEMIAH'S PROSPERITY

Generally and for the most part, those were good times on the river. Flour and gristmills were built, and deep-pit mines were dug to bring coal out of the bowels of the wooded hills and into the light of day, where it could be used to power steamboats and also shipped in barges to Cincinnati and Louisville. As everybody knows, coal burns hotter than hardwood, so the steamboats picked up five or ten miles per hour, and the rate of their explosions increased considerably. Those explosions were impressive, and you could hear them miles away, which made you instinctively look up in the sky for flying bodies, although according to measurement, none was ever actually known to fly over four or five hundred feet. But that is a considerable distance for a corpse to be tossed.

The lumber industry still throve, however—two sawmills in Brackenport were busy with orders up and down the river, and Eichenberg's brickyard was shipping out bricks in every direction to build sidewalks and houses and even barns for some of the wealthier farmers. A tannery was built below Naylor's Bluff, and a man named McGill built flatboats to float timothy hay downriver, all the way to the Mississippi and New Orleans, where the big plantations had such big herds of horses they were always in need of timothy.

In the midst of all this industry and commerce sat Nehemiah Dawes. For years he had been one of the most influential men in the community and he meant to keep it that way. It wasn't only his general store that flourished; he had shares in a number of businesses, including the tannery and brickyard mentioned above, along with one of the sawmills. The brickyard and sawmill proved to be good investments in terms of the profit they brought him, and because they supplied most of the materials he'd needed to erect a four-story building, made of brick and with a cartouche high above the street, with:

THE DAWES BLOCK
1858

engraved in letters of shadow relief.

Yes, his ship of commerce was sailing along mightily, but not all of it was smooth sailing. When the cooperage firm in Portsmouth didn't pay for the shipment of barrel staves he'd credited to them, he decided to sue. But the amount he claimed was for sixty percent more staves than he'd shipped, and the law suit became pretty lively, the way it does when lies and vilification enter the picture. One of the coopers—a man named Everhart—got so mad in court that he threatened to blow Nehemiah's brains out, right there in front of everybody, which is not a prudent threat to make in public.

Then there was Isaac. What do you do with a brother who won't work? Why, you give him a job and hope for the best. And that is what Nehemiah did, only the best didn't happen. Not even the second best. Isaac was given a clerk and his own office, but all he did was tell stories to the clerk and fill his office with the fumes of cigars and whiskey. He smelled like Biddle, only he wasn't as useful. Nehemiah had hired an accountant to replace Biddle, which left Isaac free to create broadsides and advertising posters whenever he was in the mood, which wasn't often. Nehemiah told him he wanted the name of Dawes to be known far and wide, up and down the valley; but Isaac wasn't used to listening. He seldom did, because his thoughts tended to be elsewhere.

Nehemiah would have booted the rascal out in a second, except for the fact that it wouldn't look right for him to do that to his own brother. If you boot your brother out into the cold, and it's generally understood that he's helpless, then you lose a certain moral authority. Folks are going to have trouble thinking of you as the Conscience of the Community, which was pretty much the way Nehemiah viewed himself, and desired to be viewed. No, if you have a brother like Isaac, and value your reputation in a place like Brackenport, all you can do is try to stick it out.

But Isaac wasn't the only problem Nehemiah faced, and he wasn't the most serious. There was another from an unexpected source, which had to do with his deceased wife, Elizabeth. She had two brothers. Jacob Kittle was the first mate on the steamboat *Wyandotte*, a 279 ton batwing sidewheel packet with a wood hull that had a Pittsburgh to St. Louis run. The other brother, Henry Kittle, was a farmer up in Letart Township. Both brothers were characterized by their great and abiding affection for Elizabeth, who had been their older sister and almost a mother to them, after their real ma died of childbirth fever when the two of them were still little pups, barely old enough to totter and get in trouble.

The *Wyandotte* was named for another sidewheel packet that had hit a snag and sunk above Vicksburg in 1848, when she landed on Paw Paw Island, trying to unload a crowd of drunk and quarrelsome deck passengers. Thirty people were lost when she sank, which number did not contain a sufficiently high percentage of the troublemakers, according to Henry Upshaw, one of the survivors. A man from St. Louis who had been bilked of a great deal of money by several Tennessee gamblers agreed with him one-hundred percent.

But it's the Kittle brothers who concern us here. They were not widely known as troublemakers, and if it had just been Henry, things might have been all right for Nehemiah, because Henry wasn't the fire-eater his brother Jacob was. But whenever the *Wyandotte* steamed into town, Jacob would come down the plank breathing sparks, and soon begin to work on Henry's imagination, so that before long the two of them were ready to go downtown and do serious bodily harm to Nehemiah. Often they discussed the satisfaction they would get in whipping him until he chewed gravel, or maybe throwing his body out of one of his fancy fourth-story windows to see if it would bounce or if they could maybe hit the river with it.

The source of their fury was the fact that Nehemiah had buried their sister in one of the worst spots in the entire graveyard, humiliating the Kittles. There her grave was, a disgrace for everybody to gaze upon, scarcely ten feet above the flood line. Maybe eight. But for himself, Nehemiah had bought the loftiest and most expensive plot of all, high above the river where the gravestone could look down with scorn upon the steamboats that plied and labored their way up and down the channel in their pursuit of plenty, as decreed by the gods of commerce.

And now, to top it all off, he'd buried that slave, a *darky*, no matter how light-complexioned they said he was, in that high spot on the hill, leaving their poor sister's corpse to drink the muddy floodwater every spring at flood time, because everybody knows that eight feet upslope is as naught compared to the vertical flood line in which water rises.

Jacob and Henry Kittle verged upon being two of the town's respectable citizens, in spite of the fact that neither of them belonged to a church. They certainly didn't belong to the ruffian class, and it was widely held that they showed no disposition in that direction—at least until recently, when Jacob got it into his head to start brooding over the insult to their poor sister's corpse.

They belonged to that class of men who can generally hold their liquor, but the wrong done to their dear departed sister ate at their peace of mind so much that their drinking picked up a beat or two whenever Jacob came into town. And upon those occasions when they were in their cups, they talked more than was prudent. Still, folks tended to think of their fuming as more smoke than fire, and you might say that a lot of their wrath piddled out back of the Major Enslow Tavern, with the two of them looking up at the stars while peeing together, voiding the dregs of a hard night's drinking along with long boozy seizures of plotting against the safety and well-being of Nehemiah Dawes.

One evening at the Major Enslow, however, after the two of them had drunk a glass or two of fruit punch made with a dash of Monongahela Rye whiskey, they looked up and saw Nehemiah's one-time employee, Biddle, whose first name was Eugene. It was obvious to the Kittle boys that Eugene Biddle had been drinking and was getting on to being fried, honked, sizzled, primed, and loaded. Seeing him this way, Jacob invited him over, then clapped him on the shoulder and offered to buy him a drink, knowing that Biddle was in no mind to refuse.

After the three of them got to talking, the Kittle brothers began to warm up as well. They became vociferous and profane,

35

while for the most part Biddle remained quiet, intent upon remaining in his chair, not being in the mood to chew a floorboard. Somebody in the back room was playing "Jeanie with the Light Brown Hair" on a mandolin, and two rough looking fellows in the corner were playing cards, staring at the table like two cats watching the same bird.

After the Kittle brothers had talked awhile, Biddle seemed to get his second wind and joined in the chorus. He admitted that he had been drinking too much of late, more than a man should drink, if truth be told. And he said there was only one reason for it, which was that his employment with Nehemiah Dawes had been terminated. He explained that before he was fired, he'd drunk *because* he had to work for Nehemiah Dawes, only now he drank because he *no longer* worked for him.

"And that's just the word he used," Biddle said. "He said, 'You're *terminated*, Sir!' That's what he said, all right. Clear as day."

"Somebody ought to stoke that bastard's fires," Jacob Kittle muttered.

"And one of these days, we just might do it," Henry said, nodding.

"He's a hard man," Biddle said. "But I'll tell you the gospel truth, that's the word he used, all right: *terminated*. I remember like it was yesterday."

"When was it?" Henry asked. "Last week?"

"Somewhat recently," Biddle said in a judicious tone, unable to be more precise than that.

"One of these days somebody's going to terminate *him!*" Jacob muttered.

"I was thinking more along the lines of a good whipping," Henry said thoughtfully.

"I have a wife and child," Biddle said.

"Why, Sir, so do I," Jacob said. "*Four* of them."

"Me, too," Henry said. "Only three."

"Three wives?" Biddle asked.

"No sir," Henry said after giving him a curious look. "Three *children!*" After which Jacob said, "Four."

"There's a lot of misery in the universe," Biddle commented philosophically, "and it's the Nehemiah Daweses in this world who contribute more than their share."

"Amen," Jacob and Henry said together.

Biddle laughed bitterly. "And he claims there was a crosswind that caused him to miss that bounty hunter! Boys, there was about as much of a crosswind as . . ."

Here, Biddle paused and groped for an example to measure the stillness of the air, but he couldn't bring it off.

"I remember that day like it was yesterday," Jacob said.

"It was last week," Henry informed him. "Or maybe the week before. One of those weeks, anyway. Or maybe it was three."

Jacob inhaled abruptly. "*I* know how long it was, Henry! What I'm saying is, there wasn't no more of a crosswind than the breath of a kitten."

"Why, Sir, that's exactly the expression I was going to use," Biddle said, "only I couldn't quite bring it to mind."

Henry nodded and drank from his glass of punch. "Boys, maybe we ought to lower our voices," he said in a low voice.

"Why's that?" Jacob said loudly.

"Didn't I see Nehemiah's brother Isaac come in a little while ago?"

"I don't see him now," Jacob said.

"I don't either," Biddle said.

"He's probably in the next room."

"I don't care *who* hears what I've got to say," Jacob said in a loud voice, looking all about the room.

## THE SOLEMN RITES OF HUMILITY

The next day, Jacob and Henry were as hungover as Biddle, so they decided to go and have it out with Nehemiah. They decided that the old merchant had been spared expressions of their discontent long enough. They decided, in short, that the time had come.

So they caught up with him just outside the big entrance and portico of the Dawes Building, as the townsfolk called it, rather than the Dawes *Block*, and they stopped him right there on the brick sidewalk, made with paving bricks from the very brickyard Nehemiah himself owned shares in. Nehemiah was carrying an umbrella, although the sky didn't look like rain.

It was not surprising that Jacob spoke first. He said, "Mr. Dawes, you have insulted our sister."

Nehemiah was surprised, even though he had gotten hard of hearing. "How's that, Sir?" he asked.

"Sir, you do *remember* us, don't you?"

"Of course I do, Jacob. And why all this *Mister* business and this sudden formality?"

"Sir, we are your dead wife's brothers," Jacob told him.

"She was our sister," Henry added.

"Why, of *course* she was! Don't you think I know who you are? What's gotten into you boys, anyway?"

"Sir, you have insulted our family," Jacob said formally, and Henry nodded.

"How so?"

"Having that damned darky buried up there on the hill and letting her dear dead body rot down by the flood line," Jacob said.

"Sir," Nehemiah said, "surely you know that some day I'll be sleeping down there myself."

"Yes, Sir, but damn you, you put her down there *before*!"

"Before what?"

"Before you turned your grave over to that dead nigger! You were planning to sleep your eternal sleep up there at the zenith, while our poor sister's body was festering away down near the flood line!"

"But as it turned out, Sir, I changed all that!" he muttered. "So what's all the fuss about?"

"The wish is tantamount to the deed," Henry said, using a word that kind of surprised all of them, including Henry himself.

"You boys are making a mountain out of a molehill," Nehemiah told them.

"Oh, *are* we now!" Jacob said. "Well, Sir, if that's so, then it wouldn't make any difference where *you* were buried, would it?"

"But it obviously *did*!" Henry chimed in before Nehemiah could answer, "because you bought that grand and lofty grave plot for yourself."

Nehemiah frowned and thought a moment. Then he said, "Boys, in a way you are right, and in a way you are wrong."

"How's that?" Jacob asked him, sounding uneasy.

"Don't you agree that your sister was a living saint?" Nehemiah asked.

Sniffing a trap, Jacob and Henry didn't open their mouths. At first, they didn't even move, but then they sort of nodded, Jacob first. After which he said, "Sure, but what does *that* have to do with anything?"

"It has everything to do with it, Sir. Your sister was above the vanity of funereal or mortuary ostentation. She was too good to desire as much for herself as she would have desired for another."

"What's he talking about, Jacob?" Henry asked his brother uneasily.

Jacob narrowed his eyes, and without taking his gaze from Nehemiah's face, said, "Well, Henry, that remains to be seen."

"I am talking about a woman who was holier than you and I could ever understand," Nehemiah told them.

"That may be true, but it still don't mean you haven't insulted our family," Jacob pointed out.

"Oh, yes it does," Nehemiah said, warming up to his argument. "If this had happened to just *any* woman, it might well be the insult you perceive it to be, boys. But believe me, it is not. Why? Because of the wisdom and tenderness and humility of that woman you called your dear sister and I called my dear wife!"

"That sounds like hogwash to me," Jacob muttered, although he was getting in over his head, which always tends to make a person uneasy.

All of a sudden, Nehemiah almost got violent. His eyes flared and his voice jumped an octave. "Do you dare to say that your dear sister wasn't *humble*?" he cried.

Both of them were shocked, you could tell. Finally, Henry muttered, "*I* sure wouldn't say it!"

"Stay out of this, Henry," Jacob told his brother. "I wouldn't say it, either, and goddamnit, Dawes, don't try to twist everything around!"

"Profanity will gain you nothing, Sir, when I am speaking of your holy sister."

Henry muttered, "Jesus, I never thought of her as being what you'd call *holy*!"

"She was *humble*, though, wasn't she?" Nehemiah cried, his voice getting shrill again as he dropped his umbrella and grabbed Henry's coat collar and shook him.

"Well, maybe she was, a little bit, but so what?" Jacob said.

"And humility is a Christian virtue, isn't it?"

"I suppose you could say that."

"Isn't that what the Savior taught?"

"I think he's right, Jacob," Henry said.

"Maybe, but so what?"

Nehemiah took a deep breath. "All right, then, boys, let me ask you this: what's the greatest favor you can do for some-body who's as humble as your sister was?"

"What's he leading up to, Jacob?" Henry asked.

"Whatever it is, I don't like it," Jacob said.

"What I am leading up to is simply this: If somebody is as humble as your dear sister, and my dear wife, was, then you accept the fact and *treat* them that way."

"What way?" Henry asked.

"Humbly," Nehemiah and Jacob answered together.

"Well, I'll be damned," Henry whispered.

Nehemiah sniffed. "And if you see tears in my eyes, boys, I want you to know that those are tears of affection for my dear dead wife, your sister!"

And saying that, Nehemiah grabbed Henry's coat collar again and began to pray, right out there in public, which made Henry uncomfortable, because he wasn't used to such lan-guage, and he figured this was neither the time nor the place for it. But it didn't bother Nehemiah; he just kept on going, calling on the Almighty and saying things like "thou" and "thy mercy" and saying them right out there in public, standing on the brick walk where every passerby could hear.

Several people stopped and listened for a while, and then went on. Henry and Jacob were trapped, though, because they figured this still had to do with their poor dead sister, so they had to stick around and be quiet. It made both of them uncomfortable, right up until Nehemiah got to the Amen and the two of them could make their escape.

When they were about a block away, Henry said he didn't ever want to approach Nehemiah again about something like that, and Jacob said, by God, he didn't either, although he pointed out that there's more than one way to skin a cat, which Henry kind of wondered about, but didn't bother to ask, figuring it wasn't the right time. Only he figured that maybe Jacob was talking about just thrashing Nehemiah or maybe shooting him in the head, without giving him a chance to start in talking and praying so he could confuse the whole issue.

## A SHORTAGE OF CADAVERS

In those days there was only one real physician in Brackenport, unless you counted a crazy hydropath named Fortnoy,
and a female herbalist named McVicker. Most sensible people
in town wouldn't have counted them, but they seemed to be
thriving, so somebody was paying them for their quackery.

The real doctor was a fat old Methodist named Peter Heckenwalder, and he had a young apprentice named Silas Potter. For over a year, Silas had accompanied the old doctor
on his rounds, traveling on horseback with him and listening
to his gossip and complaints and lectures as they made their
way from one case of malaria or delirium tremens or broken
tibia to another. Silas was a hard worker with a good head,
so it wasn't long before the old man told him it was time he
abandoned the apprenticeship phase of his training in order
to study anatomy.

But to study anatomy, you need a cadaver, and Nehemiah
had whipped up the religious passions of the community to
such a white heat that the chances of procuring a local specimen were negligible. In Nehemiah's view, anybody who dis-
sected a corpse was a grave robber, and grave robbers were
instruments of the Devil and about to take over the world. But
their day of judgment was coming, and then those damned
Kanawha planters would have to move over to make room for
them in the deepest pits of hell. Given the way Nehemiah felt,
the other Abolitionists had to agree with him, or they might
be thought less righteous than the merchant, who, in the long
tradition of the wealthy and powerful everywhere, had a big
part in defining the resentments of the community.

Other than slavery, was there anything more abhorrent than mutilating a poor, helpless human carcass in the name of medical science? Nehemiah viewed such shenanigans as at the least repugnant, and extending to the diabolical, and he whipped up public sentiment to such a degree that the lo-' cal preachers felt obliged to keep a close watch on Dr. Heckenwalder and his assistant, and publicly give expression to suspecting them of harboring many and various unchristian notions, the digging up of cadavers chief amongst them.

Considering this state of affairs, Dr. Heckenwalder planned to lend his young assistant enough money to travel downriver to Cincinnati, a godless city where they piled the corpses in tubs and young medical students gave them names like Mary Jane and Harry, and dug into their putrid flesh with scalpels, singing and joking as they sliced away. They said you could hear their expressions of blasphemous and profane merriment all over the city as they violated the temple of the human body, which was designed in the image of the Almighty, as attested by Scripture.

But before Silas Potter could board a riverboat downriver, Brackenport suffered a sudden outbreak of a virulent fever, and both the doctor and his assistant were kept busy ministering to the sick day and night, and all plans for Silas to journey to Cincinnati had to be postponed. Some of the more ignorant townsfolk theorized that the fever might be measles, and those more ignorant still said it might even be cholera, but Dr. Heckenwalder said it wasn't measles, unless they'd developed a new strain that was spotless. And he said it wasn't any more like cholera than it was glanders or the blind staggers, although he couldn't say for sure exactly what it was. Maybe it was a fancy new kind of bacillus that the learned physicians in Philadelphia hadn't gotten around to naming yet.

Then Silas Potter's thoughts of soon going to Cincinnati were suddenly and permanently quashed when Dr. Heckenwalder himself came down with the fever and within thirty-six hours was dead. This left Brackenport without a physician, and left Silas with little hope of ever being able to study anatomy so he could complete his medical education. Silas was not a Presbyterian, but a Methodist. Nevertheless, he had as highly developed a sense of guilt as just about any Presbyterian you could name, and he wasn't the sort to get any special pleasure from cutting into a corpse, anyway. And yet he wasn't one to back away from an unpleasant necessity, either.

Then, before the townsfolk could entirely recover from their grief over the passing of so prominent a figure as Dr. Heckenwalder, they were subjected to another shock in the form of the sudden and inexplicable disappearance of Nehemiah Dawes, who did not come to work one Tuesday morning, causing rumors to fly in all directions. His loyal cook and housekeeper, the old widow Agatha Tremblow, said that he'd left an hour earlier than usual that morning, claiming he had work to do in clearing up some overdue accounts.

The effect of his disappearance was immediately felt along the river. Everybody assumed the worst. Within an hour or two, they were talking about Nehemiah as one who had died. Most of us sink into oblivion without leaving so much as a blink and a ripple, but when a man of Nehemiah's station in life—which is to say, wealth and influence—disappears, it is a singular event, and even bums and idlers sit up and take notice.

No one was more affected than the departed's brother. The first thing Isaac did was to get sober, or at least get there within a few hours after his brother's disappearance, whereupon he began to behave like a responsible citizen, shaving and putting on a clean shirt and commenting gravely upon the various rumors that were beginning to flourish. "Yes," he was quoted as saying, "when a citizen as distinguished as my dear brother fails to show up at his own office—a man, moreover, renowned for punctuality and dependability—it is only natural that right-thinking citizens should take alarm."

People were surprised and impressed by Isaac's eloquence, and told him so, which made Isaac look even graver. People said it was almost like he'd been saving up for a moment of crisis such as this to reveal his true colors, whatever that might be taken to mean. Some said he even sounded a little like Nehemiah himself, only without the preaching and bad breath. Many claimed that it is a well-known fact that we are not awakened to our true calling until tragedy strikes.

No one had seen the great merchant arrive in his office building, and no one had noticed any light in the windows of his third floor office. The bookkeeper who had replaced Eugene Biddle, a man named Bill Hollander, became concerned shortly after nine o'clock, knowing of Nehemiah's intent to arrive early and get to work with him on the overdue accounts. So he went out to the street, where he hailed F. T. Lorry, the town constable, and told him that Mr. Dawes must be ill, or he would surely have arrived by this time.

At that moment, seeing one of the town boys loitering nearby, Constable Lorry beckoned to him and told him to go right away to Mr. Dawes' house and ask if the old merchant needed a doctor. Twenty minutes later the boy returned, and said that

Agatha Tremblow claimed that Mr. Dawes had left for work almost four hours before. She said he'd told her he had so much work to do he couldn't stay abed any longer. Now she pointed out that since he wasn't in his office, it hadn't helped a thing to get up so early, which was what she'd tried to tell him in the first place, only he never listened to her advice.

Hearing this, Bill Hollander and F. T. Lorry began to spread the word around town that Nehemiah Dawes was missing. By mid-morning the alarm was well-spread, and a considerable number of the townsfolk were already gossiping and discussing the possibility of foul play, developing furious scenarios of bloodshed and mutilation, gunshot and knife wounds, hammer blows and poisoning, crippling and drowning. As several of the fastest talkers pointed out, the great number of enemies Nehemiah had made through the years made such lurid speculations of violence not as fanciful in his case as it might have been in others.

One man was especially and unpleasantly affected by the news. This was Eugene Biddle, who was so hungover he found himself sighing a lot and contemplating the Four Last Things, with special emphasis upon Sin and Eternal Judgment. He was grumbling at his wife and groping his way around the dining table of his little house, wondering how he'd gotten to be in such a condition, since he couldn't remember being any worse than half-shaved the night before, which is to say, not so bad that he couldn't hang onto the floor without falling off. But there it was. And here he was, groaning and gazing into the darkness of a world turned sinister, seeing it out of red eyes and whiffling and soughing with the burden of staying alive inside a shaky sack of flesh wherein all his vital organs trembled and quivered. Even when he groaned, he groaned out of a mouth made foul with the decay of spirits, making it taste like a fetid swamp distilled into a half-pint measure of fulsome rot.

Who could wonder that Biddle would be affected by the news that Nehemiah Dawes had disappeared and was generally assumed dead, probably murdered? If not slain by one of the great number of those he had ruined in sharp business dealings, perhaps he'd been exterminated by one of the envious multitude. Or maybe just some damned copperhead who was tired of hearing the old man rant and rave about slavery. Or maybe some disgruntled medical student in need of a cadaver. Maybe anything. Who could tell?

Biddle was shocked and disappointed. No need to wonder why he was shocked, but the reason he was disappointed is that he himself had made up his mind to shoot the scoundrel right between the eyes and kill him dead, as he had told a dozen people during the past week, mostly while he was drunk and talking loud because he wasn't sure they could hear, otherwise.

Only now he wished he hadn't said a thing, loud or soft.

Unless, that is, he had somehow gone ahead and shot the Old Terror sometime that morning. It was possible, but if he had done such a thing, he had been too petrified and glazed from his favorite Monongahela Rye whiskey punch to remember anything about it.

## THE SEARCH

Everybody finds excitement in crisis and tragedy, else why do we go to war? Some would argue that there are ample reasons other than an adolescent itch for adventure that prod us into battle, but I say they're wrong. Put forth all your arguments for religion or the possession of land or the heritage of remembered or imagined wrongs as a cause for war, and I will counter that behind all of those drop curtains, it is the promise of the drama of battle that goads us into the folly of organized violence.

But there are crises and tragedies of a domestic kind, and it was one of those that sent so many bored townsfolk out into the neighboring countryside in search of Nehemiah Dawes. Finding him alive or dead made little difference. And what difference it did make would have tilted toward the latter, for this was a man who was feared rather than loved, respected rather than admired. Not only that, the town craved excitement, and it would be an awful letdown if it turned out that Nehemiah had only taken a sudden and impetuous notion to visit his older sister in Chillicothe.

Not everyone disliked Nehemiah, however. Agatha Tremblow was not one of that great majority who looked upon him more with cold fear than warm respect. She was devoted to Nehemiah Dawes, and was not afraid to show it. She believed he was possessed of virtues that most people didn't know about. Hadn't he taken her in after she'd been cast out of her own home way up the Muskingum River, near Duck Creek, where Nathaniel Chapman, Johnny Appleseed's half brother, had once lived? Even back then, she was old and broken in spirit, without friend or living relative, and no place to turn.

Then Nehemiah Dawes heard about her from Reverend Willis, and right away he told him, "Let her come and be the cook and housekeeper for a harmless and proper old church-going man, and I'll see that she does not starve." Those were his very words, as often quoted to Agatha by the Reverend Willis' wife, Geneva, who had a good memory for such things.

Not only that, Agatha liked to point out how Mr. Dawes had a way with taking in and nourishing the poor and downtrodden of every sort. Contrary to popular opinion, it was not only the African slaves who fired his compassion. Hadn't he taken in his own brother and *treated* him like a brother? Because not all brothers are treated like brothers, as Agatha pointed out; and she was correct in that conclusion. And wasn't Nehemiah the very pitch and soul of tolerance in his treatment of Isaac? And wasn't Isaac enough to try the patience of a Quaker?

Not only that, Agatha said, warming up to her subject, look how long Nehemiah had kept that awful sot Biddle on as his bookkeeper. Most employers wouldn't have hired him in the first place, let alone paid him wages for all those years, when most mornings he showed up tardy, and with a breath that would discourage a mule. Although you might say that considering Nehemiah's own foul breath because of his teeth and a diseased gall bladder, he could pretty much hold his own against the mouth of any creature that breathed. Still, Agatha said, that wasn't the point.

Yes, Nehemiah Dawes had funny ways, but when folks criticized his ways behind his back and said that his sympathy extended only to the plight of the African slaves and molested corpses and no further, and that his righteous wrath was limited to only two groups, copperheads and grave diggers, she would disagree, and personally testify to his kindness and large-heartedness. All of what they'd said against him was true, he was all business most of the time, and a cold man in his speech and manner, along with just about everything else. It was only natural for him to be that way, Agatha explained. That was the way God had made him. And if God had made more folks like him, the world would be a better place, Amen. In short, now that her master had mysteriously disappeared, there was no more anxious spectator of the unfolding events than Agatha Tremblow.

And yet, for the next three days, nothing unfolded. Folks searched everywhere, all through Letart, Salisbury, Lebanon, and Sutton townships, and even over the borders into Gallia, Athens, and Washington Counties. They went out on horseback and in rowboats and buggies, and quizzed every traveler in sight, especially the steamboat crews and passengers, who were seriously questioned and interviewed, as if they might forget to mention coming upon the well-dressed corpse of a rich old man floating in the river. Not that floating corpses weren't pretty common, but not many were as well-dressed as Nehemiah Dawes.

Hiram Culpepper, a farmer from Rutland, claimed he'd even ridden as far as Ross County looking for signs of Nehemiah's whereabouts. But Hiram was such a prodigious liar that nobody ever believed him, even though this time what he said was no less than the Gospel truth, which just goes to show that if you have a reputation for lying, the truth isn't a whole lot of help. It works in the opposite direction, too, which is how politicians get elected.

The change in Isaac was remarkable to behold. Everybody noticed. Some said he acted like a judge, others said a preacher, and still others voted for senator. He stayed in his office, dictating letters to his clerk and reading the reports that were coming in from all directions, and from as far away as Marietta and Portsmouth. When he walked the streets, everybody commented upon how white and clean his shirt was and how grave his demeanor. He was often seen to walk with his head down, pondering, and his hands clasped behind his back. And it was generally believed that he had not touched strong spirits since the terrible news had erupted. Which, for the most part, was true.

Agatha Tremblow hung upon every word that was spoken on the matter—rumor, speculation or report, it made no difference. People felt sorry for her. She stopped boys walking along the street and asked what was the latest they had heard, although more often than not, they'd say they hadn't heard anything at all. But this didn't stop Agatha, who kept her vigil day and night, clear until Friday, when she heard the news she had been half-fearing all along. She first heard it from a boy named Dan Schumacher, and the news almost prostrated her with grief and astonishment. Half-expecting misfortune doesn't always ease the blow; sometimes it even makes it worse.

It was a fisherman downriver who found Nehemiah's body, which had gotten hooked in his trot line. He'd pulled it up, thinking he'd either gotten a catfish half as big as a pony, or maybe he was pulling up the river bottom, but it was neither one; it was Nehemiah's corpse, all covered with mud and with a bullet hole right smack dab in the middle of its brisket. Where his body turned up wasn't too far from where Hosea's body had been snagged, but nobody noticed that fact at the time.

Even if Agatha hadn't been stopping every urchin who passed by, she could not have avoided hearing the terrible news. It spread in all directions. News like that snaps and pops like burning fuses branching outward from the center of town. It travels in all directions, upon the spokes of the great wheels of commerce, or via a railroad depot, only with the tracks hissing and snapping and flashing with the news of the death of Brackenport's wealthiest and most prominent citizen.

Agatha took it hard. At first, she could hardly believe it, and then she said she'd known it from the start. Lizzie and Prue, the servant girls, were almost as seriously affected. Prue decided to have hysterics, but then she quieted down and managed to suffer in a more sedate manner. The Dawes house may have been the grandest in all of Brackenport, but that didn't matter at a time like this, for it was now stuffed with grief. People wondered at the amount of sadness the report of Nehemiah's death seemed to inspire in those nearest to him, and some even went so far as to wonder if maybe they hadn't misjudged the man because of his fanatical raving.

When Isaac heard of Nehemiah's murder, he broke down and cried into his handkerchief, saying he had lost the best brother a fellow had ever had from the beginning of time. He swore that he could bear witness to his brother's magnanimity, for when he was destitute and broken upon the wheel of misfortune, his brother had taken him in and had nurtured and protected him in his hour of need, the way a brother is supposed to do, but hardly ever does.

Then he made a solemn promise that he would do all within his power to keep Nehemiah's many business concerns afloat. He said that nobody on God's earth could replace such a man, but he would do what he could. Hadn't Nehemiah taken him in when he was in direst need, impoverished in purse and broken in spirit, with no other place to turn? Hadn't he treated him the way all brothers should be treated, but seldom are in this selfish and ungrateful world?

Then to top it off, Isaac offered a five hundred dollar reward to anyone who could name his brother's assassin. And that was just the word he used, "assassin," making it sound like the culprit had killed some president or king or other such august person. He had posters made with the word REWARD almost four inches high, then he hired a couple of boys to post them all over town.

Several people wondered out loud where Isaac would get the money for such a reward, but the answer was not slow forthcoming: he'd already dug his hands into that pile of gold, they said, and both hands came out dripping. Several folks said that maybe Isaac Dawes had been digging for gold in the wrong part of the country; if you were Nehemiah's brother, it wasn't California where you should look—it was right here in Brackenport, on the Ohio River. And you didn't have to lift a shovel or pan water in a mountain stream to get it.

Or kill a man and have to skedaddle to avoid the hangman's noose.

## THE SEARCH BEGINS

The search for the murderer was on, and it came hot and heavy. Everybody was eager to find out who the killer was. For a while, it was practically the only topic of conversation. For a while, if you didn't talk about Nehemiah Dawes' murder, you weren't in touch with reality and nobody would do more than half listen to what you had to say. Speculation raged, and surmise flourished, and they began to feed upon themselves, so that before long you could almost have done without the murder itself, because all it took to get people excited was the excitement.

One reason there was so much fervor for capturing the killer was the fact that so many people were secretly pleased by Nehemiah's death. This wasn't just because of the natural human mixture of fear and envy of somebody who is mightier than others; there was vengeance in the mixture as well, because everybody knew that it was Nehemiah's fault that Brackenport didn't have a doctor. Everybody knew that if he hadn't been such a damned fanatic on the issue of grave robbers, Silas Potter would be in Cincinnati right now, studying the human body through the silent testimony of cadavers. Brackenport would have had another doctor by now, except for the fact that no doctor wants to go where you can't carve up a cadaver. Anybody could see that all this damned foolish talk against grave robbing was enough to scare a doctor away.

Yes, there was a lot of resentment in town. Some people who'd lost a child or mother blamed Nehemiah, claiming that he was indirectly responsible for the death of their loved one. These were folks who might not have been willing to pull the trigger themselves, but a lot of them were half-glad some-body had done it. Being glad for something like that makes you feel guilty, so it's only natural you'd want to take off and find the culprit who'd done the job for you and try him before a jury and find him guilty and string him up quick and get the whole damned business over with so you can have some peace of mind. That's the way it works, all right.

Now that Dr. Heckenwalder was dead and there wasn't a coroner around, they had to load Nehemiah's corpse on a wagon and take it up to Doctor Pritchard, in Athens County, who prepared the coroner's report. Everybody was all agog to hear what it said, and it did not disappoint them. There were those who studied it and even memorized it verbatim; how the bullet entered the chest in the center, smashing the sternum and then destroying the right ventricle of the heart, causing immediate death, and destroying muscle and lung tissue with bone fragments, with the bullet then coming out of the body just under the right scapula. The angle of the bul-let made it look like a left-handed man had fired the shot, so it was only natural that a lot of the left-handers in town be-gan to feel a little uneasy. Especially if they had said things against Nehemiah, which almost everybody had, left-handed or right.

By this time, Nehemiah's corpse was overripe, but they kept the smell down pretty well, and long enough for them to arrange a funeral befitting a man so prominent. They did it by keeping it in alcohol and then packing it in oilcloth, so that fifty feet away you could breathe pretty well, if you weren't too fastidious about such matters. The flowers helped a little, too, along with the stogies the men smoked and the perfume of the ladies.

The day after the funeral, two things happened that changed the course of the investigation. The first was when Miss Cornelia Oakum, an eccentric old spinster, went to the sheriff and asked when they figured Mr. Dawes had been murdered.

"They figure it was along about seven or eight o'clock Thursday morning," the sheriff said. "Maybe nine." The sheriff's name was Simon Tewksberry. He was good at the job and generally reckoned to be unbeatable at the polls. And unlike some sheriffs of the modern day, he was even known to arrest scoundrels upon occasion when they needed it. He was an uncommonly tall man with a serious look on his face, and he walked with his right foot turned in, like he was about to change course, even when he wasn't.

"And where do they reckon it was done?"

"No way of telling, exactly," Sheriff Tewksberry said. "Only with the current and such, and the time elapsed, the body must have been dumped in the river about a quarter mile downstream from Dawes' building. Maybe a half mile. Why, Miss Oakum, do you know something I should know?"

Miss Oakum thought a moment. Then she said, "I think maybe I do."

"And that might be?" the Sheriff inquired.

"Well, I was painting that morning you say he was killed. I like to paint in the cool of the morning, before the snakes come out and the birds quiet down, so I'd set my easel up just about where you said, and I saw a man headed downstream."

"Did you recognize him?"

"I don't recognize people, Sheriff."

"You mean, you don't look at them—is that what you mean?

"That is somewhat correct, sir. Although somewhat not."

Simon Tewksberry frowned and thought about it. Still, he wasn't too surprised by her answers. Everybody knew how peculiar she was, and how she never seemed to look a body in the face. "You recognize me, don't you?"

"I recognize your badge, Sir," Cornelia said, sounding dignified and looking about two feet above his head. "And that is all."

The Sheriff thought about that a moment. He knew she had to be handled just right, or she just might get up and skedaddle.

"Could you describe this man you saw?"

"Not in words, I couldn't."

The Sheriff frowned. "Well, Miss Oakum, what other way *is* there to describe somebody?"

"I'm sure I don't know," Cornelia said. But after she said it, she just sat there and stared above the Sheriff's head, like somebody waiting for an angel to appear.

Then he caught on. "I've heard about how you're a painter and such," he said.

She nodded.

"Could you maybe draw a picture of this man you saw?"

"I don't draw pictures, Sheriff."

"I see." Simon thought a moment. Then he said, "But you do *paint* pictures, don't you?"

"I do."

"Well, then, could you maybe *paint* a picture of him?

"I guess a body could try."

"I see. So you did look at him enough to maybe paint a portrait of him. Is that what you're saying?"

"Somewhat."

"So you did see enough of him to recognize whether he was somebody from Brackenport. Is that right?"

"But I don't recognize people from Brackenport. There are many citizens who are strangers to me."

"But do you reckon you could help us by painting a likeness?"

"I reckon a body could try."

Sheriff Tewksberry shook his head. "Well, I suppose it might help. But before you do, isn't there anything you could say about him? Like was he big or small?"

"I'd say about average," Miss Oakum said.

"Old or young?"

"About average."

"I see. Stout or skinny?"

"About average."

The Sheriff nodded. "Maybe you better go ahead and paint that picture."

Which she went home and did right away, and then brought it back for him to look at early the next morning when it was good and dry. It was a dark picture, as dark as the inside of Miss Oakum's head. And the figure she'd painted was so dark it was hard to see what it looked like. Still, from what you could see, the figure looked about average, pretty much as she'd claimed. Only that didn't help a whole lot because you couldn't see very much to begin with, and most folks figure that most people are average, else what's the word for?

Sheriff Tewksberry hung the canvas up on his wall and under it wrote, "Wanted for Questioning." He reckoned he'd have everybody take a good look at it when they came to report to him. Maybe they could see something in it he couldn't see.

That seemed about all he could do at the moment, except attack some paperwork while he was waiting for something else to happen. Enough people were out beating the bushes just for the fun of it that he didn't need a posse—not that he'd know which way to point it even if he had one.

But Simon Tewksberry couldn't get Cornelia Oakum out of his mind. She was *peculiar*, all right; if the word hadn't existed before, it would have had to be invented just for her. She was always painting pictures, only she hardly ever painted people; all she ever painted were steamboats at night, all lit up in the darkness from the oil lamps in their windows. She couldn't get the lines straight on them, but you could tell they were supposed to be steamboats. Captain Billy Jones once said that if ever a boat was built that way, you wouldn't be able to steer it. All you could do was pray.

Cornelia Oakum liked to paint outside in the fresh air, near the riverbank, with the breeze blowing her hair and the expensive dark silken robes she liked to wear. She'd paint almost every sunny day, protecting her face from the rays of the sun with large plumed hats and her arms with long gloves that reached above her elbows. Some people figured she spent almost as much time and effort getting dressed up in her finery as she did painting.

Folks also remarked upon how odd it was that she liked to paint outside in the sunshine, when all she ever painted were steamboats at night. The same thing, again and again. She painted so many of them in the same way that most people couldn't tell them apart, except for the names she put on them. But Cornelia seemed to know them the way a mother knows all her little ones, even though they all look alike to a stranger. All of her paintings were as dark as the clothes she wore, except for the white steamboat at the center of the canvas, with all its windows lit up. Somebody once asked her why that was all she painted, and she said she reckoned that a lonely steamboat in the darkness of night with its windows all glowing with lamps was the most beautiful thing on God's earth.

Nobody could argue about that, but then nobody could prove it, either. Somebody else once asked her why, if she had to paint such dark pictures, she liked to do it in bright sunlight, and she said that you couldn't really see darkness unless there was a lot of light to see it in, which also left a lot of people scratching their heads, although some claimed that what she said was deep and had meaning.

Old Henry Oakum, Cornelia's father, had left her a great deal of money, which is why people tended to think of her as peculiar rather than loony. Henry had gone to California in 1849, and was the only man from Brackenport who'd struck it rich—unless you'd count Isaac Dawes, who maybe did and maybe didn't, it was hard to say. Of the six other Brackenport boys who went out there, two died and two were never heard from again. That left two who came back with their tails between their legs, as broke and discouraged as a rusty revolver.

Henry was considerably older than most of those adventurers, nearly fifty years old, and when he got back he was fifty-one and looked like a man who has gazed into the pits of hell and confusion. He hadn't been what you'd call too sensible before he'd left, but when he came back, he had turned the corner and was as odd as a rooster in trousers. Only now, he was rich.

Six years after his return to Brackenport, Henry died of a fever, and Cornelia found that he'd invested in so much railroad stock she'd never have to worry about anything, or look for a husband, unless she decided she wanted one, which she didn't. She was thirty-one when her Pa died, with two brothers who had fled the nest long before and now dwelt in regions unknown, so there was no one she had to share the wealth with, and she could just relax and enjoy herself and be as peculiar as she wanted, and nobody would ever say a word against her, knowing she was too rich to be criticized. Although they'd talk behind her back, of course.

People said that having Henry Oakum for a father was enough to make a body peculiar. For some reason, after coming back from California, he'd got it in his head that using a knife and fork to eat with was wrong; he said a knife and fork were an insult to the memory of dead animals. This didn't keep him from eating meat, however, and it was quite a sight to sit and watch him eat a pork roast with a spoon, but somehow he managed. For one thing, he had all his teeth, clear up until he gave up the ghost and died. Yes, everybody agreed that with a daddy like Henry, you might just turn peculiar and paint dark pictures of rivers and steamboats with all their windows lit up. Cornelia always gave her steamboats the names of real ones, and one time when Judge Tanner came up to her and saw that she was busy painting a big sternwheeler, he asked her which one it was, and she said it was the *Hiram Day.*

When the judge pointed out that the *Hiram Day* had been sunk ten years previous, Cornelia said, "You can believe that if you want to, but I don't believe everything they say."

"Everything *who* says, Cornelia?" the Judge asked.

"Those who don't understand that some things are immortal," she said.

"And are you saying steamboats are immortal?"

"I'm saying that appearances are deceptive, Judge."

"I see," the Judge said, and walked away.

## THE SHERIFF ASKS A QUESTION

The second thing that happened after Nehemiah Dawes' murder occurred one morning when Sheriff Tewksberry showed up at Nehemiah's house and knocked on the door. Nehemiah had two sons still living at home, Hector and William, aged fourteen and fifteen respectively. It was Hector who answered the door, and Simon said, "Is your Uncle Isaac around?"

"No," the boy said. "He's out somewheres."

"All right, then, I want to talk with Agatha Tremblow."

"What do you want with her?" Hector asked.

"You'll find out soon enough, Hector," Simon told him, stepping inside. "Is she here or not?"

"I guess she is," Hector said. Then he yelled out her name, and Agatha came walking into the front room, wiping her hands on a rag.

"I've got a question for you," the Sheriff said. Then he said to Hector, "You can stay and listen."

"I'd planned to," Hector said.

"And while we're at it," Sherriff Tewksberry said, "your brother. I'd like to ask him a question, too. Is he here?"

"Hey, Willy!" Hector yelled, without turning his head. They heard the back door slam, and then Willy came into the front room. "I was out oiling my saddle," he said.

"Agatha," Simon said, "I want a simple answer and I want the truth. Did you ever hear Nehemiah talk about throwing Isaac out of the house?"

Agatha shook her head. "No sir. He wouldn't do a thing like that."

"Nothing at all like that?"

"No, sir. He was a good Christian man."

Simon nodded. "How about it, boys? You ever hear your Pa say anything along those lines?"

"Nope," they both said. Then Willy said, "Why?"

Simon just nodded his head. "Now, you're sure your Pa never said anything like that?"

"Nope," the boys said.

"Never any talk about what a burden Isaac was getting to be, eating your food and taking up room in your house and causing a lot of talk?"

"Nehemiah wasn't a man to complain, Sheriff," Agatha said.

"He must have been a living saint, then," Simon muttered.

"How's come you're so curious?" Willy asked.

"Well, the fact is, you hear a lot of rumors when you're sheriff," Simon said. "And sometimes it just makes good sense to check the rumors out."

Then before anybody could say anything, he got up and walked out the door.

## THE ARREST

It didn't take them long to narrow the list of suspects down to Eugene Biddle and figure that he must be the murderer. Of course he denied it and protested his innocence in a loud voice, but what would you expect? What criminal doesn't claim he's innocent? There were maybe a dozen people who had heard him threaten Nehemiah Dawes, including Isaac. Actually, maybe it was as many as twenty or thirty people, altogether. They all admitted that they had heard a lot of other folks do the same thing, but most of those were right-handed. Not only that, somehow it just didn't seem the same. For one thing, Biddle *acted* guilty, and everybody knows that it's how we act rather than the simple truth that's more important when it comes to convincing people.

Even so, it wasn't what you'd call cut and dried. At first, they looked hard at the Kittle brothers, too. Those two boys couldn't be ignored, because they were the first to tell you that they had never gotten over the insult to their family in having their sister buried so near the flood line, while Nehemiah was at least forty feet higher on the plane, and of course that darky slave was higher than practically everybody but God, in the proudest spot of all, overlooking the river like a dead king.

But the Kittle brothers claimed they had a good alibi. They claimed they didn't have to kill the old merchant because they had each other. They said it was all talk with them, and every time Jacob came into town, he had Henry to absorb his frustration and anger, and at the same time, since they were brothers and often thought alike, Henry needed a brother he could unload on, too. They claimed that all their frustration and snappishness were relieved by the way they could periodically blow off steam to each other the way a steamboat lowers the pressure in her boilers when it starts to build up. They also said that a lot of the hard things they said weren't any more than whiskey punch talking.

So the Kittle brothers reckoned that all this worked out pretty well for themselves; but what about somebody like poor Biddle, who didn't have a brother he could blow off steam to? He hardly ever talked to his wife, even, whose name was Abigail. Everybody knew that and felt sorry for the poor downtrodden woman because they knew that Biddle wasn't much better at being a husband than he was at being sensible in working for a tyrant like Nehemiah Dawes.

Then there was Sam Killibrew. He'd never gotten over building Nehemiah's shed for him and then having to threaten and cajole him for over a year to get paid. He had been so exasperated, he had almost been driven to hire a lawyer to extract his just wages from the damned merchant. Of course Nehemiah had an excuse: he claimed that Sam hadn't followed his instructions. He claimed that he hadn't put the hole for the stovepipe where Nehemiah wanted it, but Sam claimed he had, so you didn't know whom to believe.

Then there were other suspects, as well. You don't acquire the wealth of a Nehemiah Dawes without acquiring enemies along with it. Everybody knows that. It's part of the arithmetic of existence, you might say; you pay a price for everything, good or bad, and if you have any claim to wisdom, you will accept the fact, and not grumble. When you take into account the way things are, you'll realize that most of the time, the good and bad in your life add up to zero, which is the best you can hope for.

Anyway, the other suspects didn't look as good as Biddle did. For one thing, Biddle was a sot. He wasn't just your average drinker of spirits, like the Kittle brothers and many others who could be named. No, Eugene Biddle had become a committed, hard-nosed, bottle-cracking drunkard. He was a tosspot of singular attainment. And you take a staggering and whittled man like that, one who had but a single thought in his mind, which was to do away with Nehemiah Dawes, and you have a keg of gunpowder with a burning fuse, snapping and crackling like a dozen bonfires as it dances wildly on its deadly journey toward the keg.

Not only that, and to top it all, *Eugene Biddle was left-handed*!

So a warrant was made out, and F. T. Lorry, the Constable, was sent out to bring Biddle in. This turned out to be an easy task, because F. T. found him so stumbling drunk he hardly seemed to know what was happening and had to be helped into the buggy. One reason he was so drunk was worry over the possibility of being arrested, for he had not been so drunk that past week that he didn't know which way the wind was blowing. Another reason was that his long-time resentment of Nehemiah Dawes was still eating away at his spirit, a resentment that even the old merchant's death could not mitigate.

His wife, Abigail, was weeping so hard you might have thought she loved him. Maybe she did, although it would be hard to figure out why. Still, it's hard to figure out a lot of things, one of which is the female heart, while another is a loyal wife married to a no-good besotted scoundrel who is about to be charged with the homicide of a prominent citizen.

People are not always clear what they are about and don't always understand why they do the things they do or why they feel the way they do.

There is a lot of passion in our confusion, and vice versa.

## THE TRIAL

Considering that the townsfolk had gotten so fired up over who had killed Nehemiah Dawes, it only stood to reason that they'd flock to the trial to see if Biddle would be found guilty. And flock they did. People traveled from miles around to crowd into the courthouse, and if they couldn't get in, they gathered outside and peeked through the windows and quizzed the boys who were sent out on errands, taking notes to various people, and fetching logs to keep the fires blazing and bringing back sandwiches and pies and pots of coffee and jugs of cider and brandy and whiskey punch just to help keep up the strength and stamina of all those who labored within the halls of justice.

It was an exciting time, all right. And the crowd wasn't just confined to townsfolk; there were people from upriver and down, and there were law students, eager to watch the attorneys lock horns and see what happened. People said there had never been such a trial in memory, and they were right. If a vote had been taken by secret ballot, it would have revealed an overwhelming appreciation for Nehemiah's murder, just for providing so much entertainment. People would have agreed that it was better than the stage play of *Uncle Tom's Cabin*, because after the curtain went down on the play you knew it had all been make-believe, but after the trial session was over, it would be just as true as it had been an hour before, and sooner or later somebody or other was sure to get themselves hanged, which is about as interesting and serious as you can get.

The prosecuting attorney was Wilmot Chandler, who was a short, squat man with a big head and flowing locks that some said were like those of Daniel Webster. Others said he looked a little bit the way Eugene Biddle would look if he lived another fifteen years, and had more hair. Biddle lasting that long was unlikely though, because the townsfolk had smelled blood, and everybody agreed that he was kind of worthless, anyway, especially after Nehemiah had terminated his position.

Wilmot Chandler said as much, himself. In his closing arguments, he admitted that the criminal justice system was not perfect and nobody had ever said it was. And he admitted that now and then it will hang an innocent man, but that's the price you have to pay for civilization, because there are a lot of human scum in the world—assassins and thugs, dips and panders, pimps and bullies, ruffians and river rats.

Yes, now and then an innocent man will go to the gallows, Wilmot Chandler argued, but that's only the price decent folk have to pay. Furthermore, you can be sure that any man who is hanged will not be *entirely* innocent, for Scripture tells us we are all guilty. If we aren't guilty of *this*, why then we're guilty of *that*. So it all evens out, rough hew it as we may, to quote the Bard. And for all the innocent men who die on the gallows, there are ten innocent citizens whose lives will be saved because a larger proportion of the whole class of hanged men won't be around to shoot them in the face some dark night and then pluck the billfolds and pocket watches from their corpses that are still warm with the echo of life. Anybody who believes in arithmetic, Wilmot said, will have to subscribe to that argument.

By now, Wilmot Chandler had his boilers up and was going full steam ahead. If some people are born for the hangman's noose, he said, then it only stands to reason that others are born to be useful and good citizens. You don't need an oligarchy or aristocracy to provide a framework for something as obvious as that. You can adapt democracy to it, and it will do just fine. Yes, some people are just by-God more worthwhile than others. We might all be alike in God's eyes, but God is hard to figure out, no matter how religious you are, and there's no point in lying about it, for God probably doesn't appreciate liars, although we can't even be sure of that.

Wilmot pointed out that to kill a man who is moral, useful and good is a far worse crime than to kill a ne'er-do-well. Look at the weekly toll of bodies washed up on the banks of our mighty river! Most of those corpses were once gamblers, cheats, chiselers, pimps, toughs, and similar riff-raff. Can anybody claim he should lose a minute's sleep over the slaughter of such sinners? Does anybody wail and moan and cry out to the Lord for an understanding of why those rogues and miscreants have died?

Of course they don't. And why? Because some critters are just more killable than others, and deep down in our hearts, we all know it. On the other hand, if you fire your pistol into the brisket of a good and useful man like Nehemiah Dawes, you're in real trouble, which is only right and natural. Because that's not at all the same thing as killing a river rat, who may have a Christian name, but has no more moral sense than a copperhead snake that's never heard of a church.

Then Wilmot went on to say that most people would understand what he was saying, but were afraid to admit it. But why should they be afraid? Because it sounded sinful or immoral? How could it be sinful or immoral if it was *true*? Or was it because it didn't sound democratic? Well, how could it not be democratic if most folks secretly *felt* that way? Wasn't democracy based upon what most people believe deep in their hearts? So wasn't it time to be honest? And wasn't it the American thing to do to speak out for something that was as obvious as what Wilmot Chandler was saying?

He admitted that the law couldn't acknowledge the truth of his argument but that didn't mean it wasn't true. The law had to draw the line somewhere and pretend that every human being was just as worthwhile as the next; but deep down in your hearts, you knew that was just hogwash. Deep down, everybody knew it. Equality was what they call a legal fiction, because everybody with an ounce of brains knows that some people are born to be worthless, just as some dogs and horses are born incorrigible, and there's nothing anybody can do about it.

Some folks, on the other hand, are just more important than others. Killing one of them is a lot worse than killing some damned heathen who doesn't have any more grasp of the difference between right and wrong than a box turtle understands infant damnation. Everybody knows that, so why pretend otherwise? The law cannot admit to such an obvious thing, but that's nothing more than a game of pretended innocence we have to play to keep the courts under control and not overwork the hangman.

The reason so many people get all sentimental about innocent men being executed, Wilmot Chandler went on, finding more and more inspiration in his topic, is that we're right there at the hanging when it happens. We can't help but see the stricken look on a critter's face before they put that hood over his head and we can't help but see him pee his pants, which often happens, and see the trap door sprung. And we can't help but see his body plummet straight down and we can't help but hear his neck crack as loud as biting into an apple, and hear the sigh of the crowd as they watch the spectacle. And afterwards, we can't help but notice the crook in his neck, bent like an elbow, with the head to the side, as if listening to the eternal silence.

Yes, it's hard to get over seeing something like that, if you're there, which many people are, because they are fascinated and can't stay away. It's no wonder that people sometimes have strong feelings about capital punishment, maybe wondering if the poor fellow is really guilty, after all, or maybe just somebody who happened to be handy and they had to lay a crime on him for just being in the wrong place at the wrong time, and for being a criminal type to begin with.

But what about all those that fellow might kill if you let him *live*? Those are people we can neither see nor hear. We can't hear their neck bones break or see the stricken looks on their faces. Wilmot Chandler pointed out that so far as we're concerned, they have a hood over their heads right from the start, in a manner of speaking. And yet, they are just as real as you and I, and their deaths are just as ugly. We just can't *see* them, so we don't feel the full weight of their lives being extinguished, the way we do when that trap door is sprung and the body plummets straight down like the lead line from the deck of a steamboat, and the neck breaks like the crack of a pistol shot and the crowd sighs.

By the time Wilmot Chandler had finished, everybody in the courtroom was stupefied. People sat there like every one of them had just been hit over the head with an ax helve made out of ash or hickory, or maybe like they had just witnessed a miracle. Even the defense attorney was stunned. He tried to get up, but he couldn't manage, because his legs wouldn't hold him. His name was Jasper Aumiller, and he now found himself in over his head and he knew it.

Jasper's parents had come here from Switzerland, or maybe it was Austria. He was a thrifty man, and cracked his knuckles a lot, which often irritated his clients. But today, he didn't make a sound. His mouth and knuckles were silent. He was like a man who has dreamed of glory and now sees it in person. Years later, he liked to tell how honored he'd felt just to be defeated by a man like Wilmot Chandler, even to be in the same courtroom with him and breathing the same air. He felt this way even if the great man did crush and overwhelm him in argument, not to mention making him look like a fool in front of half the population of the county, along with several of the adjacent ones.

But then what would you expect? From that moment on, it was obvious to anybody clever enough to milk a cow or use a shovel that Eugene Biddle was headed for the gallows, and it wasn't likely he'd have to wait very long, either.

## WAITING FOR THE GALLOWS

So far as Biddle was concerned, the problem now was a simple one: How could he manage to be kept in whiskey right up until the moment the noose was put around his neck? Tosspots live for little else but the jug. So if he was going to be sent plummeting into eternity by such an ignoble instrument as the noose, Biddle didn't want his mind to be around to experience it any more than was necessary. There was only one thing he dreaded worse than death, and that was the thought of being cold sober when he had to climb those nine steps before descending into Final Judgment.

Biddle's concern was understandable, for the jailer was a fanatical soldier in the Cold Water Army by the name of Levi Gandy. Gandy was known far and wide for his hatred of spirits. Translated into the vocabulary of Nehemiah Dawes, strong drink was slavery and grave robbing combined. If there was any jailer north of the Ohio River who would see to it that Eugene Biddle went to the gallows sober, it was Levi Gandy. Biddle knew this as well as any man, for even a sot will eventually learn who his enemies are, so half an hour after he was arrested, he began to study the issue of how to fortify and protect himself against the terrors of Terminal Sobriety. When his loyal wife, Abigail, came to comfort him in his cell, he right away asked her to bring him a bottle on her next visit. He could tell she didn't like the idea much, but when he wheedled a little, she gave a single quick and nervous nod, which made Biddle's heart leap like a startled deer.

But sadly, it was not to be, because Levi Gandy had anticipated the move like a chess master and was prepared and waiting for Abigail the moment she was admitted to the jail's outer room, where he relieved her of the bottle, opening the east window and pouring out its gargling contents upon the brick path that bordered the wall. After which, he returned the empty bottle to her, saying that he was sure she could find a better and more wholesome liquid to fill it with.

He then accompanied her to Biddle's cell, where he addressed the condemned man as follows: "I now see which way the wind blows, and it won't help you a bit. You might as well forget your nefarious plans and learn to lead a sober and righteous life, even if it's only for these last few weeks. I am going to see to it that when you first gaze upon the Almighty's countenance, you'll see Him in all His glory. Then you'll also realize what a favor I'm doing you by keeping you from relapsing into the sinful ways you have embraced."

"Some damned favor!" Biddle muttered.

Levi heard him, and pointed out that the profane judgment of a drunkard is not to be trusted.

"I ain't any damn drunkard!" Biddle growled.

"If you're not a drunkard, then the word has no meaning," Levi said.

Biddle said he didn't care whether the word had any meaning or not, but his flippant remark was lost on Levi, who had turned his back and was walking away from the cell.

The next time Abigail visited him, Biddle told her they'd have to think of something else. She tried to advise him to reconcile himself to doing without spirits, for such a deprivation was practically nothing compared to what awaited him on the gallows.

Saying that, she pressed a small New Testament into his hand, and Biddle looked at it with such a broken-hearted expression that later Abigail said that the memory of it would always stay with her, and it was almost enough to break her heart.

So the two of them sat there for a moment without speaking, and then Biddle repeated what he'd said before, that they would have to think of something else, which made Abigail repeat what *she* had said, too. And after that Biddle agreed with her, but he looked so forlorn that she wondered if he would be able to remember his vow.

As it turned out, her doubts were justified, because there was a chink in Levi Gandy's armor. He had a sixteen-year-old son named Loftus who worked in the jailhouse, building fires in the fireplaces and keeping them burning, and sweeping the floors and changing the bed linen once a month.

Along with his housekeeping duties, it was Loftus's job to serve the prisoners their meals after Levi's wife had cooked them. Loftus served them morning, noon, and night, so he got to know the prisoners pretty well by the time they were released or hanged. His Pa had named him Loftus with the hope that the boy's thoughts would soar above the weeds of sin and confusion that have always choked the gardens of mankind.

Folks seemed to think Loftus was all right, even though he was a little bit peculiar. He was as curious as a barrel of cats, and had an odd way of expressing himself. He was afflicted with a fervid imagination, which made the town of Brackenport seem small and unimportant in his eyes. Some folks said his problem was that he read too many books—not just the Bible and law books, which his pa favored and encouraged, because he wanted his boy to become an attorney—but books of philosophy and poetry and the novels of Sir Walter

Scott and James Fenimore Cooper and the stories of Washington Irving, which he read over and over.

He was a short, stocky boy, with a head of stiff brown hair that stuck up in all directions, so much so that somebody once said he looked like a sleepy rooster. Maybe it was his swollen eyes that made him look that way, even though he was filled with a poet's passion, and had the ambition of a Prince of Commerce. He was good at figures and at his schoolbooks, which he demonstrated in the academy to the satisfaction of Mr. Postlewaite, his teacher, so that there were some among the townsfolk who predicted that he just might grow up to be a luminary of the West and maybe one day even become as successful as Nehemiah Dawes.

Not that he was tempted to go in that direction. In fact, he didn't know which direction he *did* want to go in, which is often a problem with boys. Looking back on it, you might almost be tempted to believe that it was fated for Loftus and Biddle to come together. It's true that looking back upon things often gives us the notion that they were meant to be, but that's only because they have become part of our past, and there wasn't any other way for us to get to where we are now and become what we've become, except through the things that have happened to us, and no other. But I'm talking about something more than that, because Eugene Biddle and Loftus Gandy each had something the other wanted, even if only one of them knew it.

Biddle was the one who understood this. He had faced up to the fact that he was about to die and was pretty much reconciled to his fate, even though he was pretty sure he was innocent. And yet, there had been a few times when he'd been so drunk he couldn't remember even being alive. As has been mentioned, all he wanted was to spend his last hours numbed with enough Monongahela Rye to take off the rough edges, which isn't a whole lot to ask, when you think about it. Still, the crude and practical necessities of this world tell us that anything is too much to ask if it isn't possible, which is how everything was beginning to look to Biddle.

But after he had studied Loftus awhile, he realized that here was his opportunity. Here was a boy who would serve his purpose. This boy would be his salvation. Loftus Gandy was the hole in his pa's armor. He was a sensible boy, and vulnerable to ambition and hope. Loftus was the one who could smuggle whiskey to him in order to soften his last hours—*if*, that is, *Biddle could somehow tempt him*! So he studied the boy, watching him three times a day, and asking him this question and that, and carefully weighing his answers. By the end of a week, Biddle had figured out how to get the boy to do what he wanted.

This was on a rainy evening, and Biddle was sitting there on the pallet in his cell with his elbows on his knees and feeling about as lowdown as a garter snake with belly cramps. When Loftus came to take away the tin plate and cup that his supper of salt pork, biscuits, and taters had been served in, he gathered his wits about him and started talking to the boy. First, he asked him to sit down on a stool.

"I'm not supposed to sit down in a cell," Loftus said predictably, for Biddle had asked him this several times before, always eliciting the same response.

But Biddle acted as surprised as if this were the first time he had ever been refused. "Why not? You know I'm not going to try anything."

"They say you can never tell," Loftus said.

Biddle tried a small laugh, but it didn't quite work. Then he tried it again, and this time it came out a little better. "There's something I want to talk to you about," he said.

What is it?" the boy asked, taking a half step backward.

"Whatever you do, don't start edging away," Biddle said. "Do you know something? People have been edging away from me all my life. Maybe that's why I'm sitting here in this cell. Maybe that's why I took to drink. They say that edging away will do it to somebody, and maybe that's where all my trouble began, do you suppose?"

"I wouldn't know about that," Loftus said.

"I just want to have a word with you."

"About what?" Loftus said.

"About how you can bring me a bottle of Monongahela Rye every night for as long as I'll be around to drink it."

"You know I can't do that," Loftus told him.

"All right, then. Just one bottle the night before they string me up."

"I can't do that, either."

"Why, *sure* you can. It'd be *easy!*"

"No, I can't. It's not allowed."

"I said you *can!*" Biddle said. "I didn't say it was *allowed!*"

"What are you talking about?" Loftus said, narrowing his eyes the way he always did when he started to get interested, for the distinction Biddle insisted upon verged upon being clever—especially for a devoted tosspot.

"What I'm talking about is . . . I don't think I can face the gallows without whiskey."

"You've got a Bible there," Loftus frowned.

"I know, and I appreciate it. I don't think I could do it without a Bible, either. But I've already *got* the Bible, and the fact is, the Bible alone just ain't enough. The fact is, Loftus, I can't do it sober."

"It looks to me like you don't have much choice in the matter. Looks to me like you're going to do it sober whether you want to or not."

Biddle thought about that a moment and finally said, "Yes, but that's not the same. I don't want them to have to drag me kicking and yelling stone cold sober up onto that platform. There'd be no dignity in it. I want to climb those steps quiet and dignified."

"And drunk?"

Biddled nodded. "Yep. Anything but me being dragged a-hollering and kicking and yelling up those last nine steps."

"You wouldn't be the first to go that way."

"Yes, but I've got my pride."

"Some of those fellas probably felt the same way, but one way or other, they all got there."

"Loftus," Biddle said, "you are wise beyond your years!"

Loftus thought about that and then kind of nodded. "I think this kind of job does that."

"See what I mean?" Biddle cried. "Even *that's* the observation of a man wise and mature beyond the reach of youth!"

That kind of embarrassed Loftus, and he said, "Oh, I don't know about that. Anyway, I'm not all that young. I'm sixteen."

"And you're right. I always did say that if a man's going to have any sense at all, he'll show it by the age of sixteen. Maybe seventeen or eighteen. Sometimes twenty, but usually before that."

"I still reckon I've got a lot to learn."

"That, too, is a sign of wisdom."

"I sure don't feel wise."

"*Et cetera, et cetera,*" Biddle cried. "That's the way Socrates talked! But never mind that. The point is there is something I wish to impart to you."

"What's that?"

"I, too, am not without my depths."

"What does that mean?"

"I write poetry."

"You do?"

"Yes."

"So do I!"

"I would have bet on it."

"What sort of poetry do you write?"

"I write poetry about the river."

"The *Ohio*?"

"Is there any other for one who dwells upon its august shores?"

"I write about the War of Eighteen-Twelve."

"Why is that?"

"My grandfather fought at the battle of Tippecanoe."

Nodding, Biddle pulled a folded sheaf of foolscap from his coat pocket. "Would you like to hear one of my poems?"

"I guess so," Loftus said.

Biddle unfolded one of the sheets and read the following poem:

## LONG BOTTOM

The great river runneth by day and by night
From the Appalachian crags, where dewy morn
Gloweth in robes of Auroral light.
Thus it flowed ere we were born

And will goeth forever beyond the scope
Of our poor stay here on the earth.
Our mighty river flows with Hope—
And though it bringeth death, it bringeth birth.
From Pittsburgh Wheeling clear to Long Bottom

No Babylon is here—nor Rome, nor Sodom,
For the folk of Ohio are moral and true,
And honest and helpful and happy, too.

When he finished, Biddle said, "It's only two lines short of being a sonnet, and it rhymes."

"I noticed," Loftus said.

"The last line has three words that begin with an aitch."

Loftus nodded.

"But you can only hear two of them. The aitch in 'honest' is silent." Saying this, Biddle carefully refolded the sheet of foolscap into the others and put them back in his coat pocket. "It's a poem that reaches out its hand for the touch of nobility. Did you notice?"

"I guess so."

"I like to have my verbs end in *t-h*," he continued, lowering his voice as if imparting a secret. "There's something Biblical about a verb that ends in *t-h*, don't you agree?"

"I guess so," Loftus said.

"All of these poems will be yours," Biddle said with a sigh, "if you do me just one little favor."

Loftus nodded again. "You want me to bring you some whiskey."

"That's right. If you'll promise to keep me in Monongahela Rye for my last hours on earth, I'll turn over all these poems for you to keep forever, and read for inspiration and edification. I'll ask for only one thing in addition to the whiskey: That if by some chance they are published in a book and you become famous, you will share the profit you gain with my poor dear wife."

Saying this, Biddle hiccupped and withdrew his handkerchief and wept like a poet. After a moment's genteel sniffling, he dried his face and put his handkerchief back. He gazed sorrowfully at Loftus for a while, then inhaled. "Well?" he asked. "Will you do it?"

"You know I can't," Loftus said. "My pa wouldn't like it."

"Why I *know* he wouldn't *like* it!" Biddle muttered. "That's why I have to resort to trying to make a deal with *you!*"

"Nope, I just can't do it."

"There comes a time in every boy's life," Biddle solemnly pointed out, "when he has to go against his pa's wishes. It happened to me, and it'll happen to you, some day, and now is as good a day as any. It's happened to every man born of woman, with the possible exception of the one who died on the cross. Why, I'll bet it even happened to your pa. I'll bet there came a time when he had to go against *his* pa's wishes! That's the way life is, Loftus."

"No dice," Loftus said.

"Don't the Bible say that God made man in His own image?"

Loftus nodded.

"And isn't God the father?"

Loftus nodded again.

"But does God take orders from anybody? Does he?"

"I guess not," Loftus said uneasily.

"So if a man is to be like God, he won't take orders from *Him*, will he?"

"I'm not sure."

"And it's the same thing with your earthly father—to be like him, you have to become independent and do things your own way. Isn't that so?"

"I'm not sure," Loftus said in a low voice, "only I'm not going to bring you any whiskey."

Biddle sat there and thought for a moment. Then he inhaled and thought some more. Next he stood up and looked through the bars of his window. He scratched the back of his neck and thought some more. Loftus watched him, but did not move. Biddle sighed again, then rubbed his hands together, like it was cold.

Finally, he withdrew a gold locket from his pocket and said, "Loftus, I was going to leave this expensive gold locket to my poor dear wife, but you may have it if you acquiesce like a Christian to my dying wishes." Biddle blinked and savored the word, then repeated it. "Yes, if you acquiesce."

"Nope," Loftus said. Only his eyes were caught, and he couldn't take them away from it. "Where'd you get it?" he asked.

"That is a secret. Will you listen if I tell you?"

"Maybe," Loftus said.

"Well," Biddle said, letting his breath out like a man who has climbed up a cliff, "I'll tell you, then. Do you remember the story about Elijah Boggs and how everybody figured he'd taken money from that oilcloth pouch on that poor slave's drowned body?"

"Everybody believed that," Loftus said.

"And everybody was correct. And I'd momentarily forgotten that poor slave's name, which was Hosea. Wasn't that it?"

"Yep."

"Well, do you know what I did? I went to Elijah and told him I knew he'd taken that money out of that poor darky's pouch and kept it for himself and that I knew somebody *who'd seen him do it*, only I told him that I knew a way to keep that somebody quiet. I told him I had something on that critter who'd seen him—a dirty secret. So I knew how to make him keep his mouth shut, only—like I told Elijah—I couldn't figure out how to keep my *own* mouth shut. And do you know what Elijah said?"

"Nope," Loftus told him.

"He said I was a damned liar. He said he didn't believe me worth a damn. He said I was making it all up, which was true, only I didn't like to hear somebody say it. But then I decided to take a chance. Every man has to take a chance now and then, for we're all gamblers at heart, even if we're against gambling."

"What did you do?" Loftus asked him.

"Isn't that a beautiful locket?" Biddle said.

"Sure, it's beautiful, all right."

"And valuable, too. Maybe worth a hundred dollars, do you suppose?"

"Maybe. What was the risk you took?"

"Why, I told Elijah Boggs I could *prove* that I knew somebody who'd seen him take that money out of the dead slave's pouch. But after I said that, I couldn't think of a damned thing. But then, all of a sudden, I did! Since I figured he'd pull up his trot line early in the morning, I said, 'It was early in the morning, wasn't it?'

"Elijah looked at me sharp and said, 'Sure, but that's when you *always* pull up your trot line.'

"Then's when I got an inspiration and took a chance. All of a sudden I recollected something. What's the name of the little steamboat that comes upstream every morning at that time, bringing a load of produce into town?"

"The *Lucy Baines*," Loftus said.

Biddle smiled and nodded. "Yes sir, you're right. And so was I. So I told Elijah Boggs that the critter I was talking about had seen him standing there on the bank with the corpse, waiting for the Lucy Baines to steam on by, before he picked up the oil-skin pouch and dug into it. And you should have seen Elijah's face when I said that. Right away I knew I'd hit the bull's eye."

"Then what happened?" Loftus asked.

"Then he all but come unglued and the next thing I knew, he'd whipped out this locket and told me that it was mine if I promised never to breathe a word, which I did. Later, I wondered how much money he'd gotten from the corpse, but I kept my promise and didn't breathe a word."

"That's some story," Loftus said.

"*Isn't* it though?" Biddle said. "So how about it? Will you see that I am suitably equipped with whiskey before I venture forth into the realm from which none return?"

"Nope," Loftus said.

"Well, I'll be goddamned!" Biddle said.

But that wasn't the end of it. Not by a long shot. After he'd recovered from his disappointment, Biddle said, "If a body keeps an ear open, he will hear a powerful lot."

When he didn't continue, Loftus got so curious that after a moment, he said, "What's that supposed to mean?"

"What it means is," Biddle told him, "I have come upon some information that could change a man's life. It is information that concerns a prodigy of wealth. I have heard an astonishing story, a story about gold beyond the dreams of avarice. Nothing is as it seems, Loftus. Are you aware of that fact, young as you are but wise beyond your years?"

Loftus felt uncomfortable, but he nodded anyway, because he knew it was expected of him. Biddle seemed pleased by the nod.

"And what is true of things and events," he continued, sounding even more mysterious, "is even truer of people. Folks are not what they seem. Nobody. Not you, not me, not your Pa. And not Isaac Dawes. Most of all, not Isaac Dawes."

"What do you know about Isaac Dawes?" Loftus asked, unable to restrain himself.

Biddle smiled, but it was not a happy smile. It was a distant and reflective smile, poised on the brink of a grin. "Various and sundry steamboat passengers and crew," he said slowly, "have reported seeing something odd and out of the ordinary—something they've observed downriver. When steamboats approach a certain bend, human shapes are often seen and then suddenly disappear."

"Ghosts?" Loftus asked wonderingly.

Biddle's grin strengthened a little, then subsided. "No, Loftus. Not ghosts, although some have perceived them as such. But no, not ghosts."

"Well, *what* then?"

Biddle pointed his index finger toward the ceiling. "They are made of as solid flesh as you or I," he said in a voice as solemn as the grave. "But they do not want to be seen. They are usually perceived in rowboats and do not want to be detected doing what they are doing. They do not want to be discovered. Do you know why?"

Wonderingly, Loftus shook his head no.

"Because they are looking for gold, Loftus. A great deal of gold. How do I know, you ask? Because I have been among them. I reckon there are four of us, maybe five. And Isaac Dawes is one of our number, but when the rest of us see him coming, we steal away. Why? Because he is always armed, and in spite of the reputation of his brother, he is a hard case, and a dangerous and ruthless man. Also, it could be argued that the gold in question belongs to Isaac himself."

"What gold?" Loftus asked.

"A cavalryman's valise filled with the damnable stuff, Loftus. I speak of nuggets the size of a babe's head. And that valise and its contents once belonged to Isaac Dawes. I say 'once,' because he threw it overboard one October night several years ago after he'd won too much money at the gambling table and three ruffians were approaching him on the hurricane deck with the evident intent of killing him and taking the valise.

"What happened then, you ask?" Biddle continued, widening his eyes like an actor standing before the gaslights. "Why, calm as a surgeon, Isaac tossed the valise into the water, then stood there grinning at the toughs, showing them his empty hands. It's a wonder they didn't kill him out of spite, but he figured they were the professional sort who ain't likely to do things out of passion or spite, but are motivated solely by practical concerns, and it seems he figured right. I suspect that the other three men I see searching for the money are the very scoundrels who were going to attack him, else why would they be looking there?"

Loftus said, "Why would he scare them away, now, when there are three of them?"

"I've wondered the same thing, but I reckon they knew he wasn't armed on the steamboat, but he's armed now, and anybody can see he's a dangerous man. You can tell with some men by just looking at them, and Isaac is one of those men. I tell you these things admitting that some of the details aren't exactly clear, forcing me to close a gap here and there by judicious figuring."

"Isaac Dawes," Loftus said, shaking his head.

"You can tell he's as tough as the other ones. Everybody can see that. He didn't fool the folks here in Brackenport. No sir!"

"So that's why he came here to live with Nehemiah," Loftus said.

"*My*, but you're wise beyond your years!" Biddle said, shaking his head with wonder and speaking with admiration in his voice.

"And everybody's been speculating upon where he goes when he keeps dropping out of sight."

"And now you know the answer."

"How'd you find out about this?" Loftus asked him.

"Never you mind about that, Loftus. Some secrets we have to carry to the grave. The point is, if you bring me enough whiskey, I'll tell you where that bend in the river is. Providing, that is, you give me your solemn word that you'll share half and half with my poor long-suffering wife."

"Nope," Loftus said. "I can't do it. It just wouldn't be right."

Biddle sat there and looked down at his hands that were clasped between his knees and thought a moment. He was desperate, you could tell. Finally, he played his last card. He said, "Well, what if I say I'll pray for you? Will you bring me the whiskey, then?"

"Nope," Loftus said, "it just wouldn't be right."

"Well, I'll be goddamned!" Biddle muttered, shaking his head as he tried to face up to the fact that he'd have to reconcile himself to a sober destiny.

## CLIMBING THE GALLOWS TREE

On the morning set for the hanging, however, Loftus Gandy was surprised to see that Biddle was staggeringly drunk. Loftus tried to figure out how he'd managed to get the whiskey in spite of everything, but he wasn't successful, so he assumed that this was just another of the world's insoluble mysteries. Of course, being Loftus, he couldn't help being curious. He couldn't help it because he liked mysteries; and yet, he was the kind of boy who preferred reading about mysteries in books rather than having them happen in real life. He was like a lot of people that way.

They didn't have a full-time hangman in Brackenport, because in spite of all the local skullduggery, there still wasn't that much business. So it was it was Loftus Gandy's pa who had to hang the desperadoes. This would have bothered some people, but it didn't bother Levi Gandy, who reckoned he was just helping the criminal along to his inevitable Final Judgment, which is where we're all headed anyway, sooner or later. He also shared the views expressed by Wilmot Chandler, that the fact a man has been judged guilty of committing a capital crime is in itself a pretty good indication that he's a scoundrel and hard case to begin with, and whether he was actually guilty of *that* particular crime or not, he's sure to be guilty of another probably just as bad, or maybe worse. Yes, he reckoned justice is served in that way, rough hew it as you will.

Together with a cousin who was a deputy, Loftus had always assisted his pa at the hangings, which numbered six by the time he was sixteen. Biddle's hanging would be the seventh Loftus had participated in. It sounds easy, but not everybody can do a job like that, for it's an awesome responsibility. Levi Gandy knew this, but his religion was his bulwark. He also looked upon it as being pretty much a family business, and a lot of people would agree that there are worse ways to look at something that you have to do to make a living.

On the morning that Biddle was to be the star performer, Levi was pleased to see a good crowd already gathered before the courthouse. He liked to see a good crowd at a hanging, which he looked upon as the last act of a morality play. He pointed out that there are some lessons that cannot be taught in any other way, or repeated too often. For we are stubborn and wrong-headed and bred into sin, a truth conveyed by just about everything we see around us, except maybe for such things as a mother's love and the sun rising every day.

When it came time for Biddle to speak his last words, he mumbled and sighed and maundered and driveled so much that Levi finally had to tell him to get it over with so that people could get back to their day's work. He pointed out that folks had responsibilities. Biddle listened politely, but then said something about wanting to tell a story, only he couldn't remember what it was. Years later, Loftus remembered this, and liked to point out that he figured this had to be true of everybody—there is something we all feel the need to tell about, but we can't exactly remember what it is.

Finally, Biddle said something about wanting to read a poem he'd written. He said he wanted to share his thoughts with others before stepping over the edge. Then he started patting his coat pockets, only he couldn't find the poem anywhere. Seeing this, Loftus figured he might have traded it for the whiskey he'd gotten, but who would have traded whiskey for poetry? Especially *Biddle's* poetry. It was a sobering thought.

And even if there was somebody who'd do a thing like that, Loftus couldn't figure out who it was, or how the two of them had managed the exchange. But then, maybe it wasn't the poetry at all; maybe Biddle had sold somebody on the story of Isaac Dawes' gold-filled valise.

Whichever it was, Loftus concluded that Biddle must have traded with somebody through the window, either calling down directions when nobody else was around, or dropping the sheaf of poems and then drawing up the whiskey bottle with a long cord of some sort. It must have happened late last evening sometime, but whenever it happened, either the place in the river where the valise had been tossed overboard was known by one more person, or those poems had now been turned loose on the world.

Not being able to find the poem he was looking for, Biddle muttered something about a message he wanted to leave with folks, only he couldn't remember exactly what it was, either. So he just stood there blinking and breathing heavily for a while until it finally came to him. Then he spoke more clearly than he had before, and with a little more dignity, although that still wasn't very much.

What he said was that he deserved to die, and he thanked God that he had this last chance to say it in public. "Yes sir," he said, "I am guilty, if ever a man who stood upon this earth is guilty, I am that man."

Then he thought a moment and said, "Maybe I'm not guilty of the crime I'm a-hanging for, but I'm guilty just the same. My heart has been blackened by sin!"

The tone of his voice was such that the crowd got quiet, and even Levi Gandy paid attention, and you'd think he'd heard it all by now.

But no, there was a new instrument in the orchestra, and Biddle gave it full voice. "We are not what we should be!" he cried, and somebody called out "Amen!"

"We are vermin a-crawling on the ground, and we should be eagles a-soaring in the sky! Do ye hearken, fellow sinners?"

"Oh, yes!" several folks answered.

Now, for the first time, Levi Gandy gazed upon Biddle with respect. He even nodded when Biddle repeated himself. He even nodded again when Biddle said the same thing a third time.

But three times is enough, as every orator knows, so after that, Biddle fell silent. Later, folks said that this might have been his finest moment. Everybody was impressed.

But the time finally came when Levi knelt before him and asked his pardon, in the manner of executioners from the beginning of time. With tears in his eyes, Biddle said he was forgiven, so Levi lifted the black mask and slipped it over the poor man's head.

Then something odd happened. Folks crowded up close to the scaffolding heard it, but those farther back didn't. The mask kept his voice from carrying very far, but those closest heard him distinctly say that there was something else he wanted to confide to the crowd.

That was a mistake. An orator ought to know when to shut up and hold his peace. You could tell that Levi was irritated. Biddle had spoiled everything. Then he made it even worse by crying out that he had something else to say, but Levi's patience had suddenly run out.

"Well," he said, "may the good Lord have mercy on your soul. I guess whatever it is will just have to wait for some other time."

Then he pulled the trap door, and Biddle dropped four feet and his neck cracked like a pistol shot and the crowd sighed and then gave a big cheer. Some people said it was a good hanging, but some of those who'd been up close claimed to be disappointed that Biddle hadn't had a chance to say whatever it was he wanted to say. Maybe he would have remembered a poem to recite, or broken down and cried. Or maybe he would have spoken of his mother and begged forgiveness for his sins before the Throne of Heaven.

Later that evening, Levi told his family that he was also disappointed, somewhat in the manner of those mentioned above. "I like a man's last words to be clear and to the point," he said. "For a moment there, I thought he was going to do it right. I'll confess that I liked one or two things he said. But then he had to ruin it all. A pork chop that's overcooked is almost as bad as one that's undercooked. I wonder who smuggled the whiskey to him."

Saying this, he looked long and hard at Loftus, but he didn't say anything, and neither did Loftus, who just raised his eyebrows.

## ON THE TRAIL OF A CADAVER

Long after Peter Heckenwalder had passed away, his apprentice, Silas Potter, still nourished his great ambition to be a doctor. For a long time he'd contemplated the great changes that he saw all about him. He was a local boy, and Brackenport and the scenery thereabouts, up and downriver for say twenty miles, were pretty much all of the world he knew. He liked to read books, which made him think he was more fitted than most to imagine a world beyond, but whatever that world was, it had to be pretty vague. No doubt it is this way with everybody, to a degree.

One day Silas came up with a plan to get his cadaver and complete his medical training. He went to Judge Stillman Bates and asked for a court order to have a body exhumed. He pointed out that a lot of people didn't approve of how Nehemiah had given that escaped slave the best burial plot in the whole graveyard. He pointed out that freedom was one thing, but a haughty moral pride was another. He pointed out that civilization could not exist except through compromise, not to mention the fact that the townspeople were without a physician now that Dr. Heckenwalder was well-settled in his grave.

Then he explained how all he really needed to complete his education as a doctor was hands-on experience in cutting up a cadaver. He said everybody agreed that this is the only way you can learn anatomy, unpleasant as the thought might be to many. After he acquired that experience, Silas said he was confident that he would be able to minister to the sick as well as anybody on the river, and be as good a doctor as you could find all the way from Marietta to Gallipolis. And the next time there was a murder, he could be sworn in as coroner, so nobody would have to haul a murdered corpse all the way to a place like Athens to have it checked out properly.

"I see what you're after," Judge Bates muttered uneasily, frowning and running his hand through his hair. "You want somebody to dig up Hosea's corpse so you can study it and see how all the parts fit together."

"You don't need to get anybody to dig it up," Silas told him, "I'll do the job myself."

"Surely," Judge Bates cried, "you don't expect me to consent to such a blasphemous act! The temper of the town is against it. The folks all up and down the river would find it abhorrent. I'd never be reelected!"

"I wouldn't ask to dig up anybody if Nehemiah Dawes was still alive and kicking and lecturing to the populace."

"No," Judge Bates muttered, shaking his head, "that would be a prodigious error."

"You do acknowledge the fact that we need a doctor, don't you?"

"I suppose you could argue such, although we've still got one herbalist and one hydropath who seem to be doing all right."

"I'm not talking about quacks, Judge, and you know it!"

"All right, then. And I suppose I'll have to acknowledge the fact, if you want to press the matter. But to give you formal permission to exhume a body just to cut it up and—"

"To cut it up so I can study it and learn how it works so I can learn how to heal people better."

"I know the argument. But why would it have to be a black man? Why not *Nehemiah's* body?"

"Given the way he felt about grave robbers?"

"Yes, but he was also given to self-sacrifice, wasn't he?"

"Are you saying you'd agree to my digging up Nehemiah?"

"Of course not! What a grotesque thought! But . . . but . . . well, what about Biddle?"

"I thought about Biddle, but there are a lot of people around here who'd resent it."

"Because he was hanged as a murderer?"

Silas shook his head. "A lot of people don't believe he was any more guilty of killing Nehemiah Dawes than you are."

Stillman Bates nodded. "I know, I know. I've wondered myself. But never mind that. What's done is done, and what's to be done will be done, only exhuming a grave under my jurisdiction won't be one of them, by God, not if I can help it! Case dismissed."

So that was that, you might have thought, only, Silas wasn't through yet. Not by a long shot. He went to talk with the Reverend Furman T. Willis, and gave him the same arguments he'd given Judge Bates, along with a new one. This time, the debate took a religious turn, especially when Silas concentrated on how he planned to dig up the slave.

"*Ex*-slave," the Reverend Willis corrected him.

"All right, if you want to think of him that way. After it's already done, people aren't going to be all that upset, are they? Not like they would be if it was Nehemiah. Or even Biddle."

"You mean, because the poor fellow happened to be an *African*?"

"Partly because of that and partly because he's occupying Nehemiah's grave."

"It was no longer Nehemiah's grave after he gave it to the poor wretch."

"And partly because he was a stranger. Nobody here really *knew* him, did they?"

"Well, no, of course not."

"Look at it this way," Silas Potter said, "it's just plain damned impossible for me to practice medicine without studying anatomy, and I can't study anatomy without a cadaver to examine. Now, without a doctor here, more people are going to die than if there is one."

The Reverend Willis got a severe look on his face. "Such profane reasoning is not always to be trusted, Silas."

"I'd say what you call profane reasoning is all we have, but then you'd probably counter by saying we have Scripture as well."

"I would."

"Only then I'd say that God gave us brains for a reason, and we have reasoning to take it as far as it can, and it isn't until *then* that we have to rely on faith."

"I don't see how I could agree to such a thing as you're asking."

"Let me tell you something: I watched you when they lowered that slave's coffin into the ground, and it was my impression that you didn't entirely agree with what Nehemiah did."

"Burying that poor slave there? Of course not. But not because he was a *slave*! Oh, no. It was because Nehemiah was so proud and making so much out of what he'd done. *That's* what I didn't approve of. To a Christian the place of burial is as nothing."

"I don't think Nehemiah was a good man."

The Reverend Willis took a quick suspicious glance at Silas, then looked down at his clasped hands. "Of course we don't have the right to judge another, and yet . . . well, let me put it this way: I know how somebody could say a thing like that."

"Do you realize I don't even know how blood is filtered into the spleen?"

Willis sighed and slapped both of his knees with his hands. "You know I can't give permission for you to dig up that body. I can't figure out why you're asking me in the first place, because it's not mine to give, and you know it. You should go talk to Judge Bates."

"I did, and it didn't do any good."

"So now you come to me."

Silas explained. "Well, I figured if I couldn't do it legally, I ought to have some kind of *moral* sanction, at least. I'm not sure I could do it without either one. I reckon a good man might do something illegal, but he'd never do something immoral, if he could help it."

The Reverend Willis considered that. Then he said, "Does that mean that if Judge Bates had given his permission, you wouldn't have bothered coming to me?"

"I might not have bothered."

"Then how do you explain that?"

"Well, I'm not sure I'm a good man."

This was a confession that pleased Thurman Willis so much he came near to smiling. But he managed to hold it back and look grave, which is how everybody expected him to look. Finally, he dusted his hands together and sighed. Then he said, "Well, Silas, I will admit this much: We do need a doctor, and I don't suppose there's any way I could express my disapproval, God help me, if some dark night somebody took a lantern up there and dug up one of those graves. You can see that spot from anywhere along the river, but I don't think you can see it from anywhere in town."

"I don't think you can, either," Silas said. "As a matter of fact, I've already looked. So I guess that's the only way it can be done."

"Only way *what* can be done?" Willis said.

"Oh, nothing," Silas said. "And I thank you for that, too!"

## DEEP AND NOT EASY

After his brother's death, the great change that came over Isaac Dawes was so great that nobody could miss it, partly because Isaac himself talked about it so much. It was a subject he couldn't leave alone. "I've seen the error of my ways and have repented," he told all who would listen. "I've become a new man and will never look back." He became religious and stopped drinking. He became a fanatic upon the subject of his transformation, and soon grew to be as tiresome as his brother. He became as obsessed with his spiritual conversion as Nehemiah was with slavery and grave robbing, causing some folks to wonder if maybe there was something in the Dawes' blood that caused the brothers to become fixed upon a certain topic and then worry it to death. Not to mention those around them who were forced to share in the suffering.

Some folks claimed that Isaac's transformation had been caused by the solemnity of the occasion of his brother's funeral; others, of a more cynical turn of mind, said it was because he no longer had anybody to support him. Still others, however, said that the great change that had come over Isaac Dawes was caused by reading his brother's private diary, which Agatha Tremblow came upon when she was rummaging in the attic one cold November day. She read a few pages, and was taken aback. The diary entries struck her as strange, and she was a little bit disturbed by them. She stood there and thought a moment, and then decided that since Isaac happened to be sober, this would be a good time to bring it downstairs and see what he thought of it.

"I didn't even know Nehemiah *kept* a diary!" was the first thing Isaac said.

"Not many did," Agatha said. "Your brother was a deep man. Not many understood him. He was deep, and his life was not easy."

Right then Isaac pulled a chair up next to the fireplace and sat down and began to read it carefully. When he read the previous year's entry of January 11, he almost cried out in recognition. Indeed, this might have been the entry that sparked his conversion from a ne'er-do-well into a sober and reflective Christian. It read as follows:

Do not dwell upon the Past; do not dwell upon what you have been up until this very moment, for in the Past, we find no room for Hope.

Isaac was stunned by the words. He whispered: "It's true! It's true!" And yet, if the living Nehemiah had spoken the same words to him, they would have meant nothing to Isaac. He wouldn't have listened. He would have ignored them; they would have flown past his head with no more effect than a gust of air in a cold room. But there, in the warmth of his dead brother's handwriting, those words took on eloquence. Isaac could almost hear the words spoken as he read, even though the actual hearing of them would have erased them from the reality of the moment.

Isaac leafed through the diary, stopping here and there to contemplate what was said. One entry was: "We must seek to redress the horrors without in order to silence those within." What could that mean? What horrors had his brother ever witnessed? How could a man so cold with righteousness have written such a sentence as that?

The entry for March 19 said: "Spring is coming, but what hope can it bring when I will always abide in this town, this building, this heart? Prisons, all."

For the next few days, Isaac kept the diary with him constantly, occasionally pulling it out of his pocket as if to consult it, the way a traveler does a map. There was something in it he could not resist, like the fascination of a guilty secret.

He even carried it to church that Sunday. Folks were surprised to see him, and even more surprised when he waved it at the preacher during the sermon. "Why's he waving that little book around?" somebody whispered, and somebody else whispered, "Who knows? Probably drunk."

But he wasn't drunk and he couldn't help himself.

After the service, he stood outside and stopped people, muttering, "It's Nehemiah. It's Nehemiah. He's in here and he's still alive! Nobody understood the truth of what my brother was, and I was the worst of all in my error!"

That night Isaac read this entry for May 7: "Every morning I awaken with the thought of death, but in the evening I find that I have proved too small to die." What on earth could *that* mean? Isaac pondered upon it, but it got him nowhere, and his thoughts ended as confused as they began.

Or this, for February 11: "Pigs never look up at the sky. They're like people in this regard, who never look upward within." "How could you look upward *within*?" Isaac asked himself. It was easy to understand—*in a way*—only that way was somehow not enough.

Or this, for June 20: "Today I counted seven people who wish me dead. They must see more than I can bear to look at. Saying that makes me the eighth."

Or this, for July 2: "Last night in my dream I saw the Devil and it was so much like looking into a mirror that I cried out and was awakened."

After coming upon this passage, Isaac stopped folks on the street and read it to them and then said, "And do you suppose the Devil can't put on *your* appearance? And *mine*?"

Folks didn't know how to answer that, and would walk away shaking their heads, figuring he might be sober now, but spirituous liquors had obviously permanently damaged his brain and the poor fellow would never be quite right in the head.

## THE APPEARANCE OF THE HEIRS APPARENT

But they were wrong. That wasn't how it was at all. Isaac's brain was as good as ever—in some ways, maybe even better. After that first shock he'd experienced in opening his dead brother's diary, he got quiet. Then he became preoccupied, even studious. He likened his awakening to that of Saul on the Road to Damascus. Instead of leaving town to take long walks along the riverbanks downstream, he concentrated all his energy on keeping his dead brother's business enterprises alive and kicking, figuring that they were somehow mysteriously connected with the terrible profundities hidden in the darkness of Nehemiah's soul, as revealed in his diary.

When he'd realized that there was nobody else to take over, Isaac had made up his mind to do it himself. None of Nehemiah's grown children lived nearby, and they had shown little interest in his business concerns, being involved in their own affairs. Isaac's decisive manner and resolve impressed everybody. His suddenly commanding presence was an astonishment to all who knew him. Nobody questioned him when he called a meeting of Nehemiah's employees and told them of his decision, and after he did so, he made his way directly to Nehemiah's desk, and nobody said a word as they watched him in silence. You might have thought Isaac had just been waiting for an opportunity like this so he could show the stuff he was made of.

All the clerks and workers in the Dawes Block fell into line like soldiers in the midst of battle after their commander has been killed and the next in command takes over. Yes, Isaac Dawes was assuredly a changed man, a man who spent his days studying the various enterprises his brother had had a hand in, and his evenings studying the Bible, along with other books of an edifying nature.

Nehemiah's two living sons and three daughters all returned to Brackenport on November 20 for the reading of the will. They were scheduled to gather at 9:00 a.m. in the office of Squire Tucker. You would think that Squire Tucker's office is where the drama I am about to speak of would take place, but you would be wrong, for it had happened the evening before, when their Uncle Isaac addressed Nehemiah's surviving sons and daughters in the grand parlor that had once been their father's. This parlor was uncommonly large and it was always kept dark for Sunday company and other solemn occasions. In it there were an Empire sofa made of rosewood and six walnut chairs, four of them upholstered. Next to the large window stood a Johannes Bauer grand piano—shipped there from Germany by way of Cincinnati. Nobody could ever remember anyone playing it, but it looked nice, having a richly woven tapestry draped over it in folds.

Isaac had had Lizzie deliver messages to all of them, asking them to convene in the parlor after supper, which featured baked ham, fried catfish, raw oysters, stewed carrots, succotash, green beans with pork, roast turkey with blackberry sauce, and peach and apple pie covered with slabs of cheddar cheese. He could have asked them all over the supper table, but he was capable of an ornate penmanship, and he figured that having fancy messages delivered to their individual rooms would add a note of solemnity to the occasion.

The sons and daughters all complied, and arrived in the parlor long before Isaac showed up, so they had to sit there and wait. Right away, they were suspicious; they couldn't help it. One of the daughters said, "He's going to try to dig his spoon into the casserole, but I don't think we should let him." Another daughter nodded, and then one of the sons picked up the beat and nodded, too.

After that, the five of them just sat there quietly for a while, until finally one of the sons said, "I reckon there'll be a scene trying to pry the old sinner's carcass out of here." The other son nodded and said, "Yep, he's settled in here like a hog wallowing in molasses; but by tarnation, *we'll* dig him out!" They all nodded and thought about that, and then just sat there and thought some more.

But after awhile, one of the daughters took a deep breath and said, "Only, they do say he's changed, though."

One of her brothers snorted, "Some change!"

But she stuck to her guns. "No, from what they say, he's a whole lot more genteel now than he was before."

"I'd hate to see how he was before," her brother said, and the other brother snickered.

But their sister didn't. She shook her head and said, "No, sir, I've talked with folks, and they say the difference is truly remarkable."

The other brother said, "Maybe so, but he still looks like a devil to me, with his brown skin and mangled features. He doesn't strike me as the kind of critter any proper gentleman would appreciate having to call a relative."

They fell silent after that, retiring into the privacy of their own thoughts. One of the brothers got impatient and sighed. Then he said he wondered what was taking their Uncle Isaac so blamed long. Nobody had an answer to that, so they just sat and thought some more. They had to wait so long that they began to wonder if maybe he'd played a joke on them.

Then they began to smell a strategy behind so much waiting, and tried to figure out what it could be.

But finally he showed up. And in spite of what they had said, he really did seem to be a changed man. It was true that a change had come over him ever since he'd discovered Nehemiah's diary. That diary had made the world seem different to him, and when the world seems different to you, that makes *you* different, too.

Isaac was close-shaved and wore clean linen. His hair was plastered flat with macassar oil and he smelled like a funeral. His eyes were clear; they hadn't been bloodshot since he'd first opened the pages of his brother's diary. His manner was quiet and polite. Everything was nearly perfect, except for his broken nose and twisted mouth and his hide permanently tanned as dark as a polished cabinet, from too long an exposure to harsh sunlight when he was a miner out west.

Still, his demeanor was impressive, and his voice was calm, well-modulated, polite, and judicious. His words were well-chosen. His figures of speech were startling, at first, but after they sank in, they were inspiring—a little like poetry, one of Nehemiah's sons said afterwards, and his sisters nodded, every one of them. Then, after his brother thought about it, he nodded, too.

What Isaac told them in his quiet voice was that in the long run it would be for their benefit to have him take over every one of their dead father's businesses. He said he had studied them and learned them from the ground up. He said he didn't want to blow his own horn, but he understood those affairs of business better than anybody around.

One of his nephews challenged him when he said this and asked him some questions, but Isaac answered every one of them, and his answers were sharp, clear, and accurate. Gradually, the sons and daughters all became impressed; they couldn't help it. They didn't say anything, but it was obvious. The other son asked him another question about the business, and Isaac answered it just as well. Then one of the daughters asked him something, with the same result. After all of this had transpired, they began looking at their uncle differently. He was a stranger, all right, but they were beginning to think that maybe they could see a little of their poor dead pa in his expression and mannerisms, and maybe they could, at that.

Once Isaac had brought them along that far, he changed his tactics a little. He confessed to them that he had not always been a good man or a good brother. He confessed that he had been a wastrel, but now he had seen the errors of his ways. He confessed that he had thrown away most of his life, but he was now a changed man. He had lived to regret it. He confessed that he had drunk and gambled his youth away, and had been guilty of things that would hardly bear repeating here, among his kinfolk; he told them that he had shot and killed a man in a California mining camp.

But all of that was before he had gazed upon the pages of their pa's diary. "I'll have to admit," he said, "that nothing has ever had such an effect on me. It has changed my life." After saying this, he repeated it several times, tuning in small variations upon the theme with each repetition, and then surprising everybody by asking that they join him in prayer. They didn't have the heart to say no, so they all bowed their heads.

After he'd finished and they'd all said Amen, he changed tacks again. He pointed out that according to the will they could liquidate their pa's businesses, if that's what they wanted. If they did, they would receive money right away, of course, but *then* what? He asked them what they would do with that money. He said he supposed they'd invest it, but how? And then what? He said they could invest it in railroad stock or in land or in dry goods or corn and wheat, but every one of those options had a gamble in it.

So he said, why not simply keep their pa's holdings intact, since they had *proved* to be good and profitable, right here in Brackenport where they had grown up and learned their letters and first understood what it is to be a human being, not to mention a Christian? In short, why not let their money remain invested in their pa's business and let it continue to flourish? Right about here is where Isaac brought out sheets of paper containing the recent records of their pa's enterprises, and passed them around for all to look at.

"There's no more profitable business you can invest in," he told them, "and I won't mince words by pretending to be modest, because I am not so afflicted; and I'll tell you that there's nobody who can run the business better than I can—your own uncle, your own blood relative, your own dear pa's only surviving brother!"

He went on and on like this, and finally one of the sons said, "What the hell, I vote we go along with him."

His brother and one of his sisters nodded, but another sister said, "No, I think we should go to Squire Tucker and ask him what he thinks."

"I think that's a good idea," Isaac said, which impressed everybody in the room.

So that's what they decided, and when Squire Tucker looked at the accounts and Isaac's prospectus, he said they'd be fools to let an opportunity like this pass by. He said that if shares were ever issued, he wouldn't mind investing in some himself. After he talked to them for an hour, Nehemiah's sons and daughters were sold on the idea, so he drew up papers right away.

And that's how Mr. Isaac Dawes became president of the Dawes Production and Distribution Company, Brackenport, Ohio.

# Book Two

## THE SOURCE OF BAD DREAMS

The Civil War came and it went, with many of the boys from Brackenport and the vicinity shedding their life blood for the Union, although truth to tell, more were carried off by measles and the flux than died of gunshot wounds. Yes, it was a morbid looseness of the bowels that did most of them in, which is not bloodshed, as it is usually defined, but something entirely different. Still, the body needs all its vital fluids, and such niggling distinctions are no more than a trifle when the roll is called up yonder, or after enough time has passed by, because you're as dead from one as you are from the other.

The dark shadow of the Confederacy was never far away from Brackenport in those years. You could see it in that part of old Virginia across the Ohio River, before it became the state of West Virginia, and folks often stared and wondered at how great a division a river can be. Yes, the Confederacy often loomed over their thoughts, and with John Morgan's raid, it descended like the darkness of night upon the Ohio shore. It was then that the war came knocking on their door, you might say, and loud enough that the summons could be heard all the way from Steubenville to Cincinnati. Everybody knows the story of how Morgan and his men invaded southern Ohio, biting off more than they could chew, as it turned out, because the local boys chopped down trees and bushwhacked the invaders up and down every road and path, wherever they could.

Their invasion was a taste of our own medicine, as the Rebels thought of it. You could almost hear them saying that *now*, by God, we knew what it was like to be invaded by an army! Whatever the issue of that argument, everybody knows the story of how the forces of Judah and Hobson finally gathered and closed in on Morgan, capturing or destroying most of his force at the battle of Buffington's Island, which is not many miles upriver from Brackenport.

Morgan was a great man, in his way. And you couldn't find anybody who didn't agree that he had a courage and resolve worthy of a nobler cause. But the rascal was eventually caught and hamstrung and imprisoned in the Ohio Penitentiary in Columbus, where he wasn't penitent very long, because he kicked up his damned heels and escaped and was once more as free as a bird.

For all those years, and afterwards, Silas Potter was the only doctor in town, unless you count the herbalist and hydropath, which most sensible folks did not. During that time, Silas was also becoming more prosperous and influential. Maybe he'd never be as prosperous and influential as Nehemiah Dawes had been, but then whoever could attain to such heights? And who would expect as much? But Silas prospered about as much as a wise man should ever want or need to, because money is never an unmixed blessing. More often than not, it turns out to be half curse.

Silas got married in 1864 to Victoria Wickstrom, a sweet-faced woman with her left leg slightly shorter than her right, so that she walked leaning over a little, as if listening to something down below that nobody else could hear. She was superstitious and had such an irrational fear of Wednesdays that she often referred to them as either Tuesdays or Thursdays, which added a certain interest to the weeks, not to mention confusion. But Silas didn't mind a great deal, because he loved her even more than he did the practice of medicine;

nevertheless, these two loves were near-enough in his affections that when one became tiresome, he could always turn to the other.

Everybody agreed that Silas was overworked, but then he was joined by a young doctor named Caleb Eckert, who came directly from the fleshpots of Cincinnati, where he had completed the prescribed course in medicine, carving up a score of cadavers, it was claimed, without ever once breaking into song. Young Eckert had three facial moles and was a freethinker. He had pale hair and a round face covered with freckles, along with the moles, and a loud tenor voice, which he exercised every Sunday in the church choir. He was a Methodist as well as a freethinker, which is not all that strange a combination, when you think about it. Some say it's as easy for a Methodist to be a freethinker as it is for a dog to scratch fleas. But like a lot of things, it depends pretty much upon your definitions.

Things seemed to be turning out pretty well for Silas, except for the fact that along about the time when Caleb Eckert appeared on the scene, he was beginning to be troubled by bad dreams. Actually, those bad dreams didn't just start with Caleb Eckert's coming to town; off and on they'd troubled Silas for years, only now they picked up tempo and began tormenting him in earnest. Before Caleb came, Silas had been too busy to brood over them long enough for them to make him uncomfortable, let alone miserable. That's the way it is with busy people, and that's why they tend to be happier than the other kind.

But once Caleb Eckert started taking over some of his practice and lifting some of the load from his shoulders, Silas began to relax, and it was then that his chronic fever stepped up its pace, and with it the horror of an old memory came back and kept him from sleeping. When he did sleep, it would torment him—disguised as this and that, the way it is with dreams. Some people say that if ghosts exist anywhere, it's inside our dreams, and maybe they're right.

That's how it was with some of the soldier boys after they came back from serving in the OVI regiments in the Civil War. While they were fighting and rifle balls were flying and cannon shells were bursting their eardrums and they were climbing over stinking, bloody corpses all mussed and twisted in their clothes, they hardly had time to be scared. But after the war was over and they came home, the things they'd seen began to open up while they were asleep, the way nocturnal flowers open up and bloom at night. Yes, there's no place like sleep for that darkness in which ghosts find their true dwelling place. It was like this with Silas Potter, only it wasn't the horrors of battle that came to haunt him, or even all the cadavers he'd sliced into—it was only the first one, done in a spirit of crime. It was the memory of digging up the grave of that poor slave at two in the morning, and lifting out the stinking body and wheeling it away in a wheelbarrow in the black of night and taking it almost two miles to the shed in back of his house, hoping every step of the way that nobody would see him. He made it all right, even though it was so dark that the wheelbarrow almost turned over a couple of times from the holes and ruts in the road, so that Silas had to keep his cussing down to a whisper, which made it even harder, because it was a pretty heavy body and the wheelbarrow was rickety, having been discarded by a stone mason named Amos Purefoy because it wobbled too much for hauling stones.

Silas could remember lifting that corrupt and stinking body up onto a table made of pine boards laid over two carpenter's horses in his shed in back, and placing a lantern up next to it and dousing the putrid corpse with alcohol and then starting to work, cutting down into the fetid flesh, determined to see what things looked like inside, instead of how they were supposed to look according to the crude woodcuts and marbled prose of Dr. Heckenwalder's old anatomy textbook.

Silas's bad dreams didn't have to do with just any kind of bodily corruption, such being common enough and part of a doctor's daily experience; it had to do with guilt at the memory of how he'd learned his anatomy by stealth. And how it was the body of a poor slave that had instructed him in the art of anatomy. Illegally digging up a corpse all alone at night, and doing it by stealth, isn't like digging one up by day while surrounded by friends and fellow workers. Silas knew this, and reminded himself that there had been idealism in his motive. It wasn't like digging up a woman's corpse to steal its diamond ring, the way common grave robbers liked to do it, if they weren't medical students.

And yet, how were those motives different, after all? Didn't Silas intend to *make money* as a doctor? Didn't he intend to become wealthy and influential? And was it right and ethical to dig up the corpse of a poor slave who'd yearned for freedom, only to be killed—who instead of finding freedom, found the grave? And then cut into his body so as to gaze for the first time, by the flickering light of a coal oil lantern, upon the liver, spleen, and vermiform appendix? And stand there for a moment contemplating the fact that this man was just barely a man at all, but more a boy, maybe no more than fifteen or sixteen? But never mind how young or old he was, for the question remains the same: can the end *ever* justify the means?

Sensible people know that this kind of questioning gets you nowhere, which is exactly where it got Silas. But then, nobody's sensible all the time, especially when they're dreaming or in the kind of thoughtful mood where you wonder about the mystery of what we're doing on this earth. Two-month-old puppies chase their own tails; we don't have tails to chase, so we ask imponderable questions.

There were two things that made his dreams such a torment. One was how he was sickly in those days. He couldn't seem to recover completely from his malaria, no matter what he took for it. Quinine seemed to bounce off it the way a floating tree limb bounces off the hull of a steamboat. Everybody knows how a fever can stoke nightmares, and being a physician, Silas knew it better than most, only knowing it didn't help a whole lot.

The other thing that turned his dreams sour was the way Silas remembered how he'd actually been a little disappointed when he'd carved up that poor boy's corpse. He didn't learn as much as he'd expected. He found it was all pretty much familiar territory, which meant that Dr. Heckenwalder's grubby old anatomy textbooks hadn't been so far off, after all.

Nope, as it turned out, it hadn't really been worth it. The only thing he had learned was how much a rotten corpse could stink, even after all that time.

# CAPTAIN BILLY JONES AND THE J. P. RICKETTS

At about this time a local steamboat captain named Billy Jones entered the picture. Captain Billy regularly hauled sand and gravel up the Kanawha River to Charleston in his sternwheeler packet, the *J. P. Ricketts*, which had a wood hull, and was one hundred and nine feet long, with a nineteen-foot beam and a five-foot draft. The *Ricketts* didn't handle very well; she had a morbid and neurasthenic inclination to drift to the starboard and nudge into shore away from the channel, like some critter with a notion to go home by an overland route. But in spite of her shortcomings, she was rugged and dependable.

So was Billy Jones, who was a chunky old man with a sharp nose and filmy white hair that floated around his head like a halo. Maybe he didn't exactly deserve a halo, but he was a square shooter, with a wide streak of decency. He smoked a pipe and enjoyed reciting poetry whenever the opportunity arose, or even when it didn't. He also had a habit of referring to himself in the third person, so that strangers who happened to overhear him might suppose he was talking about somebody else. But he wasn't. The local boys tried to make fun of him and imitate his ways, but it didn't work, because Captain Billy didn't have any idea of what they were trying to do. He was like most of us and couldn't hear himself the way others heard him—he was no more aware of the way he sounded than a crawdad broods over the question of free will.

Captain Billy had once suffered from lumbago and rheumatism of the joints, and he'd gone to Silas Potter for relief, whereupon his suffering was considerably eased. Afterwards, he was grateful to Silas, partly because he was a Mason, which is also what Captain Billy was. Captain Billy was the only son of a Methodist circuit rider who had never taken a stand against liquor. Captain Billy hadn't, either, and now he liked to drink an occasional glass of Monongahela Rye with Silas, whose occasions were not all that occasional, as people liked to say when they were in a mood to criticize a doctor.

One such time was an early evening in March, and the two of them were sitting in the Major Enslow Tavern, situated on a high bank above the Ohio, where you could see half a mile downriver, and almost two miles up. They were drinking a hot punch made from a whiskey recently imported from a Morgan County still, and feeling mellow and comfortable. There was a hot coal fire roaring and snapping like popcorn in the stove. It was a cold and blustery day, and the wind was blowing white caps on the water out in the channel, which they could see through the tavern's leaded glass windows.

Captain Billy was talking about how much Silas had helped his lumbago, and how he wanted to make it up to him in some way.

"You don't owe me a thing," Silas told him. "You pay your bills, and that's good enough for me. Especially considering the size of the population hereabouts who do not."

"That's not enough when you've suffered the way old Captain Billy suffered," Captain Billy said. "Captain Billy will not have anyone classify him among those about whom the poet Wordsworth wrote: 'Alas, the gratitude of men hath left me mourning.'"

"Forget it. Quinine and iodide of potassium is all I prescribed. Any doctor would have done as much."

But Captain Billy wasn't listening. "Captain Billy always pays his debts," he stated, his internal fires whipped by the winds of gratitude.

"Dammit, Billy, you're not listening: so far as I'm concerned, you don't *have* any debts!"

"That's not exactly what Captain Billy was talking about, Doc. No favors for Captain Billy, unless it's a quid for a quo. Fair trade is fair trade, in his language, even if it's something different. A nickel is worth half a dime, or a penny five times over. As for suffering from lumbago, it's something I never *did* like to take lying down." Saying this, Captain Billy thought a moment, then laughed halfway into his pipe, hard enough to make it puff a cloud of smoke toward the ceiling. The old man was feeling pretty good, you could tell. And he appreciated the fact, which was what he was trying to convey to his friend, Silas.

Silas quietly considered all this for a moment. Finally, he drew a wet circle on the oak tabletop with his index finger. Then he took a deep breath, after which he cleared his throat and said, "Well, maybe there *is* something you could do, if you insist upon it."

"Name it," Captain Billy told him.

"It's not really important. It's just this old business I think about every now and then."

"Name it," Captain Billy repeated.

Silas inhaled and then breathed out. "For some reason or other, I've often wondered about that escaped slave Nehemiah had buried in his own grave plot."

"You're wondering about Hosea? What about him?"

"Oh, nothing special. I've just always been sort of curious about him. That's all. You know, I just wonder what he was like, what sort of critter he was . . . things like that. It's just the kind of thing a body wonders about, now and then."

"Well, Captain Billy can tell you this much: that poor boy's mother is still alive and living in Charleston."

"Hosea's *mother*?" Silas asked.

Captain Billy nodded. "Everybody knows about her. Her name is Sarah. She's living with a daughter named Padgette, along with her Bible and a little dog about the size of a Norway rat. His name's Poke. And when she isn't patting her Bible, she's patting Poke."

"I assume she was one of Lysander Crenshaw's slaves."

"A slave in more ways than one."

"Do you mean what I *think* you mean?"

Captain Billy paused, gathered his memory together, raised his index finger, and quoted in his preacher's voice:

I would not have a slave to till my ground, To carry me, to fan me while I sleep, . . . And tremble when I wake. . . .

"For God's sake," Silas interrupted, stretching out both of his arms, like a man embracing the air. "Don't start in spouting your poetry, or you'll never get to the main course! What do you mean, she was a slave in more ways than one?"

"She goes by the name of Sarah Crenshaw. She took her old master's name."

"So what? That's what most of them did."

"Sure. Only sometimes Captain Billy tries to visualize how slender she must have been when she was young, and how pretty. But, oh, how the years exact their toll upon our mortal flesh!"

You could almost see him grope for a quotation; but it was no good, and his net came up empty.

"You talk like you know her."

"I do. She washes Captain Billy's laundry when he does his Charleston run. She must have been mighty pretty years ago! And it appears the stories Captain Billy heard turned out to be true. In fact, she as much as admits it herself."

"Admits *what*, dammit?"

"Don't pretend that you don't know what Captain Billy's saying: Lysander Crenshaw was the boy's father. That old sinner was Hosea's pa."

For a long while, the two men sat in silence and stared out the window. Finally, Captain Billy said, "Not only that, this Lysander Crenshaw sired another son in the dark soil of her living flesh. That one's still walking the earth, living somewhere in Charleston, the last I heard."

"So when Lysander Crenshaw set his bounty hunters loose to fetch Hosea and bring him back, he didn't just want to retrieve an escaped slave he looked upon as his *property* . . . he was trying to get *his son* back."

"That's how you have to look at it," Captain Billy said, puffing on his pipe. "Although it's hard to think of it in those terms. Captain Billy can't imagine how Lysander would think of Hosea as a *son*, exactly."

"Why not? That's what he was!"

"Yes, but not in the way you and Captain Billy think of our sons."

Silas shook his head. "No, I don't suppose it's the same. But Lysander would surely *know*, wouldn't he? And if he *knew*, it couldn't be the same as if that young buck was just another whelp living back there in the slave cabins."

"No, I guess it wouldn't be like that, either. And Captain Billy agrees that it's all mighty curious. You have to wonder how Hosea thought about it!"

"Maybe he didn't think *anything* about it. It's been my observation that not many people go around doing any *thinking at all*."

"Could be. Nobody seems to remember much about the boy, anyway.  Not even his mother. She just says he was a wild one and liked to kick up his heels and snort."

"The boy would have had to know, too, wouldn't he? And that would have made a difference."

"Oh, I don't know. There are a lot of people who would never bother their heads with a question like that."

"But he did escape, after all. And he did cross the river, at least. That's more than most of them managed to do."

Captain Billy nodded and frowned over his pipe. "Maybe he did escape, and then again, maybe he didn't."

"What are you talking about?"

Captain Billy shook his head. "Oh, I don't know. Sarah isn't so sure about that part, but she has her ideas."

"What are you talking about? Everybody *knows* he escaped! How do you think he got *killed*?"

"We know he got away," Captain Billy said, "but we don't know he *escaped*. We don't know *how* he got away. Or why."

"I see what you mean. But I still figure there's only one way. And one reason."

No, there are two ways to do it: you can wiggle under the fence like a fox getting away from the dogs, or you can just walk off the plantation some night with your pocket clanking with gold and silver coins that your Pa gave to you."

"Well, I'll be damned!" Silas whispered. "They did say some money was found on the corpse when it washed ashore."

"And that clever scoundrel Elijah Boggs squashed the rumor right away by saying that a story like that insulted the dead fellow, since he was a darky, and the only way he could have gotten the money was by stealing it, so if people went around repeating their suspicion, folks would naturally think they were damned copperheads and thought of all Africans as thieves."

Silas rubbed his hand over his eyes. "But now we know of another way a slave could get that much money."

"Amen," Captain Billy said.

"So she thinks Lysander Crenshaw gave her boy money so he could escape!"

"That boy was his boy too, don't forget."

"But if he did something like that, why would he set his damned bloodhounds on him?"

"Captain Billy asked her that, too, but Sarah says she'll never understand the ways of men, let alone white folks."

"But after all this time she'd have *some* notion about why Lysander would sic his men on his own son, after he'd given him money to escape."

"No, Sarah says it didn't happen like that. She says there was no way Hosea's escape could be kept secret, and as soon as the overseer got wind of him taking off like that, he fired the starting gun, in a manner of speaking, and they right away set their dogs loose on him before Lysander Crenshaw could stop them. Supposing he had a mind to stop them."

"What are you talking about? How can you figure he'd have a *mind* to after he'd given the boy money so he could skedaddle?"

"Those bounty hunters weren't just hired by Lysander Crenshaw alone. All those Kanawha planters banded together and hired men to go and get any slave who escaped. So when Hosea took off, the machinery was already running and nobody could have stopped it. And by the time the bounty hunters had been set loose, Lysander had to keep his mouth shut, because they were all in it together, those planters, so as to protect what they looked upon as their *property*!"

"Human property is the devil's invention, if there ever was one!"

"You know that, and Captain Billy knows that, but history tells us that slavery has been with us from the beginning of recorded time."

"Like every other kind of evil."

"Amen."

"So she thinks Lysander gave Hosea the money so he could escape."

"Well," Captain Billy said, "she does and she doesn't. She hardly knows *what* to think. But it's plausible, ain't it? That boy was his own son, after all, no matter how ill-begot. And nobody's ever explained how that oilskin wallet he was carrying got filled up with all those gold and silver coins."

"Somehow you don't talk as if you're so sure, Billy."

"Well, Sarah says that Lysander had a lot of gambling debts. She reckons the plantation must have been in pretty bad shape."

"You mean, she doesn't think Lysander had enough money for giving some to the boy?"

"She had no way of knowing something like that, but she reckons he must have had some pocket change, at least. Maybe enough to get the boy as far as Lysander's brother, who's a doctor in Lancaster, and then he'd be on his own."

"Very curious," Silas muttered.

Captain Billy nodded. "But there's also something else. Captain Billy reckons that if she couldn't be sure that Lysander had given him the money, how'd she know the rest of it, unless Lysander came right out and told her? Or Hosea, as the case may be. But she claimed they didn't."

"Oh, I think there'd be other ways of figuring it out, or at least coming up with a theory about it. Living alone like that, she could spend a lot of time going over the past."

"Maybe, but that would hardly make what she came up with true."

"No. But do you know something? You've got Captain Billy interested in this business."

Silas said, "I was just kind of curious, is all."

But Captain Billy was only half-listening and said, "It's curious, all right."

Silas shook his head. He couldn't help but wonder how big a can of worms he'd opened by saying anything to a good-natured old windbag like Captain Billy Jones.

# THE GHOST

That night, after supper, Silas was feeling malarial, but he knew he had to go visit a nine-year-old boy with scarlatina. This was Charlie Fitch's boy, Ben. They lived on the road that goes upriver to Long Bottom. So after his second toothpick, and after he'd loaded and primed his horse pistol, which he always carried in case he should run into trouble, Silas stuffed his silver flask into his leather bag, harnessed up Bessie, his little mare, and they went trotting off into the moonlight, headed out of town on the River Road.

By the time he arrived at the Fitch house, the boy was dead and all of the family were sitting around praying and crying. Even Charlie, who never went to church, was weeping copiously, with his empty boots lying on the floor beside his feet. The house was too warm, and it smelled of fever and catfish fried in lard, which they'd had for dinner. One reason Charlie was so distraught was that little Ben was the second son he'd lost to sickness, and still another one had been drowned. Not to mention a pretty little daughter named Josephine, who'd died of the flux. Charlie Fitch was born to be unlucky, and he was smart enough to know it, which made it all worse.

The atmosphere in that little house was miserable, and by the time Silas wrote out the death certificate and expressed his condolences to the family and got outside, he was ready for a drink of brandy from his flask, just to make the human condition seem tolerable. When he untied Bessie and climbed into his buggy, he was thinking what a beautiful world it could be at times. Like now, for instance, with the moonlight flooding the wagon path ahead, where it led to the Long Bottom Road, and the dark moon shadows, deep as ponds under the trees . . . and here was the corpse of that poor innocent little boy inside the house. Such a beautiful world without, but how cruel within!

And what if the others in that family were infected? And what if *he* was infected, too, and brought the contamination back to Victoria and their own children? This would have been an especially frightening prospect for her, given the fact that this was a Wednesday. Still, he'd done what he could, and that's all you can hope for. Treating the damned thing with carbonized oil and soda baths and quarantine could only do so much, but they were all you had against something like scarlatina. And what good was quarantine, anyway, if you were a doctor and had to break the seal every time you got near enough to treat the patient? And were further weakened by a case of malaria that hung on like Original Sin?

It's no wonder that such thoughts drove Silas to his silver flask, which was as handsome as any he'd seen, with the design of liberty holding up the flag incused on the surface, and filled with copper. A Gallia County merchant named Willoughby had brought it back from Cincinnati one time and gave it to him as a reward for helping him through pneumonia when it didn't look like he was going to make it.

But that was a long time ago. Maybe ten years, and how many folks had died and gone drifting down the River of Time since then! There were periods when the fevers came and deaths seemed to outrun the births, making Silas realize he was fighting a losing battle and in this sense all humanity was doomed. Caught up in the mood of darkness, Silas drank from his flask and shivered and cussed. He snapped the harness to wake up Bessie, who was trotting at such a lazy pace she must have been half asleep.

Then things began to get hazy and his mind began to drift, helped along by the drumbeat of Bessie's hooves. And soon he found himself in a miserable and feverish fog, half from the old malarial infection and half from his frequent trips to his brandy flask. It was one of those times when there was a lot of it he couldn't remember afterwards, which somehow made it all seem worse. For example, after he'd gone to bed, he couldn't remember arriving at his barn and climbing out of his buggy and taking care of Bessie. He couldn't remember going into his house and speaking to Victoria. He couldn't remember how she'd greeted him. He couldn't remember whether he'd bothered to tell her that the Fitch boy was dead by the time he got there, and for all he knew, the scarlatina that had killed him was climbing into bed with him.

Later, all of those things were gone. Clean as a whistle. Everything.

But the dream that he had that night wasn't. In the dream he was back in that grave he'd dug late at night, standing on the coffin lid and trying to pry the damned thing up with a crowbar. Since he'd just dug straight down, there wasn't any place for him to stand, so he had to pry against the coffin lid while he was standing on it, doing all he could to split the wood.

He'd been feverish then, too. He could remember going over it all in his mind, making his plans on how he would manage it. The only way was by placing his coal oil lantern at the edge of the grave and then digging down until he hit wood and then prying at the top of the coffin until the solid board split, and then splitting it again and again with an ax, and then chipping the slivers away until he was able to squat and reach down into the coffin and tie a rope under the arms of the corpse.

He remembered how he had to work up his nerve for it. He remembered how he couldn't tell how much of his shaking was from malaria and how much from nervousness over what he was doing. Now, while he was lying in his bed and trying to forget what he'd seen in the dream, and trying to go back to sleep, he could feel himself slipping back into the dream, the way a wagon will skid in mud and you can't stop it, but know for certain it is headed for a ditch or maybe down a river bank. At first he knew he was dreaming, but gradually it all seemed more real than being awake, even though everything was murky in it.

He could feel himself back down in that grave, and for some reason he couldn't climb back out, and even though he couldn't see the body clearly by the light of the lantern, he somehow knew that something wasn't right. And sure enough, when he prized up the wood, there wasn't anything but a wad of dirty clothes stuffed there in the coffin, as if the body had taken off somewhere. But if it had escaped, where could it have gone, except where he kept seeing it in these dreams he had over and over again?

Yes, that was the only place, and even though that's where they were, they weren't exactly there, after all. It's like seeing a human figure made out of smoke and you know it's not real, only it's still human, somehow, and still *there*. And that's the way ghosts exist, and the only place where they last on, where you don't know where they are, exactly, only you know that they last on, somehow, and the fact that you can't see or hear them makes them more potent than exploding steamboats or thunderstorms, and sends a chill into the heart deeper than the coldest winter when the trees crack at night and the wind is as still as Eternity, for the winds of Time have ceased blowing and there you are and know it.

## THERE'S A LOT WE'LL NEVER KNOW

Two weeks later, when the two of them met at the Major Enslow Tavern, Captain Billy came out right away and answered
the question Silas had asked two weeks before: "She pointed
out that the other boy was only twelve at the time. Hosea was
four years older."

"Only sixteen?"

"Many of our soldier boys were no older, don't forget."

"Of course. But it still seems awfully young."

"About the other boy, . . . well, Captain Billy had a thought."

"Which was?"

"Captain Billy wondered if maybe he wasn't the other slave
who escaped with Hosea."

Silas raised his eyebrows. "Really? I thought you said she
told you the other boy was living in Charleston."

Captain Billy nodded. "That's right, she did. But that doesn't
make it true. Captain Billy thinks that poor old Sarah is a bit
touched. Demented. If you could have been there and seen
her petting Poke and listened as she answered questions . . .
well, she struck Captain Billy as being a little unbalanced."

"Hardly any wonder, when you consider what the poor old
critter has gone through in life."

"No, hardly any wonder."

For a while, the two men sat and thought. Captain Billy
puffed on his pipe and Silas kept turning his glass on the tabletop, turning it so hard you might have thought he was trying to screw it down into the wood. Someone in the next room
was playing "My Old Kentucky Home" on a harmonica. Then
later, he changed tunes and started in on "Old Dog Tray," a
sentimental favorite if there ever was one.

Finally, Silas said, "What are Sarah's thoughts about Lysander—other than as a man his ways are inscrutable to her? How does she feel about him? Does she forgive him or hate him or what?"

"If Captain Billy had to choose one of those verbs, he'd say she hates him."

Silas nodded. "Understandable, I suppose, considering he twice got her pregnant and she had to bear two of his sons, without having much choice in the matter, being considered his *property* and everything."

Captain Billy shook his head. "No, that's not exactly the way it is. Captain Billy could be wrong, but he reckons she looks upon her boys as *her* boys, no matter who happened to sire the critters. They say that women can think that way. No, that's not it at all."

"Well, what is?"

"What she *can't* seem to forgive Lysander for is how he sent her boys away from her by letting them escape and even giving them money to accomplish the fact. But she says that even if he didn't, he was part of the group that got one of them killed."

"Didn't she know that Nehemiah Dawes killed him?"

"She does know that, but she reckons it was just a mistake. To her way of thinking, what *wasn't* a mistake was how her boy got to be sitting in that boat out in the river so that he was in the way of the rifle ball. You see, even if the boy had escaped alive, she would've never heard from him again. And how's something like that different from death?"

"A great deal, I'd say."

"Well, Captain Billy might agree. Only, there are those who think differently. I speak of women."

"I see what you mean," Silas told him. "And she claims the other boy's living in Charleston?"

"So she claims. And he doesn't amount to much, from the way she talks."

"But you think he might have been the one who escaped with him."

"It's possible. Although it's odd that there's no gossip on the matter. Those Kanawha Valley folks are full of news, but nobody seems to know about the younger brother . . . whether he's the one living in Charleston or maybe he got away and is living in Canada. Or maybe he escaped but then changed his mind and came back to his old home, now that slavery has been done away with."

"I'd find that pretty odd."

"Maybe, but I don't doubt it's happened upon occasion. Anyway, from what they say about the Charleston man who may or may not be Lysander's other son. . .he's a nasty piece of work."

Silas thought a moment. "A lot of folks think it was a mistake we ever bothered to free the slaves."

"Well, Captain Billy doesn't happen to be of their number."

Silas nodded. "No, I don't guess I am, either. Slavery was a losing proposition, no matter how you looked at it."

For a moment they sat and thought. Finally, Captain Billy said, "There's a lot we'll never know, Silas."

Silas sipped from his glass. "No doubt."

They sat thinking, then Captain Billy said, "Speaking of how gossip flies up and down the Kanawha, she did say something that kind of surprised me. She said if you ever came up the Kanawha, she'd like to meet you and talk with you."

Silas didn't try to hide his astonishment. "With *me*? Why would she want to do a thing like that? How does she even *know* about me? *You* didn't mention me, did you, Billy?"

"Captain Billy didn't have to mention you, Doc. She doesn't know any more than everybody around here knows . . . that you dug up her boy's corpse so you could learn anatomy."

"Well, I'll be damned!" Silas whispered.

"It's not much of a secret, after all."

"But I thought it *was!*"

"No. Everybody knows and nobody minds."

"But how come I've never guessed it?"

"Why, folks respect your *feelings*, that's why. And they don't want to scare a doctor away with scandal, when there are only two of you in Brackenport. Not only that, you've been so busy with other things you probably haven't been paying attention to how folks might have given it away that they knew your secret. You've been laboring with your spirit elsewhere, as the poet says."

"Well, I'll be damned."

"Folks hereabouts wanted to protect you, so they kept their mouths shut."

"So they could keep that monstrous secret from me, even though I couldn't keep my secret from them."

"Folks are willing to be practical and forgive and forget. If they'd taken you to court for bodysnatching back in those days, and you'd been convicted, where'd we have gotten another doctor?"

"I guess that's one way to look at it. But it's a shock to realize that Hosea's old mother, living all the way down in Charleston, would know all about it, when I didn't even think folks around here knew."

"Well, it's water over the dam. By now, nobody much cares. And you've turned into a mighty good doctor, that's all. You sure have helped old Captain Billy's lumbago."

"I take the compliment kindly," Silas told him. "But why would she want to talk with me?"

"That is something Captain Billy can't figure out. But if you ever get to Charleston and talk with her, Captain Billy would like to know what the two of you said."

"I don't ever get to Charleston," Silas muttered.

"Well, it's only a hop and a skip and a jump, when you think about it. And you're welcome to come aboard the *J. P. Ricketts* any time she's headed that way."

"But I don't have any reason to go there."

"You do now, don't you?"

Silas thought a moment, then said, "Well, maybe I do, at that. We'll see."

Once again, Captain Billy went back to what he remembered of his long conversation with Sarah Crenshaw, and what a strange life she had lived and was still living.

# Book Three

# LYSANDER CRENSHAW'S DIARY

*Cloverland, Sunday, Feb. 1, 1857*

On this Sabbath day, I, Lysander Crenshaw, having painstakingly numbered exactly 100 sheets of foolscap in the upper right-hand corners, take up my pen to start a journal, so that if Posterity should ever bless me with grandchildren & further descendants, they may read what I have written. I refer to any among that ghostly population who may be related to me by blood and may desire to have some idea of their ancestor and the life he lived.

I am getting old & I am a widower. My wife, Lydia, passed away 9 years ago, thereby so darkening the world that I doubted it would ever brighten. I have no inclination to take another wife. Whatever my sins & failings (& they are indeed great), I was the most uxorious of men & fondest of husbands. There could never be a replacement for the wife I loved & still cannot help but love, as if her Death is nothing more than a great Interruption & Irrelevancy. As if.

Shortly after we were married, my father died, whereupon as the eldest son I inherited Cloverland, a plantation on Virginia's Kanawha River, consisting of 1600 acres, along with thirty-two family slaves. My younger brothers were Robert, who drowned in 1839, & Ziba, who moved to Lancaster, Ohio, joining an uncle there (our mother's brother) in order to study medicine. After learning the art, he stayed on & continues to live there with his family, where he practices as an allopathic physician.

I now live alone at Cloverland, with my son, Ransom, & four house servants. When last heard from, my eldest son, Abel, was living somewhere in or around Washington, the Nation's capital. I seldom hear from him & often wonder if he is still alive. He is, I am saddened to admit, an utter libertine—as dissolute & irresponsible as his father once was; but I see little evidence that he will come out of it, as I finally managed to do, with the help of God and my dear wife, along with whatever inscrutable forces may be thought to influence our human destinies.

I am of average height, but heavier than most—weighing somewhat over 200 lbs, without being ill-proportioned. My hair is naturally red, though now turning gray, and my face is wildly freckled, with the sort of skin that ages badly, so that it is now unfortunately gutted, mottled, and badly wrinkled. My features are irregular, mostly because of a badly broken nose, earned by too many violent & vulgar drunken brawls when I was young. There were times when I would fight for almost any reason, or none at all. My body is even less winning because I am covered by a generally hirsute haze, the pale hairs thick on my legs & forearms & my skin everywhere freckled. In compensation for these flaws, I was born with great physical strength & there was a time in my youth when I could grip an apple in my hands & break it in half with a single twist.

But now I have arrived at the age when the weight of years has descended upon me. My health of late has been irregular & indifferent. One of the reasons for this is my habitual application to spirits through the years. My favorite is the brandy made from our own peach orchards & distilled right here at Cloverland. Although it is boastful of me to say so, I will claim that it is the best peach brandy I have ever tasted. Occasionally I make an effort to moderate my drinking, but such efforts seem to have little effect & are at best short-lived.

In brief, I am afflicted with the aches & pains that men of my age should expect, along with a recurring malaria that troubles me upon occasion. Passing water is increasingly difficult & my sleep is often interrupted by a recourse to the chamber pot. It is often noted that the children we once were continue to lurk within us, no matter how old we have grown or what claim we can make of maturity & wisdom; if so, it is no doubt some version of my younger self who wants to cry out that I am too young to suffer from an old man's maladies. No doubt something like this is essentially true of all who have lived more than a half century upon this troubled earth & find their thoughts turning toward Things Eternal.

My sins are many & should be listed. I am headstrong & my sympathies are limited. I am impatient & intolerant of others. I lose far too much money at the gaming table, & often run up such debts that I have to turn to the rich harvests of Cloverland to amortize same. I am given to drink & occasional bouts of drunkenness—a fact too shameful to admit in society, but one which should be confessable within the privacy of a journal, knowing that I can burn its pages any time I want, thereby erasing the record of my sins & failures, as if such records were facts themselves, and not their shadows.

Trained as a lawyer, I have never practiced seriously or for any length of time. I still read Latin for pleasure & some Greek, though the latter comes laboriously & with less pleasure. I love music & horses. I also love the glance, voice, & presence of women, in spite of which I have for the most part lived a celibate life since my dear wife's death, as if in penitence for all those times before when, I now tremble to confess, I was too often unfaithful.

Indeed, though my trespasses have been great, my history is not entirely one of unrelieved wretchedness. The 2 happiest periods of my life were my days as a law student at the University of Virginia & a period of years after my return to Cloverland, when Lydia was still alive, young, and beautiful.

Sometimes I still find myself talking to her in the crepuscular dimness of the hallways. How much this habit may amuse the darky house servants, I have no idea. Indeed, their African gift for the marvelous & the supernatural might lead them to believe that I am actually conversing with my dear wife's ghost, which is a fantasy I cannot help but find somewhat congenial.

There, now. I have written enough for a start—three times as much as I'd intended, filling both sides of 2 foolscaps & spilling over onto a 3rd. Such verbosity might well recur in future entries. It is wrong to waste good paper, but perhaps worth it in order to get certain basic facts down in writing to start my journal. I think of this beginning as winding up a clock & I like to fancy I can already hear it ticking. Such a beginning requires something almost like courage, but now that I have begun, it does not seem so great & intimidating a venture as I had feared.

Furthermore, though I've already in this one entry used up almost a week's allotment of words for a diary, the journal I intend is not so evenly divisible into days & weeks that I cannot allow some entries (like this one) to grow into pages, while others might occupy no more than a sentence or two . . . or, indeed, be omitted entirely, for not all days are worthy of notice, any more than all people are.

Having written that, I have of course revealed my aristocratic prejudice & Tory proclivities, but if these pages are not the place for such revelations, what is? Our convictions need to be aired, if only in the private pages of a journal, which may never be read. Indeed, that thought itself is an invitation for candor.

Now, I only pray that I will have the heart & motivation to continue & eventually find it possible to discover & articulate something of the mysterious center of my Life, for both my sake & yours . . . whoever you are, descendants carrying a fraction of my blood or utter strangers; & whatever your reason for reading this may be.

*Cloverland, Monday, Feb. 2, 1857*
Today, after 4 or 5 weeks of enduring his solicitations upon the subject, I finally gave Mr. Denbow permission to hire an extra assistant, a 15 yr old boy from a nearby hill farm, named Tommy Byrd. Mr. Denbow is our Overseer, thus inexpendable for the prospering of Cloverland, & he earnestly assures me that the boy is a quick, industrious, & likely lad. Mr. Denbow's approval is good enough for me, because he is after all directly responsible for the successes & failures of Cloverland. In fact, I have admitted as much to him.

Charley Dugan is Mr. Denbow's other assistant, & when I asked him if Charley approved of our hiring Tommy Byrd, Mr. Denbow assured me that he did, indeed. In fact, he said it was Charley who'd first heard about Tommy & recommended him to us, in order to assist Mr. Denbow in his many varied & onerous duties.

So now there are 2 white men & a white boy, riding herd on all the working slaves. I haven't counted the darkies of late, but it's hard to put too high a number on the results of their casual & irresponsible manner of propagating their kind.

Occasionally when I decide to sell a couple, they become the very stuff of dreams and have a way of vanishing. At any rate, Mr. Denbow—who is a brave & sturdy man—confessed that he will feel more comfortable, now, with one more white face to look upon.

When he told me that, I pointed out that some of our mulattos were scarcely darker than he & I, but he didn't seem to find the jest funny—which of course it wasn't. No doubt I should try to cure myself of the habit of trifling with the help, whatever their color. Jesting has never fit in comfortably with prestige & a stance of authority.

I told Mr. Denbow that we might think about selling some of our overstock of slaves after the spring planting. I dislike the thought of breaking up any of their "families," of course; but then most of them have no more family sense than a rabbit. Indeed, the majority tend to have little if any notion—much less, concern—of who their sires are or were, although they all tend to know their mammies, of course—a privilege their women guard with remarkable passion and tenacity.

I can still hear the day's offering of fiddle & banjo music from the slave quarters this evening, as if in mocking answer to all of my more rational & civilized deliberations concerning their Fate.

If it weren't so expensive, I'd have their quarters moved a quarter mile away. Or better yet, several thousand miles, to the African continent.

Why was this dreary, nasty, & unprofitable slavery business ever begun? One cannot help but wonder, & regret its damnable history & dismal heritage, although it must be confessed that a place like Cloverland could not function for a week without their labors.

*Cloverland, Tuesday, Feb. 3, 1857*
Sick today with a damned fever & ague. The dark pewter color of the clouds to the north is a perfect mirror of the world as it presents itself to my morbid sensibility at this moment.

The fever's onset was sudden, and yet I find myself trying to remember the instant I felt it—the instant of recognition when you suddenly realize that you're sick & have been for a while without full awareness of the fact. Why this seems so important to me, I can't explain. Although it might have something to do with our need to measure our lives with the utmost precision, and to understand where one part ends and the other begins.

So now, shaking with fever and wrapped in a comforter, I try to think of what I was doing when I first felt the sickness as a sickness, rather than one of the more-or-less chronic discomforts a man is obliged to feel at my age.

I remember explaining to Ransom why he should always be careful with his mother's locket, as he fondles and plays with it like a child, which indeed he is in all but appearance and stature.

This gold locket with Lydia's image in it is my dearest possession, the most tangible link with her vanished presence. How I wish I had a photograph of her! But there is none—only this small pen-and-ink sketch done by an artist in Richmond, when we visited her cousin there many years ago. It is a good likeness, indeed; but hardly possessed of the remarkable fidelity of a photograph.

In spite of my endeavor to concentrate, it's impossible for me to search out that thin dividing line. I cannot remember when it was that my self-government officially announced the return of the fever and ague, inflicting its loathsome presence upon me. My foggy memory is no doubt partly caused by the fever itself, perhaps in the same way that a trauma destroys some nerve cells precisely as it triggers the sensation of pain in those cells that survive, so they can signal the brain that some part of the body is in trouble.

And we would never want to miss out on something as necessary as *pain*, would we?

*Cloverland, Wednesday, Feb. 4, 1857*
*Cloverland, Thursday, Feb. 5, 1857*
*Cloverland, Friday, Feb. 6, 1857*
Generally recovered from what Tommy Byrd & his poor ignorant white brethren refer to as "fevernager," & am able to get back to work on the damned accounts.

Talked with Mr. Denbow early this afternoon, & told him to get one of the workers busy in building steps to the woodhouse. He said he would, then assured me that things are generally going well & that he's looked into the granaries & can vouch that we have enough seed corn for a bumper crop.

I told him that was all very good, but then reminded him that it's the tobacco crop that deserves our closest care. I reminded him that any year when we don't fill our curing barns is likely to be a year of serious financial loss.

He answered that he understood the fact very well, & considered the prospects for the tobacco crop good. Contingent, as always, upon the gods of weather.

It is a great & abiding curse to be a farmer. As well as a great blessing.

Sometimes I think that of all my gambling habits, continuing in my labors to make Cloverland prosper is the most dangerous gamble of all.

154

*Cloverland, Saturday, Feb. 7, 1857*

Dreamed last night of the boy, Hosea, who was shot & killed last summer while being rowed across the Ohio River. Two of our hired detectives, Mr. Timmons & his accomplice, had recovered the boy on one of their incursions directly upriver from Brackenport, & were returning him to Cloverland to collect their bounty, when a shot was fired from the northern bank, killing the boy immediately & dropping his corpse into the river. Probably, the shot was intended for Mr. Timmons, who was rowing the boat, or possibly his assistant, who they say was sitting in the prow with his rifle across his lap.

The story is that it was a merchant named Nehemiah Dawes who, in aiming for one of the white men, murdered the boy. I asked Mr. Timmons to find out what he could about the matter. I consider it essential that we know without a doubt who pulled the trigger. I haven't heard from Mr. Timmons since, but I expect to at any time, whereupon something must and will be decided.

The boy was a fine & handsome quadroon, quiet & sensible & powerfully built. His mother was one of our mulatto house servants. I was the boy's father.

According to my reckoning, as I was responsible for his life, I am now responsible for his death, insofar as I devised & planned his escape. I will never forget that late evening last summer when I called him into my office & told him to sit in the chair beside my single-stem Duncan Fyfe table, & listen to what I had to say. The house had not yet cooled from its daily absorption of heat, but it was comfortable enough for me to light the oil lamp.

At first, the boy was naturally reluctant to sit, but when I told him a second time, he sat down on the edge of the small slat back chair beside the table. The lamp cast his features in such a light that one who didn't know him might have thought he had no Negro blood at all.

I said, "You know who I am, don't you?"

He nodded.

"Then you know who *you* are, don't you?"

He nodded again.

"You can speak up, you know."

"I reckon," he said.

"There'll never be anything for you here at Cloverland," I told him.

He glanced at me uneasily, then looked down at his hands. So far as I know, he'd never sat in one of the house chairs before. At that moment, there was a great strain between us, which was perhaps only natural. But the feeling was intensified because of the thickness of the air, which was heavy with moisture because of a rain brewing. I sipped from my glass of brandy.

"I think it's time you get out of here," I told him.

He looked up at me in surprise, then back down.

"Did you hear what I said? I think it's time you took off. Escaped. Skeddadled. Pulled up roots."

He seemed stunned.

"You're not stupid, goddamn it! *Look* at me!"

He lifted his face.

"Do you understand what I'm *saying* to you?"

He nodded.

"There's not a goddamned thing for you here at Cloverland, & there never will be. But maybe up there, someplace, you can find something to do. Maybe you can build a new life. Look up at me when I'm talking to you."

He looked up, then looked down at his hands again.

"You've already thought about it haven't you?"

When I said that, a sort of ripple seemed to pass over his body.

"You've already thought about escaping, haven't you?" I paused a moment, hearing myself breathe heavily as I thought. Finally, I said, "I know goddamned well *I* would've thought about it in your place. Are you my son or aren't you?"

He thought a moment, then nodded.

"I guess most of you think along those lines, don't you?"

He shrugged.

"I want you out of here," I said. Right away I knew that didn't sound right, but for some reason I couldn't think of how to change it.

"I'll give you some money," I said. "And a message. You can take it to my brother, Ziba, who's a doctor in Lancaster, Ohio. I'll draw you a map so you can find Lancaster. When you get there, you can ask around for him. People up there won't care much whether you're a nigger or not. Can you remember what I'm saying?"

"Sho, I remember."

"You *want* to get out of here, don't you?"

"Sho do," he whispered.

Hearing him talk like that was almost enough to make me sick, but it was something that couldn't be helped & it's one of those things best not dwelt upon in the memory. I stood up and began to pace back & forth in my study, from bookcase to bookcase—which is to say, from wall to wall.

I told him not to say a word to anybody, & he nodded again.

"Don't even tell your Mammy," I said. "She shouldn't ever know about it. She's got to be as surprised as anybody else. Not only that, she'd probably try to talk you out of it."

He nodded.

"You've got to promise me. You've got to say it. Go ahead: say it."

"I promise."

"It'll be one hell of a gamble, you know."

He looked up at me.

"They catch more than get away. And sometimes they kill them, which doesn't make any sense, because none of you are worth anything dead. But I think they get mad & frustrated & lose control. I think that's when some of you get shot. You understand?"

He nodded.

I closed my eyes a moment & thought. Then I recommenced my pacing & said, "We'll have to turn our bounty hunters loose on you. And I'll pretend to go along & yell as loud as the next man, although I might be able to delay them in some way. If I can, I'll give it a try. But you ought to know the risk. Understand?"

He nodded.

"I want you to understand that you might get killed. There's no way I can hold Mr. Timmons & his men back after we've hired them to do what they do. You'll be just like any other escaped slave who's tried to fly the coop. Do you understand?"

He nodded.

"So it'll be a considerable gamble, but if you want to do it, I'll write a letter & I'll put it in code, so if they catch you, they won't know what it says. There'll be something else in it, too— something for Ziba. It doesn't concern you. And I'll pack the letter and a Bible in an oilskin pouch so they'll stay dry, even if you have to swim the river. You can swim, can't you?"

"A little bit."

"Well, you know how to do it, anyway. Just grab a log and hang onto it & keep your head above water & kick your feet and push your way to the Ohio shore. You won't drown that way. You're not afraid to take the risk, are you?"

"No, I ain't afraid, Massuh."

"Don't call me that, you understand?"

He nodded.

"You don't ever have to call me that again. Or no other man. You understand?"

He nodded.

"You'll eventually be going to Canada, you know. My brother will speed you on your way. And when you get there, I want you to learn to read and write so maybe some day you can write me a letter."

He nodded, & then I gave him the oilskin bag, containing the Bible & enough money to get him all the way to Toledo, if he wanted, not just to my brother's house in Lancaster.

That was the last I saw of him. The next morning when it was discovered that he had escaped during the night, there was a great hue & cry all up & down the Kanawha, & my voice was not the least among them. We all bayed like a pack of hounds when a fox is scared out of the brush.

Mr. Timmons & three men took off immediately, & while I cheered them on, I gave them a false lead, saying I had an idea he'd headed downriver, not upriver, or across it to Syracuse or Brackenport.

It turned out, however, that news of his capture was not as great a personal disappointment to me as it might have been, because the next evening—almost exactly twenty-four hours after his escape—I looked for the gold locket with Lydia's portrait in it, and I was astonished to realize it had disappeared. I had always kept it in my study, lying there among the clutter of books & papers on my single-stem Duncan Fyfe table.

But clearing everything away this evening did not uncover it, and for a long while I concentrated my memory, wondering where it could be.

And then it came to me: the bastard had stolen it while we were sitting there, and I was pacing back and forth lecturing him. If it had been anything else of value, I could have forgiven him—even laughed about it; but the son of a bitch took the only thing I have of my dear wife to remember her with. My wife, but not his mammy.

For the rest of the evening I sat there drinking brandy, wishing I could have believed in some kind of hell so I could have pictured the son of a bitch frying in it forever.

*Cloverland, Sunday, Feb. 8, 1857*
A gloomy Sabbath, with naught to tell.

*Cloverland, Monday, Feb. 9, 1857*
Today Mr. Denbow sent one of the gangs out to chop down trees in order to extend the road bed to the back orchard. All day, when the wind was from the east, I could hear the distant *thunk, thunk* of axes, sounding like distant gunfire. It reminded me of the hunting season in autumn, when we're on a stand & the darkies are driving game before them, & suddenly the deer break out of cover, & 20 or more of us are waiting there and begin to shoot, while our house servants reload for us so that we can keep on shooting.

2 yrs ago there was a kill of 94, although last year's was only 56. Plenty of venison, nevertheless, & taken with a minimum expenditure of time & effort. It is altogether a fine adventure, especially when the sun is bright & there's a cold early winter chill in the air—just enough to make a sip of rye whiskey welcome.

Sometimes things go wrong, of course. 4 or 5 years ago Seth Kemp was killed when a stray rifle ball passed through his back & upper intestine. He bled to death in minutes. One more now enlisted in the mighty legions of the dead.

It seems to me that we killed over 100 deer that day, although I can't remember the exact count.

*Cloverland, Tuesday, Feb. 10, 1857*
Mr. Denbow informs me that in his view, hiring Tommy Byrd was a wise move, for the boy is proving a great asset. He is a hard worker, bright & honest. In addition, the darkies seem to like him—a fact of great importance, if one expects to get enough work out of them to pay for half their upkeep.

Though feeling sluggish, I had Tomaso saddled & I rode through the orchards. The south 20 acres off the hillside is filled with trees that badly need pruning, a fact which Mr. Denbow readily acknowledges, though he isn't sure when he can turn a crew loose on them.

I don't know what reason he has for delaying at *this* time, but I was patient & did not choose to confront him with my doubts. He is too valuable an Overseer to nag about small matters.

*Cloverland, Wednesday, Feb. 11, 1857*

Today I received a letter from Ziba. In it he informs me that he, his wife, & children are all of them well, living in their big house in Lancaster, up north in Ohio.

When I visited there 8 or 10 yrs ago, I must confess that I found the citizenry polite & amiable. I told Ziba as much & went on to say that they would be just like home folks if they would only ignore the salvos of those firebrand New England Abolitionists who keep sending out their hateful pamphlets & come forth to lecture with a self-righteous pretense of idealism & piety, with no tangible result beyond stirring up & poisoning the minds of the populace.

Ziba was quiet when I talked in this vein, so I playfully slapped him on the shoulder & said that he should pay close attention to his older brother & always do exactly as he says.

I instantly regretted my small attempt at humor, for it was as a younger son that Ziba had left home 23 yrs ago. Cloverland had naturally passed on to me as the eldest & from his earliest years Ziba understood that there could be no future for him here. But if he had not been forced to leave to make his way in the world, would he have been inspired to study medicine & become a successful & locally famous allopathic physician?

That was all long ago, of course. And now his letter is most welcome, for it assures me that he & all his family are well & that his brotherly affection for me remains unshaken & enduring in a world of perfidious change.

The boy Tommy Byrd seems to be working out well. His left eye isn't quite straight, which I keep forgetting, so that it surprises me a little when I happen to notice it. As today, when he was talking to me about one of the carriage horses. But in spite of his strabismus, he is a good-looking lad & smart as a whip, as Mr. Denbow assures me.

*Cloverland, Thursday, Feb. 12, 1857*

I find that for every day, there is a presiding Idea, a dominant Notion. The dominant Notion for this cruel & murky day, with a cold river wind that gropes & gnaws at the bone, is simply that the human creature was not made for wisdom & happiness. We cannot tolerate an enduring satisfaction. So we survive by feasting on the scraps that fall from some inconceivable Celestial Table that looms over us, as transparent as sky & as nebulous as clouds. Like *all* of our larger realities, perhaps & alas.

I think of this somewhat as the Greek pantheon—almost as if the gods still exist & exercise their occult influence upon us in ways far beyond our awareness & understanding. Except in some such blind groping as this in which I am now indulging myself. But maybe the little that can be gathered in such moments is enough. Sufficient unto the hour is the morbidity thereof.

Mr. Denbow informed me that they are nearly through pruning the upper orchards. I reminded him that the pruning should have been finished at least a week ago. I could tell that he thought I was wrong, but was polite enough—or prudent enough—not to argue the point.

Then, after a moment's silence, he reminded me that the severe winter had delayed pruning. After which exchange of reminders, I ended the matter by my final observation that it should not have delayed us as long as this, whereupon he once again remained judiciously silent.

What I *didn't* remind him of was the fact that without a good crop from the orchard, what hope is there to keep the brandy still working at full capacity? But he probably needs no such reminder as that from me.

The above disagreement notwithstanding, I think Denbow is not only an altogether competent overseer, but in some ways a remarkable one. He handles the darkies with rare tact & skill, which is a necessity if you're going to cut through their 1000 & one rituals of foolish dalliance in order to get a teaspoon of productive labor out of the exasperating rascals.

Passed water dolefully this evening, standing in the male stance before the chamber pot for what seemed a quarter of an hour, waiting for the exiguous drip to relieve the pressure . . . the full comfort of which I was denied.

What a miserable damned way to live. Or die.

*Cloverland, Friday, Feb. 13, 1857*
Why do they call this an unlucky day? Because it is said that the Last Supper came on a Friday, and there were thirteen present, the thirteenth being Judas.

Today, Ransom once again asked about his mother, & I once again explained that she was in Heaven, where her spirit was watching over us.

He thought about that, as he always does. Sometimes I think of changing my answer, but then decide that this would be a senseless & cruel trick, for even if he forgets virtually all he's told & has to keep asking the same questions over and over, it's surely possible that *something* is retained in his mind, & it would be unkind not to preserve & nourish whatever that small continuity might be. Or at least, this is what I suppose;

**164**

although I must confess that I find my poor son's mind a profound & terrible darkness.

*Cloverland, Saturday, Feb. 14, 1857*
A fairly good evening over the gaming tables tonight on my weekly visit to Charleston. Not enough to crow about, much less to discharge any significant part of my recent losses.

A drinker who gambles is a fool & a gambler who drinks is another. That spiritual arithmetic, therefore, tells me that I am 2 fools enclosed in one painfully aging body.

But to hell with such gloomy thoughts & to bed, judiciously numbed with brandy.

*Cloverland, Sunday, Feb. 15, 1857*
Shortly after the new century, my grandfather bought over 4000 acres in the wild Kanawha Valley & built Cloverland. I have only dim memories of him, for he died when I was only six years old. My Papa took over from him with what I now see as hardly a pause in the growth cycles of crops & animals. In this way, they were both instruments of the estate that they owned, thus both owners & owned, because of the intensity of their preoccupation & dedication to our land. Even so, we have managed to be happy & productive & proud of our horses.

In contemplating them & the history of Cloverland, I think of how it has changed. For Grandpa, everything was work & growth & survival. And in the early years, it was the same for Papa. But there came a time in his life when he envisioned some escape from it, or some transcendence, perhaps. This was never mentioned directly or discussed in my presence, but I know it must have been so, for he sent me over the mountains to the University of Virginia, so that I might study law & pursue my rightful duties as a gentleman.

He said to me, "Lysander, when you are a lawyer, you will be able to manage Cloverland far beyond the abilities of either your Grandpa or myself—poor ignorant farmers that we are."

Other than the "poor, ignorant" part (for Papa spent his cold winter evenings reading poetry & the classics), I half-believed his words—& still do so, for here I am, & here is Cloverland, thriving to all outward appearances.

Nevertheless, there are times when it all seems to me as insubstantial as time itself & constructed mostly of appearances, for I am hardly able to see beyond the next payment of bills. A condition that is hardly alleviated by my chronic gambling debts. God help me, deserving or not!

*Cloverland, Monday, Feb. 16, 1857*
Dreamed of Lydia all last night & have been thinking of her off & on all day.

There's certainly nothing unusual in *that*, but the intensity & frequency of my dreams lately seem greater than usual.

I remember a dream several months back. In it, Lydia & I were sitting in a room talking about the horses. I remember that she was sitting in the walnut rocker, rocking & sewing the hem on one of her dresses. I remember her pausing & saying, "The moon won't be full until Thursday."

I remember that it was late summer & a moth was flying in odd ellipses around her oil lamp. I remember the sound of crickets.

Then, I was suddenly aware that Hosea was in the room next to ours. I couldn't see him, of course, but I knew that he was sitting in the darkness and listening to us.

Then Lydia spoke very slowly & in a very soft voice. "I'm worried about Sarah," she said.

I wondered if Hosea could have heard her & the thought that he might was strangely disturbing.

The memory of that dream often comes to me, & although there is something very disquieting about it, I feel something almost like gratitude in the notion that this is something of Lydia that is left for me. I will never be able to get closer to her than in her sudden, unexpected visitations in my sleep.

I often wonder if dreams are not the origin of the widespread belief in ghosts that flourishes among the ignorant & superstitious—a class that, from a strictly philosophical viewpoint, will surely be found to include all of us.

Indeed, I know that I am half among them, in spite of my skepticism regarding the Bible & its message. And yet, how can we know that the beloved dead do not await us in some unfathomable realm, beyond the dreams of time & matter?

*Cloverland, Thursday, Feb. 19, 1857*
Missed two entries due to the fact I've been sickeningly morbid & melancholic these past few days, brooding upon old wrongs & guilts & disappointments, which I trust would prove a sufficient cause for any philosopher worthy of the name. Indeed, I could not—*physically* could not, I say—lift my pen.

Given such dolorous declivities, what good is the great physical strength I have always prided myself upon? Only to mock the impotence & fecklessness of the moment. Indeed, we die in parts & pieces, outlasting our faculties one by one in the slow progression of our temporal decay.

Part of the problem is that my thoughts keep returning to the dead boy. I keep going over the reports I have gotten of how those scoundrels across the river buried him high & mighty in the loftiest spot in the graveyard, overlooking the river. Not that he didn't 1/2 deserve such an honor, of course. Or perhaps, to be precise, 3/4—which is to say, his proportion of Caucasian blood. But whatever that proportion—"what price glory?"

After breakfast this morning, Ransom asked me what the stars were made of, & I explained to him that it is said they are great balls of fire in the Heavens, so distant that their enormous magnitude is lost upon our senses. My answer quieted him for a full minute. No doubt he was filled with wonder during that time, as well he might have been; although he would not have thought to question my answer, for he seems to have little or no critical sense & therefore accepts virtually all that is said to him as Gospel.

While this was the first time he'd asked me that particular question, I know it will not be the last. When a question occurs to him & takes over his imagination, there is no silencing or ending it. He will ask it & ask it, over & over, & I will answer & answer; the same every time. It seems the poor boy can no more remember my answers than forget the question that has alighted upon his poor weak mind to trouble it.

Sometimes the slyer rascals among the darkies come near to having fun with him, but with their superb instincts for self-preservation, they never quite cross the invisible line. They feel the shadow of Mr. Denbow's whip over them, no doubt. Or sense the impact of my own anger, should I hear about it . . . which they of course realize would swiftly translate into the whip. Or worse.

I consider his question about the stars a more interesting one than many of those asked & asked & asked again by my handsomely quiet son who celebrated his 22nd birthday only two weeks ago.

Lydia understood that poor Ransom was destined to be slow before his first year was out, & she fastened upon him with a fiercely protective & compensatory maternal passion. The fact that he was destined to be an imbecile was lost upon me; but women have ways of knowing such things that are far beyond our ken. Oh, God, but I miss her!

How different poor Ransom is from Abel, in whom his mother & I had once reposed so much hope. It's been over a month since I've heard from our Scapegrace son, & I can't help but wonder if he's still alive in his ardent pursuit of gambling & all the dark pleasures of the flesh as a Young Blood in Washington. It seems that being a gentleman from the West requires a far more ardent application to certain gentlemanly ideals & licenses than if one is to the manor born (which is to say, one of the bloods who come from Philadelphia or Richmond).

Did I just imagine I could almost hear him solemnly pronounce the sinister word *hon-uh?* I think I did.

Death has spared my beloved Lydia of so much, for which I cannot help but rejoice.

And yet, oh, how I miss her!

Enough. No more self-pity. To bed, that dark garden where dreams can pullulate like weeds and thistle in my sleep.

*Cloverland, Friday, Feb. 20, 1857*
A dull & worthless day. Bilious with a touch of *katzenjammer,* achieved by serious & sustained application to what I am proud to boast is the best peach brandy west of the mountains.

I tell myself that if one is going to suffer the distempers of profligacy, one should do it with elegance & style.

Mr. Denbow claims that Tommy Byrd is already working harder than most of the darkies on the gangs—as if there could be much cause for pride in that. But to be just, it must be admitted that motivation has a great deal to do with the invidious comparison of the African's capacity for work & the white man's. No matter how hard a slave works, he'll see nothing in it *for himself.* Perhaps we would all be just as shiftless in their place, although for one who has worked with them for any length of time, it is hard to conceive of such a possibility. Still, beyond question, the possibility exists.

Today's presiding mood: a draught of misery, with a dash of exasperation.

*Cloverland, Saturday, Feb. 21, 1857*
As usual, I had the boy, Flip, throw the harness over Lady Gwenn this evening & I trotted her into Charleston for my weekly entertainment with cards at the Kilbourne House—a ceremony I have yet to describe fully. Judge Beeker, Cornelius Laidlaw, Colonel Gault, Squire Paige, and Isaac Krober were all in attendance, as expected.

Living in so uncertain & capricious a world, how I have come to cherish my weekly ritual at the gaming table. I do believe that we require such humble continuities for the preservation of our spirit. Indeed, perhaps our identities.

And yet, how can the gambling passion be thought of as a "continuity"? How can I manage to find stability in courting uncertainty & caprice in the very arena of chance? Truly, we are enigmas to ourselves. The Delphic Oracle's prescription for self-knowledge was beyond our attainment, eluding even the wise Socrates, by his own admission. And indeed, I've always thought, eluding Plato's grasp as well, according to his own testimony as filtered through the Sage of Athens.

Before leaving the Kilbourne, I stopped off at one of the other gaming tables, where I quickly managed to lose over $200 at faro. Exactly how much was lost is uncertain, since I was not "entirely lucid," as I used to say to my beloved Lydia upon those occasions when I was deep in my cups.

How I wish there were some way I could make it all up to her! How I wish I had proved deserving of so good, chaste, and wise a woman!

Today's presiding mood: futility. Along with a sudden realization of the futility of this stupid business of pinning a label upon each & every day.

*Cloverland, Sunday, Feb. 22, 1857*
The birthday of the Father of our Country.

Surely, we have betrayed the trust invested in us by that great & magnanimous man, our Cincinnatus of the New World.

A colt was found dead this morning. But as if in compensation, another pickaninny was born to a woman they call Nyburnia. The child was a boy. I know his momma slightly, & from what I know, I can fancy that she is as proud of her part in bringing another baby into the world as if it had required great resourcefulness & talent from her & were an accomplishment such as had never before been witnessed in human history.

Verily, the blackamoors have raised irresponsible breeding to an art. You have to wonder at their obsessive rhythms, at why they love to sing hymns—& you have to wonder at their savage distortion of Christianity.

*Cloverland, Monday, Feb. 23, 1857*
Lately, I have been reflecting upon the word "honor," a word that in these exiguous times turns bitter in the mouth. This reflection prodded me into remembering my days at the University & some of the tense, dangerous, arrogant, & posturing *gentlemen* of my acquaintance in those long-departed days in the beautiful town of Charlottesville, where we studied, quarreled, gambled, drank, & complained to one another under the watchful & lofty regard of Mr. Jefferson's Monticello.

I remember writing the following doggerel about my classmates—which I was prudent-enough to keep private, lest I would be challenged to fight so many duels I would have surely been carried off in one of them eventually . . . if not the 1st, then the 18th or 22nd or 43rd:

> At nights the gaming tables hold the feasts
> Of planters' sons, those Gentlemen of Beasts.
> Each keeps a loaded pistol by his bed
> In case he feels insulted by something said
> By another gent, if only in a dream.
> It needn't be an insult, only seem:
> Which is enough, as any one'll tell you
> Before or after he's contrived to kill you.
> All day they boast of they-uh precious "hon-uh";
> What place but Charley-ville can boast such fauna?

And yet, even while pillorying them, I was aware that I was pillorying a species I understood too uncomfortably well, being of their grotesque kind by only one remove. Not only that—in spite of all their disgusting & high-flown rhetoric, what would we ever be or do *without* honor in some version or other?

Such thoughts remind me of that old couplet comparing the eastern Virginians and those of us in the wild & rude regions of the tramontane West:

The western cocks are poor but do not know it;
The eastern cocks are rich & always show it.

Still, for all the confusion & silliness & pomposities of those days, my memories of them are among the few that sustain me now that the world has darkened. For all my scorn and contempt for the superstitions of the Bible, I can only agree with its insistence upon the notion that we are a corrupt & fallen species. All of us, darkies and whites, Germans and English—and for all I know, Australian aborigines and Chinese mandarins.

Such cynicism & self-pity always partake of something that is base & disgusting, but perhaps here in the privacy of my journal I may indulge it in its guise of Truth.

*Cloverland, Tuesday, Feb. 24, 1857*
Today, alone, I "celebrated" my birthday, two more than Pa was given to celebrate, & 8 more than my dear Mother.

Here in the privacy of my diary I will confess that the event was somewhat less celebrated on a nationwide scale than that of 2 days ago in honor of the Father of our Country.

For what, exactly, am *I* the father of?

Do you await an answer? Well, here 'tis: today Ransom asked me 4 times if it was my birthday, & each time I assured him that it was, until finally I roared out, "Yes, goddamn it, Son, *it is my birthday!*"

Right after getting so angry with my poor imbecile, flesh of my flesh, I found my vision blurred & I had trouble getting my breath, so I went to my room & damned near fell into a fit of weeping, but finally managed to get control of myself & behave like a man.

With the help of a glass of brandy, to be sure.

*Cloverland, Wednesday, Feb. 25, 1857*
Mr. Denbow informs me that the silage is running dangerously low, so I told him I'd immediately ride into Charleston & see how many wagonloads I could purchase on credit.

Which I did as promised, having Flip saddle Tomaso, which the boy finally got around to doing after his usual extended dim-witted commentaries on life & the inscrutable ways of God & the white man.

After which, of course, he did not get the cinch tight enough, a fault I was forced to remedy so I wouldn't spill out of the saddle before going a mile down the road & break an arm. Or a disaster far worse to contemplate, my brandy flask.

I often contemplate the appalling fact that through my own wretched & sinful appetite, our Crenshaw bloodlines have been spilled into that black tide of cosmic ineptitude & worthlessness. But when I am visited with such dark thoughts, I contemplate how achingly beautiful my mulatto princess, Sarah, was, & strangely, somehow *continues to be*—& how handsome were the 2 quadroon sons she gave birth to, before the better of them was shot & killed by those pious & insolent Bible-spouting Villains north of the River.

But enough of that. In Charleston, Mr. Ballard told me he will accept a sixty-day note for twenty wagonloads of barn-cured alfalfa, to which I of course agreed.

I'm not sure where the money will come from, but maybe I can sell some of my yearlings if the stockyards can pay a better price than last year's. Or maybe a couple of niggers, if we don't flush them into the woods before we can throw a rope over their worthless heads. Although I am convinced that niggers are nothing but brutes, scarcely more than mules in wit or character, I nevertheless have to admit that Hosea was far better than my own 2 sons who've grown up into one halfwit & one scoundrel. As for our only grown daughter, she's married to a little redheaded, self-centered runt with the face of a fox & no more affability than a ferret.

*Cloverland, Thursday, Feb. 26, 1857*
Today, I rode over the entire estate with Mr. Denbow in attendance, although I was aware that he would have preferred seeing to the plowing & other chores. It is only proper that he wants to know if the mules are properly taken care of & a thousand other things that always need attending to.

Once, in a reflective mood, I remember telling Mr. Denbow that in maintaining Cloverland we were sustaining an honorable tradition, for great landed estates such as ours were known to the ancient Greeks, 2000 years ago. I explained to him that they called theirs *oikoi*, a fact that did not at first seem to excite his imagination greatly. But when I told him that the Greeks also had slaves, I could almost see his mind come alive.

"Do you mean to tell me them Greeks had *plantations?*" he asked.

"Indeed," I said. "Although they didn't call them that, of course."

Mr. Denbow frowned & shook his head. "You're talking about Plato & Socrates & those fellers?" he asked.

"Yes, I'm talking about the Greece they lived in over two thousand years ago."

Again he shook his head, this time remaining silent. Contemplating the wonder of it all, perhaps. Although with our good, sturdy, reliable Mr. Denbow it would be hard to tell.

Charley Dugan was kicked in the upper thigh by one of the trotters, but his injury seems minor. Mr. Denbow says it was Dugan's own fault, so we trust he will learn from the experience.

*Cloverland, Friday, Feb. 27, 1857*
Once again, at 10 o'clock at night, with pen & paper & inkwell & brandy bottle, I sit down at my handsomely carved cherry desk (brought over the mountains from Richmond) in order to create from memory this additional day I have survived to add to that long string of days that constitute the duration of my life.

As for this one: another 16 hours of hard work, with far too much to do & far too much left undone.

Still, *Labor ipse voluptas*, as I quote to my Africans when I join them for a while & we all work together. Mr. Denbow never responds, but the darkies stop to play their games— to exclaim & marvel at my learning & laugh & shake their heads, while Mr. Denbow waits & blinks, puffing philosophically on his pipe until he can get on with the work, freed from Latin.

Lydia will have been dead nine years, next Thursday; and her death is a chronic pain in my heart, and will ever remain so. I am obsessed with the thought that the son she took with her to the grave would have been the splendid fulfillment of our marriage—the son & heir we had always dreamed of. Unlike the 2 who survived—the one feeble-minded, and the other a hopeless cad & scoundrel. . . utterly so, without the least whisper of that damned & precious *hon-ah* referred to so often by the gentlemen in Mr. Jefferson's University at Charlottesville.

God help me for writing such a cruel truth. But why pretend otherwise?

Ransom was quiet today, even for him. Sometimes his marmoreal contentment pleases me, & I am almost tempted to envy him for inhabiting a simpler world.

He & "our African brethren," as the New England firebrands think of them, are often much alike, in this respect . . . *if*, that is, one ignores the significant differential in the noise they make.

*Cloverland, Saturday, Feb. 28, 1857*
A very bad adventure with the gaming table this evening. A loss of a great deal of money—how much, I am not only afraid to write down on paper, but afraid to *know*. I should be winning far more than I have been lately—&, of course, losing less.

A man who drinks & gambles is a fool compounded.

Having lost so heavily at the Kilbourne, my faithful Lady Gwenn brought me safely home. At least I *suppose* she was the one, although I can't be sure, for my spirit was not present during that hour's ride by moonlight.

If there was a moon, that is.

I owe Squire Paige a great deal of money. I have it written down somewhere, but am reluctant to look for the paper where I've listed it.

Arriving home, I was scarcely able to pass water. Old age, no doubt. But if, along with retaining my water, I have retained any of my youthful ambition to become a philosopher, I should be able to withstand such physical discomfort & inconvenience.

Since the Ancient Philosophers could face death with such admirable equanimity, surely a man in our enlightened age can face the reluctance of his bladder to dribble.

*Cloverland, Sunday, March 1, 1857*

No recent intelligence from Abel. I can't help but wonder if: 1) he's still alive, & 2) if living, still in Washington, & 3) if he is living the life of dissipation that he learned so well from his father—without, it seems, bothering to emulate any of my virtues. Assuming that I have any of measurable importance.

Since his mother is dead, I have assumed the worry over Abel & his commitment to a life of dissipation. But even if she were still alive, our son would provide enough worry for both of us—with four grandparents, if any were alive, & a host of aunts & uncles thrown in.

Not at all like our other son. Ransom is seldom any cause for worry, but then he's seldom any cause for pride, either. Poor Ransom is seldom, God forgive me for saying it of my poor boy, *anything at all.*

*Cloverland, Monday, March 2, 1857*
Somewhat improved in health & spirit, I had Flip saddle Tomaso & I rode for two hours, at a fair gallop in stretches. His wind seems good & unless I imagine it, he's not as hard a rider as he used to be. Either that, or I am less sensitive, becoming numb in my fundamental and proximal nether extremities.

A bright day, with the willow trees along the river starting to bud. A month or 6 weeks from now, Cloverland will reveal herself in all her Arcadian splendor.

*Cloverland, Tuesday, March 3, 1857*
Dreamed of Lydia all last night, then awakened to a darker world, though I managed to make my way through my dungeon of hours until supper and brandy.

*Cloverland, Thursday, March 5, 1857*
Why have my thoughts so often of late returned to reflections upon my university days in Charlottesville, that beautiful little town nestled in the mountains? Assuming my stance as *laudator temporis acti*, I regard my days there as among my happiest. And yet, there are times when I seem to remember that period as being the very opposite. Still, even when my memories seem darkest, I realize that I never once failed to understand what a fine & noble heritage it represents. One of my regrets is not having had the singular opportunity to meet the renowned Mr. Poe, but he left three years before I arrived upon the scene.

Still, three years is as nothing relative to that profound & morbid genius. Everybody still talked about him, speaking as if he'd been gone for only three weeks, rather than three years. His enduring legacy was one of equally fabled fame as a talker & one committed to reckless dissipation, especially as regards the gaming table & his dark thirst for wine & a passion for working codes & ciphers, whose intricate mysteries were inevitably disclosed under the effulgent lamp of his fierce though febrile intellect.

How I would have liked to meet him! No doubt all my classmates felt much the same way, but I cannot help but feel that this ambition had a special pertinence to me, for I shared his passions for poetry & ideals & beauty & melancholy & the gaming table—as well as an addiction to wine & spirited liquors, alas. As all my friends would testify.

This affinity was noted by all at the university. My old friend, William Chapman—an underclassman when Mr. Poe came upon the scene—liked to call me Edgar the 2nd, saying that if there was a dynasty of genius, I was next in line for the throne.

I was flattered, of course. But now I cannot help but ask what such gifts as I might have laid claim to so long ago . . . what they have amounted to.

Here, too, I am tempted to indulge in self-pity, brooding upon all that has passed away. My return after graduation to Cloverland beyond the mountains was, it now turns out, my destiny. With my father dying & a tobacco crop in the ground & no one else to take over the affairs of our dear *ager fluvialis* . . . this, I tell myself, was as grand & noble a curse as any philosopher might aspire to.

*Cloverland, Friday, March 6, 1857*
A day of mud & misery. Or misery & mud.

One or the other. Being gifted with free will, I have a choice between the two.

Once again I suffered a seizure of self-pity, surely the most disgusting & degrading of human emotions. Even so, I gave way to it, thinking of the gold locket that Hosea stole. How I miss the dear image contained therein! And after all this time! It was so little to possess, you would think; and yet even that little has been taken away & is probably lying somewhere in the muddy bottom of the Ohio River.

*Cloverland, Saturday, March 7, 1857*
I won over $300 at the Kilbourne this evening. It's about time the cards smiled upon me.

In celebration of which event, I returned sober enough to contemplate with remembered leisure the splendid hands delivered to me by the Gods of Chance.

Lady Gwenn must have been puzzled that I held the reins & talked to her all the way home. She's used to me tying the reins & snoring the hour away under the moon, while she trots busily toward the barn, where Flip will be waiting to rub her down.

This evening, I had a rare glimpse of happiness, even while I contemplated the dark truth that life itself seems to promise nothing more in the way of certainty than a gaming table. And no matter how heroically the Mr. Denbows of this world strive to make our affairs orderly, we all know deep down that there's no way to win.

*Cloverland, Sunday, March 8, 1857*
Another cold & dreary Sabbath, the sort on which I pray to God he will forgive all of us Atheists of our many sins.

*Cloverland, Monday, March 9, 1857*
Mr. Denbow & I rode the south border today. All seems satisfactory.

I spent this evening thinking of the dead boy buried in the graveyard high on the bank over the Ohio. *My son*, God help us!

How odd to think of him that way, for it was in the nature of things that I would hardly know anything about him. In this sense, you might say, he was hardly any different from any other son. Because what do I know of Abel, for example, except that he has shown nothing but a determination to pour his life down the Drains of Dissipation?

Of course, there is always poor Ransom. But can I really say I know him? Who could solve such a mystery? For the most part, his mind seems to be nothing but a profound silence. But I keep reminding myself that silence does not indicate absence. As the old legal Maxim states: "Absence of any evidence of guilt is not evidence of the absence of guilt."

Now that I think about it, I wonder if that is indeed a maxim, or simply something I've dreamed. No, I think it exists, somewhere. But I won't go to my law books to find it. The requirements of a diary should never be that demanding. And I find that my entries are often more those of a diary than of a journal. So be it.

*Cloverland, Tuesday, March 10, 1857*
It seems to me beyond the reach of a white man to understand the shallows of the nigger's childish & clownish brain. About a month ago, Sarah stole a handful of ribbons from my dear Lydia's dresser. Damned if I didn't *see* the wench take

them! And damned if "my mulatto princess" could have failed to *realize* I saw her!

But what does such witnessing matter? What are facts to her? Nothing at all, as measured against *feeling*. She looks upon such knowledge as cold & unemotional & would never allow it to inhibit her infinite capacity for self-deceit & self-indulgent surrender to feeling. Today, she actually denied it, when I brought it up to her. Insolent. Stupid. Exasperating.

Anyone who knows niggers knows this about them. They have no more sense of truth than a field mouse or turkey. This capacity to ignore all that is inconvenient at the moment is the source of their legendary fecklessness & irresponsibility. Their simple-minded ignorance of Truth is infinite. For them, truth is nothing other than a *feeling*; it is no more than a notion of what they want to believe at any particular moment. No doubt this is connected with their fabled ability to be happy under conditions of servitude & wretchedness that would make a white man miserable.

Indeed, it is their childishness that makes the thought of their emancipation so bewildering & hateful. All of us can understand this in a way, for we remember that when we were children, we were like this. It is the tactic of children to lie their way out of a difficulty & deny any responsibility for what they have done. Finally, in claiming their lie so fervently, they eventually *come to believe it as surely & fervently as if it were true*.

So today when I mentioned the ribbons, Sarah was distraught. It was as if by mentioning the fact I was somehow breaking a rule. Then she became so indignant & angry that for a moment I thought she might scratch at my eyes or spit on my vest. Instead, with another bewildering reversal of mood, she started hiccupping, then worked her passions up into a full-scale weeping fit, filling the house with her dolorous echoes.

I know her well, & can say that beyond any doubt, she is now utterly convinced of her *innocence*! How could a white man ever understand such a critter? Only by remembering our own behavior as children, when the word "truth" was no more than a noise grown-ups made.

Speaking of insolence, I've noticed that Sarah treats Tommy Byrd worse than Mr. Denbow treats the worst of her people. Scorn & arrogance combined. I suspect that this has nothing to do with the proportion of white or Negro blood in her, but something far more profound—the flaw of being human.

*Cloverland, Wednesday, March 11, 1857*
Still busy with the tobacco crop. Planting season is so hectic & busy that even with Mr. Denbow's industry & foresight in managing things, I have little time for guilty memories & the prolonged morbidity of self-recrimination.

Ransom wandered off today, no one knows where. Now & then he does get the urge to walk off somewhere, usually to wander through the orchards or hills in back; although one time last August one of the slaves saw him clear across the river, walking on the Charleston road, & I had to go fetch him in the buggy. On our way back, I asked him where he'd been headed, but he didn't answer directly. Instead, he talked vaguely about wading in the river to cool his feet.

I said, "But you were walking on the road *alongside* the river."

He seemed to think about that.

I pointed. "The river's over there. You can see it."

He looked where I was pointing, but still didn't say anything.

"You weren't really headed for the river to cool your feet, were you?"

He thought about that, but didn't respond. I chucked our little mare Nausicaa along, and she picked up the pace, making the buggy bounce faster over a rough section of the road so that Ransom and I kept bumping our shoulders together.

Then I told him I didn't like the idea of his wading in the river, anyway. I said if he wanted to cool his feet, he could cool them in a bucket of water, or if he felt like wading, do it in Spill Creek. I pointed out that there was quicksand in the river.

He thought about what I said, then asked me if it was true that we were going to have to sell Cloverland.

"Who in the hell told you that?" I yelled at him.

"Nobody," he said. "I just heard it."

"Well, dammit," I said, "if you *heard* it, somebody had to say it."

When he didn't respond to that, I gave up & concentrated upon Nausicaa, who for some reason was trotting at a slant, as if she wanted to throw a shoe.

By suppertime, everything had returned to normal, so I decided to ask him again where he'd been headed when I picked him up on the Charleston road. This time, he told me he'd been headed for the south orchard, which might be true, even though he'd already passed the wagon road that leads to it.

Sometimes he just says whatever comes into his mind at that moment, & seems to believe it. Very much like our darkies.

As yet, judged morally, no better than Abel.

*Cloverland, Thursday, March 12, 1857*
The tobacco planting is going well, in spite of one sick mule & 2 sick niggers.

Mr. Denbow had 2 of them horsewhipped today (I do not refer to any of the sick) & when he explained why, I told him that he had done the right thing. Absolutely and without question.

I don't see any alternative to what our Northern brethren see as "gratuitous cruelty."

If those pious nincompoops *only knew!*

But I find a direct correlation between distance from the facts and moral indignation. The sentimental hogwash about the mistreatment of Indians, for example, is largely confined to the East Coast, where most of the people have never *seen* a wild Indian. But I've never heard of anybody in the West subscribing to the popular belief that Indians aren't savages at all, but simply downtrodden Methodists who like to wear leather britches with the bottoms cut out.

And so it is with all the outcry against the southerner's keeping African slaves, only this seems to me far worse.

And yet, having said that, I will admit that slavery is a vicious & stupid & woefully inefficient institution, judged by almost any standard.

But granting that, what alternative do we have? None at all. Doing away with slavery & releasing these savage & ignorant blackamoors upon the land would be like releasing great armies of locusts upon a field of wheat.

*Cloverland, Friday, March 13, 1857*
Thrice out of four, when Friday the 13th falls in February, it will recur in March. I told Mr. Denbow this, after which he

waited frowningly for the pertinence of my remark, which I did not provide. Finally, I told him it was a simple observation & no more. Whereupon the good fellow nodded & went about his tasks.

Altogether, the tobacco planting seems to be flourishing, & if the weather holds for a long-enough growing season, we'll do well. We won't get rich, of course; but we'll do well-enough.

But since good weather for me is good weather for others, that which increases our yield will increase the yield everywhere & lower the price. It's the planter's eternal dilemma. Still, with luck, I should be able to borrow enough within a month to see us through the year, pay it all back, pay off my gambling debts, put money aside for next year & bank the goodly sum that remains.

Last week I'd invited the Wilsons & VanKeeps & Tylers to come for dinner this evening. Tildy cooked some of the venison, catfish, & pork roasts that we'd salted away in the cookhouse. As side servings, we had succotash, hominy, baked potatoes, buttered yams with raisins, molasses, applesauce, baked corn muffins, & jugs of cider, & Catawba wine. For dessert, we had peach cobbler with thick cream.

The table talk was mostly of nigger uprisings & the damnable Abolitionists, after which we settled down to happier discussions of our prospects for a decent tobacco crop. All were sanguine that this will be a good year. Mrs. Wilson seemed merry enough, although she has been poorly of late.

After dinner, we had more peaches, but these soaked in brandy. With their permission, we gentlemen smoked our cigars before the ladies. Then we again turned to the eternal question of slavery & abolition & politics—all of which we discussed & debated for a while, then I brought in Flip and had him play the fiddle so everybody could dance. I took a turn with all the ladies, & it was a lively evening.

Mrs. Tyler & Mr. Van Keep sang the soprano & baritone duet of Papageno and Papagena from *The Magic Flute,* with Flip tagging along pretty well, although he didn't know the piece. Mr. Van Keep's voice is firm & resonant, but Mrs. Tyler's high notes are uncertain. Many singers have excellent areas within their range, but it is only the truly exceptional whose ranges are consistently equal & consistently of the same tone texture. Still, the two of them did enough justice to that beautiful piece for the rest of us to enjoy it.

Flip was on his good behavior, this evening. I'll have to admit that there are times when the damned rascal acts almost human. He's almost coal black, but Lydia always claimed he had white blood in him, somewhere. Maybe so, but I can't see much evidence of it.

Now, getting ready for bed, I miss Lydia more than ever. I shall never get over her being taken from me so long ago. Somehow, even the thought of recovering from her death strikes me as a betrayal of her, and therefore evil—a thought rendered even more profound insofar as I don't otherwise believe in evil, or even—the benefit of Scripture notwithstanding—quite understand why evil should exist at all, or even know exactly what it is, if it does exist.

My guilt & love for her are therefore deeper than explanation can probe.

*Cloverland, Saturday, March 14, 1857*
After supper, I found I was so tired that I decided not to go into town for my weekly bloodletting over the cards. Instead,

I decided to stay home & get politely drunk in private.

Things were peaceful for a while. I sat with my brandy bottle & listened to the fiddle & banjos in back, somewhat irritated that I had no choice in whether I listened or not, for there is no quieting them in the evening. They'll have their music or die . . . which I sometimes feel I'd prefer, but in truth it would be too much trouble to bring about the death of so many who are so ostentatiously helpless.

No, you might as well try to put a stopper in a volcano as prevent them from playing what they call their music & dancing & laughing & signifying in their multifarious games to establish pecking orders & courtships that turn out to be as ephemeral & meaningless as the courtship of fruit flies.

Eventually, my mind somehow managed to block it out, whereupon I got to thinking about our Abolitionist talk last night & how—if those poor deluded, self-righteous New Englanders had to live & work with their beloved & saintly niggers for a week—they might wake up & repudiate their highly principled ambition of civilizing them & calling them neighbors. Most of the few liberated darkies who've traveled north as a display are convincing enough to make all of Massachusetts & Connecticut think the whole savage race is deserving of citizenship in a civilized country. But it's all fakery & hocus pocus, a swindle & a wangle got up to make the New England Yankees feel righteous & morally superior to their Southern brethren.

I should know, for I'm half-Yankee myself, insofar as my dear Mother came from Vermont & met my father under such strange circumstances that I hope some day to write the history of their courtship. That will have to wait, however. Like so much.

189

Now, to come back to earth—or at least to my present circumstances & my troubled existence here at Cloverland, with Sarah fastened to me like a leech. . . . I should never have let her join the house niggers all those years ago. But having done so, I should never have climbed into her bed.

Lydia had to know of it, & I shudder to think that somehow her knowledge might have hastened her death. This is sentimental nonsense, perhaps, but it is part of my thinking & it would be dishonest to deny it.

If any man ever deserved to fry in hell, I guess I am the one.

Oblivion is the most I can hope for.

Sometimes I think that my whole life has been a mistake.

Mr. Denbow informed me today that there are bores in the peach trees & another yearling has died.

*Cloverland, Sunday, March 15, 1857*
Sick & bilious today. Also drunk.

Or perhaps the other way around.

Several times I thought about praying, but had neither the conviction nor motivation.

*Cloverland, Monday, March 16, 1857*
Still too sick to bother.

*Cloverland, Tuesday, March 17, 1857*
Still & again.

*Cloverland, Wednesday, March 18, 1857*
Feeling a little better. Good enough to work, but not to bother with *this* damned chore of *writing down my thoughts* after a long day of hard & tedious labors.

*Cloverland, Thursday, March 19, 1857*
Work, work, work.

Fell into bed with my boots on last night & slept almost until 6 this morning.

Once again Ransom asked if his mother was dead & I was too tired to answer. All I did was stare at him, then shake my head & walk off.

I wonder if he wondered at my not giving him an answer.

Surely, there's *some* task he could undertake, something to help out with the 1000 things that need doing. He's no taller than I am, but as stout as any man I've ever seen. But what of it? A mighty vessel of physique is worse than useless without the light of Understanding in the pilot house.

*Cloverland, Saturday, March 28, 1857*
More than a week gone by without an entry. Too busy & too tired at day's end to do ought but remove my clothes, bathe, & fall into bed. I've even been too tired to get drunk.

Thank God, the tobacco's in—tucked into its beds & all covered with muslin. We should be able to transplant it into the fields sometime in May.

Lost pretty heavily this evening while laboring over the gaming tables at the Kilbourne. Exactly how much, I am not sure. While I have been drawing very poor hands, I will have to admit that I do not play as well as I could if I were only to drink just a little less. Maybe 1/4. Or—who knows?—maybe drink a little more.

But one more manifestation of my flawed character is unimportant compared with the fact that, by mid-September—by God—we should be—by God—*rich!, by God!*

*Cloverland, Sunday, March 29, 1857*
A quiet day working over the accounts. Mr. Denbow reported
to me & all is well.

For some reason, today my memory has kept returning to
an episode when I was a student at the university. There was
a gambling den on the turnpike just east of Charlottesville
called the Eagle Nest. The proprietor was an elegant old fellow named Ned Fairwinkle, who wore more gold on his vest
than some people might see in a lifetime. I remember late one
evening when a customer asked Ned if his son intended to
follow his trade as a gambler.

And old Ned, who must have been sixty, answered, "No, but
my nephew shows a gift for cards." Then he paused & thought
a moment, after which he said something I'll never forget. He
raised his own experience to the level of a universal law, as
surely as if he were a philosopher. He said, "It's never a gambler's son who follows his trade; it's usually a nephew."

I've often thought of that, & in the private dialogues in my
head have often called those poor bastard quadroons of mine
"nephews." I do this partly in memory of what I heard Ned
Fairwinkle say all those years ago, and partly in the spirit
of those cynical & arrogant old Renaissance cardinals who
liked to call their bastards "nephews." They did this, comfortable in the knowledge that they possessed so much
power that no one would dare question their conferring such
a bland & innocuous title upon the living products of their
unconscionable lust.

*Cloverland, Monday, March 30, 1857*
If Melancholy were a Presence, I could give it a name & fight
it. But it is only this appalling Absence of Something. But of

what? The will to live? Yes, but that is more its result than its nature. And yet, can an Absence *result* in anything?

I can't follow the trail of that thought, getting tangled up in my Nomenclature, something Philosophers have always had to guard against.

As for Melancholy: Mr. Poe, I believe, sensed its Presence almost as a tangible Entity, as material as a horse or walnut table, and as loathe as any material thing to reveal the secret of its inner life.

This evening at supper, Ransom talked about his horse, Tuck, who's been acting up, lately—bucking & kicking. For all his limitations, Ransom sits well in a saddle, but he hardly knows what to do when Tuck gets snuffy, so if Ransom isn't thrown (which has already happened twice) he simply dismounts & stands there holding the halter & stares at the beast without moving or doing anything. Charley Dugan once told me that he saw the boy standing there for almost half an hour, eye-to-eye with Tuck, both of them as motionless as statues. And, I would add, as inscrutable.

While I refer to his horse as "Tuck," Ransom has informed us that after long deliberation, he has decided to rename him "Savior," which strikes me as verging upon the blasphemous, but I have said nothing, knowing how little right or authority I have to pronounce upon blasphemy or indeed any other moral issue.

Still, I am uneasy. There is something a little unsettling in renaming any creature. Or, indeed, anything. We crave continuities in our lives more & more, the older we grow. And names provide continuities for us.

I will not, of course, trouble poor Ransom's mind with my thoughts on the danger in renaming things. I think of his mind as an under-furnished room, wherein even the smallest change can have consequences beyond the reach of our more complicated calculations.

I have seen this happen before, several times in several ways. I think of it as related to his need to ask the same question over and over, and indeed I sometimes think the very simplicity of his mind gives it a strange kind of dignity and solemnity, in the way a map transcends in its lucidity the territory it represents.

*Cloverland, Friday, April 3, 1857*
My first entry in four days. Mr. Denbow is ill with a Fever. Tildy cares for him in what I take to be a spirit of sullen maternal compulsion. Or perhaps, from the perspective of the darky mind, she is merely being practical.

My Africans fear & hate Mr. Denbow, as well they might. It is no doubt inevitable in view of his immediate & unquestioned power over almost every detail of their lives. And yet, there are times when they seem to be almost fond of him, in spite of the shadow of the chain & whip they live under.

Whatever else he is to them, Mr. Denbow is an instrument of order. And we all crave order—even the Africans, whose exuberant & emotional lawlessness is for the most part incomprehensible to the white man. But while the need for order is universal, the urgency of that craving is obviously far greater among our kind than among the darkies.

As for the character of *their* inner lives—that must forever remain a mystery to me.

*Cloverland, Saturday, April 4, 1857*
In spite of work, biliousness, & melancholy.

Which usually obtrude—if, indeed, an Absence can obtrude—only in my moments of relative idleness.

I find it unsettling that it can have the arrogance & power to come & stake its claim even while I am busy.

Maybe it is a positive force, after all. One of the smoky gods, perhaps.

Then, again, perhaps not.

Tildy informs me that Mr. Denbow is improving. I went to see him, & he informs me that her sanguine prognosis is correct.

For which small comfort in a dark & uneasy time, I should express thanks.

But just the thought of giving thanks in any direction leaves a bitter taste in my mouth. Thanks for *what?*

*Cloverland, Sunday, April 5, 1857*
I dreamed last night of snow.

Too much brandy. All that fire within & all that coldness without. I spent the day feckless & dispirited, muddled in mood & a trifle melancholic. Thank God for the succor of work, whatever it might be.

*Cloverland, Monday, April 6, 1857*
Today, at last, a letter from Abel arrived. He informs me that he needs money for an investment that will "carry him over the top," and asks that I forward a thousand dollars to him.

I note that his reference to paying me back is judiciously vague, but I will send the money, anyway, having enough left from my recent loan that I can supply it for his comfort, convenience, & *hon-uh*. More painful to me than the casual &

lordly attitude of an aristocrat that he has assumed toward re-payment, is the utter lack in his infrequent letters of anything remotely suggestive of sadness or regret over the passing of his mother. All he needs, it seems, is a periodic replenish-ment of funds from Cloverland.

Sometimes I am overcome with bitterness: two sons, as different from each other as it is possible for two humans to be; and neither of them *right*. Such thoughts ignore the two bastards who will never be allowed to call me their father—whelped by my house nigger, Sarah, who lives beautifully & elegantly inside her polished mahogany complexion, and seems as simple-minded as a puppy . . . & yet, upon occasion, as unfathomable as a she-scorpion or eagle.

Mr. Denbow has recovered. And the corn has been plant-ed in the bottom seventy, on the river. I'm always grateful to get it in the ground down there, superstitiously convinced that once the corn is deep in the bottom loam, the rest of our planting will go smoothly. After that, I can relax to some extent, held hostage by the weather while we hope for a bumper crop.

A month from now, Cloverland will be green & beautiful.

Last night I slept with a loaded pistol by my bed. I keep it there for two reasons, one of which is obvious & prudent. I speak of protection against all but the mind's phantasms.

The other for a reason I do not wish to put in writing, be-yond acknowledging that it exists. Otherwise, it should not be dwelt upon even here, in the privacy of this journal.

*Cloverland, Friday, April 10, 1857*
The 3 missed days are due to the fact that we've all been busy working the fields. Usually, work drives away gloom, but this

time, even in the midst of planting I have still somehow managed to get whiffs of my old melancholia.

Why should I work so hard at making Cloverland thrive, when there is no son to leave it to?

Speaking of which, at supper this evening, Ransom asked me once again if his mother was really in Heaven.

For the hundredth, or perhaps thousandth time, I told him that if anyone was in Heaven, *she* was.

That seemed to please him, which in turn pleased me. The poor boy needs constant assurance about his mother, as would I, if I had no memory & could believe in the Heaven of the preachers. But the important thing is that Ransom misses her, which is perhaps enough. Not at all like my other son, indeed.

Speaking of whom, Ransom was quite upset when I read Abel's most recent letter aloud to him. He remembers his mother well, as indicated by his chronic anxiety over the state of her soul, but I sometimes think he has only vague memories of his scapegrace brother, who acts as if he had no soul at all . . . which may be true enough in itself, but that is hardly justification for not *acting* as if he did.

God help us, everyone. God save us. Sinners all. (With, of course, the possible exception of poor Ransom, whose innocence will never depart from him. And my dear dead wife as another exception.)

*Cloverland, Saturday, April 11, 1857*
I met with Mr. Denbow this morning & he reports that all the crops are in. But another mule has died, leaving only eight that have survived our planting season.

I asked him how many we'd begun the season with, & he looked at me sharply before answering, "Nine."

Sometimes I get the impression that *he* gets the impression that poor Ransom & I are more alike than my position would suggest.

If this is so, Mr. Denbow fails to realize that my poor son's absentmindedness is precisely an absence of mind; whereas mine is . . . what? A terrible remoteness in my life that will not depart from me for a minute.

Now, with the grand organ sound of that paradox, I will end this entry.

*Cloverland, Sunday, April 12, 1857*
Last night, Jocko, a big & dangerous lout who is the most quarrelsome & violent of the field hands, struck Sarah in the mouth with his fist, knocking two teeth out and horribly mutilating her lovely face.

I must confess that for a moment I thought of shooting the rascal in the head, but then decided to leave the punishment— or lack thereof—to Mr. Denbow. Some of my neighbors let their Africans do whatever they will with one another, so long as they do not cross those invisible lines dividing the races. Mr. Denbow is of that same mind, now & then. Although he is not consistent, & everyone knows that consistency is of the utmost importance in the treatment of children, mules, dogs, & niggers.

What Mr. Denbow will do in this instance is unknown & I care not. (In fact, I found myself yawning as I wrote that last sentence, although it is late enough at night for yawning & the lamp is burning low.)

As for Sarah's beauty of yore . . . I no longer care much about it. The fire in my loins is not entirely out, but it is not the raging conflagration it once was. I haven't touched her since Lydia died. As if in penance, indeed; but for other reasons, as well.

And yet the insolent wench occasionally acts as if she's mistress of Cloverland & flounces before me, knowing how profoundly conscious I am of the fact that the two of us share a long & profane intimacy.

I wonder if she'll stay in hiding now that her face has been permanently twisted out of shape by that brutish imbecile, Jocko.

*Cloverland, Monday, April 13, 1857*
Mr. Denbow informs me that he has given Jocko a good whipping. He further informs me that Sarah had the good taste to resist the brute's advances, while continuing to tease him until the dim-witted creature lost all control & smashed her in the face.

*Cloverland, Tuesday, April 14, 1857*
Not a drink all day. I wonder how long it will last this time.

*Cloverland, Wednesday, April 15, 1857*
Another day. One day at a time, as the saying goes.

Sometimes at night I half-awaken to find my fingers clutching the gold locket. Then I realize that it is only the sleeping half that can grasp it, and I am left to wonder how much of our lives is like that.

Misery, whatever the answer to that conundrum might be.

If I still possessed her dear image, would it ease my days? Or would that only bring her nearer to me, thus intensifying the loss?

There's no way of knowing such a thing, of course; although I cannot imagine my loss being any greater than it is now. Maybe the sense of loss is itself part of her remoteness from my life?

An unsettling thought, & I'll try not to think on it.

*Cloverland, Thursday, April 16, 1857*
I suppose we should have foreseen it. Today at a little after two-o'clock, Jocko turned on Mr. Denbow & menaced him, whereby Mr. Denbow was forced to shoot him with his pistol, killing him outright.

Mr. Denbow had come upon him in the #2 curing barn & reproached him for his treatment of Sarah, but Jocko was having none of it & began raising his voice & stomping back & forth under the burden of his resentment & sensed humiliation. The story is that at first, he wouldn't even look at Mr. Denbow, but moved restlessly back & forth. Then he grabbed a perfectly good gunny sack & in an ecstasy of frustration started to rip it apart in his mighty hands.

Mr. Denbow ordered him to stop the foolishness, but the damned fellow ignored him. Mr. Denbow told him again, & this time Jocko looked him in the eyes for the first time & told him to go to hell.

Mr. Denbow then told him he'd get a whipping for his insolence, & Jocko yelled out: "You think I care 'bout dat? Ain' *no* whip gone quiet down Jocko!"

Mr. Denbow said, "Well, damned to hell if we won't just *see* about that!"

Right then, Jocko was in such a rage that he started toward Mr. Denbow, making threatening gestures, whereupon Mr. Denbow pulled out his pistol & told him to stop. But Jocko had worked himself up into an ecstasy of rage & kept on coming, whereupon Mr. Denbow calmly shot him in the face & the brute dropped dead at his feet.

There was an immediate outcry, then dangerous murmuring throughout the slave quarters. At first I expressed my concern over Mr. Denbow's violent reaction. But he defended the act by saying that Jocko's insolence & arrogance & shiftlessness were such that he was worthless, at best, & Cloverland would function far better without his disruptive presence.

I reminded him that a man's life is more than a "presence," but when I said that, Mr. Denbow just stared at me a moment, & then he said maybe so, but it was *Jocko's* presence he was talking about, & he could assure me that the work gangs would accomplish far more without Jocko around to keep them agitated & stir up their smoldering discontent.

I told him that was not the point. Then to demonstrate it, I cupped my hand to my ear & said, "Do you hear that?"

"Hear what?" he asked. "I don't hear anything."

"I do," I said. "I hear a low murmur from the slave quarters. It almost sounds like growling, & it's bound to get louder."

Mr. Denbow nodded. "I get your point," he said. "But, trust me. If I'd let that insolent black bastard live, we'd be a lot worse off than we are now."

I thought about that a moment & finally acknowledged that in spite of all the unfortunate implications of the act itself, there might be something like merit to his argument.

*Cloverland, Friday, April 17, 1857*
A quiet night, which fact does not bring the comfort one might expect.

Since we're so greatly outnumbered by the slaves, I suppose it's only natural that the owners and their families & overseers in the valley are occasionally wary. Although he has his faults, Mr. Denbow is a brave man. He is not the sort to blink, eloquently demonstrated by his killing Jocko.

At breakfast this morning, Ransom asked me for the sixth or seventh time why Jocko was killed. He has enough trouble remembering anything I tell him, but he finds the unpleasant things the most difficult to keep in his mind. In this, he may not be so different from most of us. But so far today I've managed to be patient & give him the same answer, over & over, using all my imagination in an effort to understand how my words don't seem to leave any trace in his memory.

"Tildy's mad at me," he said after a moment's thoughtfulness. "Why is Tildy mad at me?"

"Ransom," I said, "she's not mad at *you*. In fact, she's not mad at anyone. She just feels bad about Jocko."

The poor boy nodded & closed his eyes a moment, thinking. Then he opened them & said, "Why was Jocko killed?"

Once again, I tried to explain it to him, trying my best to hang onto my temper—with both hands, a cuss, and a goddamn prayer.

*Cloverland Saturday, April 18, 1857*
Last night was quiet again, disturbed only by the faint whispering of a light though persistent rain, lasting from midnight to daybreak.

Jocko was buried this afternoon in the slave graveyard beyond the orchard. I advised Mr. Denbow not to attend, as his presence would be inflammatory to the darkies of all shades and color. He agreed, and I attended in his place. This was more honor than I would have accorded Jocko under any other conceivable circumstance, but it seemed prudent at the time and for the occasion.

A preacher from Charleston showed up & preached the sermon. His skin was the color of dark mahogany & he had sharp features and thin lips for a Negro. He's also small for an African, and I suspect he has some Indian blood in his veins. He preached a far more decent & respectable sermon than a loud & ignorant brute like Jocko deserves. The preacher waxed poetic, saying life is a river and we surface for only a moment, and then we are pulled back down into the Channel of Darkness, where our Ancestors are, their line extending all the way back to Abraham and Moses. This reference reminded me of how a great number of darkies seem to think they're directly descended from the Prophets of the Old Testament. Many of their spirituals proclaim this, to be sure, but those I speak of seem to believe such nonsense literally.

Sarah's back in the house, working. She is silent & won't look at me, which is the way it should be, or at least the way I would normally prefer it. I wonder how often she thinks of our dead son. A thing like that, however, is something I will never know.

Her face remains badly mutilated, her beauty evidently gone forever.

Not a word from her about Jocko. Was she glad that Mr. Denbow killed him? Or does she resent the fact, even though one might say it was done indirectly to avenge what Jocko had done to her?

And yet, could she look at it that way? Or did she see it as simply one more brutish act on the part of Mr. Denbow to maintain his control over the slave quarters?

There's no denying the fact that killing Jocko was a damned imprudent thing to do, no matter what the provocation.

When I contemplate our history, I curse the slavers who brought the first Africans to our shores. What a misery they laid upon the land. And what utter folly for so many to think that all those million slaves would make us prosper.

And what a mockery that the New England Abolitionists assume that all slaves were captured and brutally yanked from their peaceful villages by evil slavers! The fact is, as anybody knows who knows anything, slave markets were a thriving business in Africa long before the first European stepped foot upon the dark continent. These markets were operated by Arab traders as well as sub-Saharan Negroes, & so it was that the overwhelming majority of American slaves, or their ancestors, *were not captured but purchased as slaves!*

This evening while reading in my favorite chair & under my favorite lamp, I suddenly stopped, aware of the unnatural silence from without. Then it came to me: I have not once heard Flip play his fiddle since Jocko was killed. I've caught glimpses of the rascal down by the quarters, but not a glance from his direction & not a sound from him.

Tildy is quiet & will hardly look at me as she ostentatiously manufactures an appearance of busy-ness in my presence.

Sarah walks up & down the halls with the dignity of a princess. Her face is clearing up, but will be forever marred by her broken nose & two missing teeth. What a blow he must have delivered with his fist, & she as small as a child to him.

In spite of all the ominous signs, Mr. Denbow calmly assures me that the darkies will get over it. They always have, he points out.

Which is true enough, I guess. So far, at least.

I wonder how my son Hosea would have reacted if he were still alive & still here.

What a terrible *division* in the poor lad, & what a division in myself, as I contemplate the poor bastard's hybrid existence.

*Cloverland, Sunday, April 19, 1857*
While reading this evening, I was startled to hear the sound of a fiddle.

Flip is once again playing, & once again all seems well at Cloverland.

News arrived today that Mr. Findlay has died of pneumonia. He was forty-eight years old, reminding me (as an old man with authority to pronounce upon such things) of why pneumonia is called "the old man's friend."

Ransom has twice asked why he died, & twice I have tried to answer.

I vow to be patient, but can't help but wonder how many more times I will have to answer the same question. Of course, it's probable that tomorrow he'll have forgotten that Mr. Findlay is dead at all. Or that he had ever lived.

What chronic anxiety the poor boy must feel, having to ask the same question over & over, never quite understanding the answers I give.

Not that *any* of us can understand, of course. But we somehow manage to sweep our perplexity under the rug, so that we can function & get from day to day without going mad.

It's too bad my poor Ransom doesn't have a rug.

*Cloverland, Monday, April 20, 1857*
Mr. Denbow reports that the planting has gone better than in the past five years. The weather, the condition of the soil, & not as much sickness among the mules & darkies as in past seasons.

*Cloverland, Tuesday, April 21, 1857*
I heard the most extraordinary thing from Tommy Byrd this evening. He said he was sitting in the stable, hunkered down in the straw of one of the stalls & mending saddle, when he heard 2 of the black men talking in the next.

As Tommy interpreted their discussion, the slaves all blame *me* for Sarah's disfigurement & Jocko's death.

Their argument? Because I'd bedded Sarah & made her bear 2 of my sons she was alienated from all the other darkies, & they hate her for it. And they think that it was because I had taken possession of her that she had resisted Jocko's advances for years, no matter how ardently he pursued her when the mood was upon him.

Apparently they don't blame me for bedding her so much as for not protecting her from the likes of Jocko. Up to a point, they seem capable of accepting the fact that one of their women belongs to a white man; but they think that given the fact that since she does belong to me, she should have my protection. There's a certain crazy logic in that view, but what would it have meant in Sarah's case? Should I have set her up in a separate cabin & declared it off-limits to any buck nigger? Evidently, the two philosophers Tommy Byrd overheard did not address that issue.

Usually, it appears, Jocko was content with several of the other women in the slave quarters, along with a high-yeller wench from Van Meter's plantation, who managed to meet him in one of the corn cribs that border our properties when the weather was favorable. But Jocko could never get over Sarah & the way she acted as if she was too good for him, & it was during their final argument that he struck her & changed her appearance forever.

From what Tommy learned, most of the slaves hated Jocko, because he was a stupid & particularly mean bully, even among the niggers. He was impossible for anyone to get along with. They eventually understood that while his constant arguing with Mr. Denbow seemed to make him feel important in the eyes of the other darkies, in the long run, it just made more work & trouble & misery for everybody at Cloverland, blacks & whites together.

For whatever else we are or might be at Cloverland, we are a community. Like it or not.

*Cloverland, Wednesday, April 22, 1857*
Dreamed of Lydia last night. For the thousandth time, I would guess; and yet she seems more & more distant after every successive dream.

I will never forget her, to be sure; but I have had the thought that the time will inevitably come to pass when no one alive will know that she ever existed. This thought is almost a torment I cannot bear.

*Cloverland, Sunday, April 26, 1857*

My old nemesis, John Barleycorn, has returned with bells jangling & his horses prancing & his bottle held high. I have therefore missed 3 days in my diary.

Headachy all afternoon, with only a moderate intake of peach brandy to keep my head from bouncing off the floor, where I might step on it & get my face dirty. The megrims run in my family, so I can hardly complain of having my share of headaches, because blood will tell, whether for good or ill, & to a great extent it is our fate. As for the remainder? That is the arena wherein our character is tested.

A heavy rain this afternoon, which brought the work gangs in from the fields. The sound of much singing from the quarters. They're dancing, too, of course. But then they always dance. It is hard for a white man to know what in the hell so much dancing means.

Probably not a great deal. Something of a neural itch, I suppose, like a dog scratching fleas, & nothing more.

*Cloverland, Monday, April 27, 1857*

The Kanawha is up & some of the low spots are already flooding.

*Cloverland, Tuesday, April 28, 1857*

Shortly before noon today, Ransom wandered off & now (8:00 P.M., as I write under my oil lamp) he is still missing.

*Cloverland, Wednesday, April 29, 1857*

Our neighbors all up & down the river have been told of Ransom's disappearance. In spite of the roads flooded upstream.

*Cloverland, Friday, May 1, 1857*
Ransom's body was found this morning at about 10:40 by two of Van Keep's slaves who were pulling upstream in a skiff.

*Cloverland, Saturday, May 2, 1857*
Ransom now lies buried in the family plot up on the hill by the lower orchard, near his mother.

I've managed to write a letter to Abel, informing him of the tragedy, but I hardly know if I can reasonably expect an answer from him—busy as he no doubt is in his pursuit of the pleasures of the flesh.

No one seems to know how the boy drowned. Or what he was doing down by the river when he fell in. Or jumped.

His corpse was found tangled in the limbs of a sunken tree on the northern mouth of Spill Creek, just where it meets the Kanawha.

God bless our poor boy & goddamn me for surviving his simple goodness.

I am distraught & cannot write any more.

*Cloverland, Sunday, May 3, 1857*
In addition to the manor house with its 19 rooms, Cloverland boasts 4 storage barns, 2 stables—one each for trotters & riders—a blacksmith forge, 2 cookhouses or "summer kitchens"—1 for the manor house & 1 for the slaves—9 huts in the slave quarters, 2 spring houses, a cistern shed & 6 miscellaneous storage sheds, one of which is so dilapidated that I think I'll have Mr. Denbow put the torch to it.

I count my possessions & try to remember exactly how it was that I once took pride in them.

The flooded waters have subsided, & it appears that the loss in corn & tobacco is very slight. Elsewhere, the crops seem to be doing well.

All the darkies tell me how sorry they are that Ransom is dead & somehow I'm tempted to believe them. Sometimes their good-heartedness is enough to touch your own heart—& break it, considering the world we live in, a world in which a person as innocent & inoffensive as Ransom could drown.

For he lived his life without ever harming anyone or anything. How many could boast as much? I certainly couldn't. That is a bad-enough confession, but it is a far worse one that I wouldn't *want* to live harmlessly, for how is that possible if you have power? And who can live without wanting power? Other than Ransom, that is.

I fear I share this passion with too many, alas—including even my slaves, no matter how deep their affection for the poor boy & their sorrow over his death.

Would *Jocko* have grieved? I cannot conceive of it. Jocko never once thought of anyone's good & comfort but his own.

Then is it possible that Jocko & I have more in common than I would be willing to admit, outside these private pages?

I don't even want to think about it.

*Cloverland, Saturday, May 8, 1857*
Slowly life at Cloverland seems to be going on, somewhat as before.

Only I miss his repeated questions & long silences.

*Cloverland, Sunday, May 9, 1857*
Thinking of his death, I cannot help but compare it to Robert's death so long ago & remember the great sorrow it brought to my mother & father.

I have not been drunk one time since Ransom died. I think it might be better if I could get drunk. But that is hard to say.

*Cloverland, Sunday, May 10, 1857*
Once again, the Sabbath.

As good a time as any to join Lydia.

# Book Four

## PEACE AND PROSPERITY DESCEND UPON THE LAND

For several years after the Civil War ended, Isaac Dawes lived a settled and comfortable life. He had taken up residence in his brother's big handsome house, and was now living in affluence, elegance and ease. Agatha Tremblow had died of a stroke in 1862, when she learned that the son of her first cousin, a local boy named James Woltz, had been killed at Shiloh. After her death, she was replaced as cook by a woman named Mary Polking. Lizzie and Prue were still alive and serving as maids in the house.

This was a period of rapid growth in Brackenport. Two more physicians came to town and set up practice, and six months later, folks wondered how they'd ever gotten along with only two doctors, let alone just one. Shortly before they arrived, a boiler on the *J. P. Ricketts* exploded some eleven miles up the Kanawha while she was plying her way down south to Charleston. The old boat burned and sank, carrying four men to a watery grave, although Captain Billy Jones managed to swim ashore.

Isaac had expanded Dawes Enterprises in several directions, and all but one of the original businesses he took over prospered. The only failure was a grist mill Nehemiah had invested in about eight miles up Snag Run, managed by a man named Purefoy, who suffered so much from malaria that he got so he could hardly lift his spoon to eat a plate of corn mush, let alone run an active grist mill.

Two of the retail branches that Nehemiah had opened in the 1850s were dry-goods stores, one in Brackenport and the other downriver in Gallipolis. The Brackenport store was flourishing, while the Gallipolis store was just managing to hang on. Still, it was making a small but steady profit—which in the view of many folks wasn't too bad for those times.

And yet, the times could have been much worse. War is invigorating, as everybody knows. Heraclitus said it was the father of all things, and in a way, he was right. Maybe so, but you have to wonder if the best part of it might not be the peace that follows. Then again, maybe war and peace need each other, the way a man needs a woman, and vice versa. Who can know? But whatever the answer to that conundrum, the War of the Rebellion had been awful beyond description, and when it ended with Appomattox, peace settled on the valley as quietly as a soft snowfall in the night, transforming the world in which you awaken. You could feel it. Folks all up and down the valley woke up and began to taste the peacefulness. The specter of rebellion no long cast its dark shadow over Brackenport.

People had long ago ceased to marvel at the change that had come over Isaac Dawes. Now he was as admired as he'd once been scorned—as much respected as his brother had been. Not only that, he was *liked,* which doesn't often happen if you're rich and mighty. The fact that his businesses were flourishing meant that he had to hire a considerable number of people from Brackenport, and that raised him still higher in public esteem.

Of course, nobody's perfect, and that included Isaac Dawes. While people admired his success in whatever he turned his hand to, they had trouble understanding why he had to be so damned tight-fisted. He could be as narrow and hard in a bargain as his brother had been, and that was considerable; but there were some who said he was even worse, only without all the fanaticism. Maybe you have to be stingy to get rich. And maybe the stinginess was in his blood.

One of the men Isaac hired during his period of expansion was Loftus Gandy, the jailer's son, who was so dependable and quick with figures that after six months he was made a chief clerk. Some liked to say that Loftus was within reach of Biddle's old job. Others said that he was already that high, considering how much the Dawes enterprises had spread out and changed.

Isaac was so busy that he didn't travel much, but one day he took the *Shawnee Maid* downriver to Cincinnati. He'd been planning the trip for some time because of the elegant fancy gold locket he owned. Inside the locket was a pen-and-ink drawing of a beautiful woman. She was so beautiful, he couldn't get over it. He was as obsessed with that little picture as he had been with Nehemiah's diary. But from the way he felt now, he didn't think he'd ever get over that little picture. He figured it would stay with him forever.

He wanted to have the locket duplicated, and have the second hold an image of his own face in it, so that he'd have the two together in what you might call a sort of marriage. He could picture how they'd look. In Cincinnati there was an old German jeweler, named Adolf Smeltzer. Everybody had heard of him and said he was the finest artist in gold anywhere in the entire Ohio Valley. So Isaac figured that Smeltzer was the only one who could do what he needed, because the locket was as fancy and delicate-looking as a snowflake, and it would take an artist to match it.

One reason he'd put off going until now was a young widow named Anastasia Eckert. Her husband had been a wealthy Columbus dry-goods merchant who had joined the 40th OVI and then rose to the rank of brevet major just two weeks before he was killed at Chickamauga, leaving her well-off but drowning in tears. His name was Henry, and Anastasia had loved him about as much as it's possible to love somebody. Upon hearing of his death, she grieved so much that it was feared she might not survive the ordeal of her bereavement.

But there's an old saying that you can get used to anything but hanging, so the time came when Anastasia Eckart lifted her pretty head from her pillow of bereavement and looked into the mirror and saw that she was still comely and then looked around to see that there was a world waiting for her. One direction she looked was Brackenport, where her widowed sister lived, a woman by name of Geneva Hartzler. Geneva hadn't lost her husband in the War; he'd died of pneumonia in St. Louis in 1859, and his remains had been shipped back to Brackenport where they were laid to rest not over thirty feet from those of the wife of Nehemiah Dawes.

Considering how devoted to each other Isaac and Anastasia Eckart soon became, there were a lot of folks who wondered why they didn't just make up their minds to get married. The two of them seemed made for each other. They were both well-off and levelheaded. And yet, nothing happened. They just kept on seeing each other and going to church together, but so far as you could tell, that was the sum of it.

One explanation was that Anastasia had sworn eternal fidelity to her dead husband, Henry, and that included fidelity to his memory. Another story was that Isaac couldn't bear the thought of sharing his wealth with another person, even if she was also well off, not to mention so pretty the average man could hardly look her in the face to talk to her or even sit down in her presence. It was odd that Isaac wasn't affected that way, considering his swarthy skin and mangled features, although perhaps the fact that he looked like a ruffian might have been in his favor for some reason or other. Sometimes it's hard to tell a blessing from a curse.

But since her dazzling beauty tended to scare men away, maybe she was relieved just to have a man look her in the eye and talk to her in a normal voice, even if that man did happen to look like the assassin in an opera or maybe a retired river pirate. And the fact that Isaac had gotten to be even richer than she was, might have helped make him pleasant in her eyes, because not even a simpleton would figure he was courting her for her money. And she was far from being a simpleton.

Whatever the secret of their relationship, the two of them seemed suited to each other. Maybe their courting, if you could call it that, was more amiable than a lot of marriages. Maybe it was as stable and dependable as you can expect in a changing and perfidious world. Some folks said that Anastasia was one of the reasons Isaac had become a pillar of the church, but it would be hard to judge how to divide the credit between her and Nehemiah's diary. In the evenings after supper, Isaac still liked to read parts of the diary aloud to Anastasia in the parlor. He invited the cook and maids to join them, after which they all prayed.

Everyone commented upon Anastasia's beauty, and upon occasion Isaac would show somebody the pen-and-ink drawing in his gold locket and ask if that wasn't as close a likeness as anybody could ever imagine. He claimed it was as true as if Anastasia herself had sat for the artist. Some folks agreed, and some didn't, the way it usually is when you try to convince people that somebody looks like somebody else.

When folks exclaimed over the beauty of the locket, he told them how he'd gotten it from Eugene Biddle only a couple of days before he was hanged. He told them most of the story, but he didn't mention that he'd paid for it with whiskey that Biddle wanted so he could oil the wheels of his approaching death by hanging. Isaac figured it was all right to leave that part out, because the Isaac who'd smuggled whiskey to Biddle by tossing a rope up to the barred window and letting the condemned man pull the bottles up was not the same Isaac as that of today, having been transformed by reading his brother's diary.

## ISAAC FINALLY REACHES THE GREAT CITY OF CINCINNATI

Eventually, in spite of all the delays, on the first of October, Isaac bade Anastasia good-bye and bought a ticket on the General Grant to travel downriver to Cincinnati. He stayed there for three days in the Golden Eagle Hotel. He told people he wasn't going to leave that locket out of his sight any longer than he could help it. He told Adolf Smeltzer that he'd wait for him to finish the duplicate to his satisfaction.

Nevertheless, he did manage to enjoy himself while he was there in the city. Every evening he dined like a prince at Sauber's Restaurant, in the section they called Over the Rhine. Sauber's was famous for its *Sauerbrauten und Kartoffelsalat,* along with its German music, played on violin, accordion, and tuba. One afternoon he went to a wax museum, and that same evening attended the theater and saw one of the cleverest productions of *Rip Van Winkle* ever performed over the gaslights.

Everything went pretty much as planned. But after he returned to Brackenport, Isaac ran into difficulty. There was a hitch. Something went wrong where he'd least expected it. He hadn't shown the original locket to Anastasia because of his plan to surprise her after having it matched. He'd wanted the pair of lockets to be a surprise for her. He figured that the likeness of the woman contained in the original was so much like Anastasia that nobody would ever know the difference. He had grandiose notions of the effect it would have on her sensibility.

So on the day after his return, while they were sitting in her parlor at her sister's house, he slowly withdrew the lockets from his breast pocket and showed them to her. Anastasia's sister was sitting in the sunroom next to the parlor, knitting. They often spent their time together in this way, being proper and refined and intent upon keeping their names free from the least breath of scandal among the local populace.

"What's this?" she asked when he opened the first gold locket and placed it in her hand.

"It's a locket," he said.

"Well, I can see that," Anastasia said. "But *who* is it? Whose likeness is it?"

"That doesn't matter," Isaac said. "What matters is the fact that she looks exactly like you." He held up the other gold locket he'd brought back with him. "I plan to have my own likeness made and put in this one. That way, the two of us will be together. As good as a marriage."

"As good as a *what*?"

"A marriage."

Anastasia was quiet a moment. She seemed to be thinking as she continued to hold the locket and gaze at it. "Who is it?"

"Don't you see, my dear? *Who* it is doesn't matter."

"Oh, but I think it does."

"All right. It's some woman who lived down in the Kanawha Valley."

"You say 'lived'; is this woman dead?"

"Yes. But isn't that a remarkable likeness of you?"

"I'm not sure."

"Everybody thinks so," Isaac said, stretching the truth a little because he could feel himself getting nervous. "Everybody says it's an exact likeness of you."

"Well, even if it does look like me, it *isn't* me."

"Why's that so important if it *looks* like you?"

"Are you asking me why the *truth* is important?'"

"Truth has nothing to do with it," Isaac said. "Don't you see?—if you'd sat for this same picture and it had been drawn by the finest artist, it still wouldn't be *true*; it'd just be your *picture*!"

"But, Isaac," she cried, almost in tears, "it would be a picture of *me*!"

"But a picture is never *true*! It can't be. A picture is a lie. If somebody draws a picture of an apple, you can't eat it because it's just a *picture*! You can't bite into a *picture*, can you?"

"No, but it has to look like an apple instead of a peach, doesn't it?"

"Exactly, and this looks just like you. Everybody says so."

"Maybe some people think so, but it *isn't* me."

"Of course it isn't you! It's a *picture*!"

"But it's not a picture of *me*!"

Isaac thought a moment. "Look. What if somebody drew a picture of you but it didn't *look* like you? What if it looked more like some other woman than it did you?"

"It'd still be my picture, wouldn't it?"

"How *could* it be if it didn't *look* like you? What's the point of having your portrait made if it doesn't *look* like you?"

"Are you saying it doesn't make any difference that it was supposed to look like somebody else? I don't know how you could ever forget a thing like that. And I find it shocking that you should even suppose that I could accept this likeness of a complete stranger as my own."

"What I can't figure out is what difference it makes if it *looks* like you?"

"I know. You keep on saying that."

"Yes, and you keep on ignoring it."

"But I'm *not* ignoring it."

"If you're not ignoring it, my name isn't Isaac Dawes."

She thought about that for a moment. Then she said, "Well, there's one other thing."

"What's that?"

"I'm not sure how much it *does* look like me."

"Why, like I've been trying to tell you all this time, it looks *exactly* like you! *Everybody* says so."

She was silent a moment. "When you say 'everybody,' does that mean you've gone around and shown it to all sorts of people?"

"I wouldn't say I've gone *around* and shown it, only . . ." Isaac stopped and shook his head and started over. "Well, it's like this," he said. "What I wanted was for it to be a surprise."

"Then you've succeeded very well. You might say that I'm very surprised. Very surprised, indeed."

"I didn't want you to be surprised that way," Isaac told her miserably.

"I can very well see that. Only, how *did* you want me to be surprised, Isaac? Perhaps I can accommodate your dearest wish, if it is somehow within my power."

"Damn it, Anastasia, I just wanted . . ." Isaac stalled and tried to think. Nothing was turning out right. Everything was wrong. He opened his mouth to say something else, and then closed it. He didn't know what he wanted to say. He didn't know what he'd been thinking. He didn't know what he was thinking now. For some reason, he was ashamed and flabbergasted and embarrassed, altogether, and he couldn't figure out exactly why.

Finally, in a miserable voice, he muttered, "I just thought you'd be pleased, Anastasia. That was my intention."

"Well, I'm sure your intention is all that matters," she murmured, looking away from him.

"What in the hell does *that* mean?" Isaac cried out.

"Whatever you wish it to mean. If you wish to superimpose your own sense of my appearance upon that little portrait in your locket, I'm sure there's not a thing that I or anyone else could ever do to stop you."

"Look, you're taking this all wrong!" Isaac said, waving his hands and raising his voice. In the silence that followed, he just sat there and breathed hard and imagined he could hear an increase in the tempo of her sister's knitting needles as they clicked away in the next room. Not only that, they seemed louder, like drumsticks snapping away at the rim of a snare drum while a band marches past in a parade.

He lowered his voice. "What I mean is, you're taking this all wrong."

"That's what you just said, Isaac."

He raised his voice again. "I know, and I meant it. You're taking it all wrong!"

"And in exactly what way do you propose that I *should* take it, pray tell?"

By now, Isaac was practically beside himself. Along with being confused, he was tired. He felt that he'd been played like a fish and was ready for the net. He was lost and dumbfounded. In the last few minutes, he had learned things about Anastasia that only an hour before he wouldn't have believed. She had led him over his head somewhere into deep water, and he couldn't figure out exactly where the shore was.

Thoughts like that are discouraging to a man. They tend to leave him frightened, confused and a little bit furious. Considering this, it's no wonder that Isaac lost his temper and lurched to his feet. It may have been unfortunate, but it was not surprising. "By God," he shouted, "I'll just go ahead and have the goddamned thing done, anyway!" Then he charged out of the house.

Later, Anastasia told her sister that she had never heard him use profanity until that moment. Then she said that his departure had been like that of "a wounded buffalo." Those were her very words, only you'd have to figure she didn't have any more idea of a real wounded buffalo than she could picture a zebra in trousers. Still, it's the thought that counts, as the saying goes.

Anastasia also pointed out to her sister that Isaac had forgotten to take his hat with him. She said that she viewed this as eloquent testimony of how angry and confused and upset he must have been. The thought seemed to please her, and her sister joined in and seemed just as pleased, although the two of them didn't break out in laughter about it, the way two men would have done it.

Still, they were pleased, all right.

## HOG-TIED TO ORGAN MUSIC

Well, that was that. Isaac figured it was all over, so far as Anastasia was concerned. He thought about it and thought about it. He reckoned that Anastasia was prettier than any woman has a right to be, and she looked as fresh as a young maid. Looking at her, you wouldn't believe that she was almost thirty. She had a dewy complexion and a face that could wreck a man, and that face had almost wrecked Isaac before he got a glimpse into the sharp and dangerous rocks concealed beneath the surface. He had seen behind the mask of her beauty and glimpsed something awful.

Yes, he was lucky to be free of her. To live with a woman like that would be like having a tame panther or mountain lion in the house. They're beautiful animals, all right, but you'd never be able to figure them out or trust them worth a damn. No matter how tame they'd act, they'd never be tame all the way. They're not like a good faithful dog or some man you're having business dealings with.

Not that a man won't try to cheat you, but you know the rules, somehow, even when it comes to cheating. You can figure a man out, but not a woman. Some men discover this truth to their grief, others to the satisfaction of their craving for adventure and excitement and love. Some accept it for the last reason, and live with a woman happily, with the conviction that for all their oddity, a woman is a man's other half, and we're incomplete without them. Loftus Gandy was one of those who looked at it this way.

But Isaac wasn't. He couldn't handle a truth like that. He couldn't tolerate the realization that there would always be something untamed about a woman, no matter how soft and beautiful she was. Isaac had had his brief glimpse into the jungle of the female heart, and he reckoned that one glimpse would by-God do him for a lifetime.

He was thinking he might even stop attending church regularly, especially if *she* kept on showing up. He concluded that Anastasia Eckert was more of a mystery than any human being has a right to be, even a woman. He tried to picture how it would have been if they'd gotten married: Anastasia might be sitting there smiling one minute, and the next she'd have you trying to explain exactly how it was you were sitting there across from her and not sitting somewhere else. And before long, she'd have you feeling miserable and guilty, no matter what kind of answer you came up with.

So that was that. He decided he'd just go ahead with his plan for the locket anyway, but the problem was finding an artist. There were maybe a half dozen in Brackenport who looked upon themselves as artists, and he thought about all of them. But the one his thoughts kept returning to was definitely the worst one, Cornelia Oakum. He knew she was a lunatic, but that was all right. Weren't artists supposed to be eccentric? Even if Cornelia was as crazy as everybody said she was, there was something about that portrait she did for Sheriff Tewksberry that wouldn't leave him alone. Everybody had laughed about that painting and said it was too dark to make out much of a human figure at all, if that's what it was. Of course they were right. You couldn't deny it. And yet, once Isaac studied what she'd painted, something in his mind got tangled up in it. There was something mighty odd about that dark figure. Not only that, wasn't his *own* skin too dark in the view of most people?

So he went ahead with his plan and showed Cornelia Oakum both of the gold lockets, one with a woman's portrait in it and the other awaiting his likeness. He told her that he wanted as close a match as she could make, his portrait done in pen and ink so that the two of them would be mated, in a manner of speaking.

Cornelia listened politely to what he said, then told him she didn't do pen and ink portraits.

"I've heard you don't," Isaac said, "but I figured if you can do a painting you can do a drawing."

"I paint steamboats," she said, the way a woman might point out that she does needlework when somebody asks her if she breaks wild horses.

"I am aware of that," Isaac told her, "but I figured that since you did a portrait once, you might do it again. And you might do a pen and ink drawing. It can't be that much different, can it?"

"It can and it can't," Cornelia answered with a faraway look in her eye.

"What does that mean?" Isaac asked, beginning to feel a mite uneasy.

"Money is of little concern to me," Cornelia said.

Isaac drummed his fingers a moment and thought. He thought of Anastasia and reckoned his approach had been wrong then, and it might be wrong now, with Cornelia Oakum. Maybe flattery would do the trick. "I sure liked that portrait you did of the unknown man," he finally said.

"It wasn't Mr. Biddle," Cornelia said.

"What?"

"The man I saw was not Mr. Biddle."

"Are you sure?"

"I notice things," Cornelia said.

"But I heard Sheriff Tewksberry say you claimed that you *didn't* notice things. In fact, that's what he said you said. He said you said . . ." Isaac hauled in his sails at this point and decided to grope his way more cautiously. Then he started over. "When Sheriff Tewksberry asked you to draw a picture of the man you'd seen on the day Nehemiah was killed, didn't you tell him you don't *notice* people?"

"I do and I don't," Cornelia said.

"I see."

Isaac drummed his fingers some more. "Well, I sure liked that picture you painted well enough, and I figured that—"

"Yes?" Cornelia asked.

"Oh, never mind," Isaac told her. "To hell with it. I don't think I want my picture in that goddamned locket, anyway! What's the point of it? What's the point of having your picture *anywhere*, come to think of it?"

Isaac jumped to his feet and stared at her, gripping and ungripping his hands, like a man who wants to choke something or somebody. And yet, he wasn't surprised that Cornelia didn't answer. Everybody knew she was unhinged. What bothered him was the way she just sat there and smiled at him. *He* was surprised by the way he was acting, but *she* didn't seem to be surprised at all. Not only that, he couldn't figure out what her smile meant.

When he thought about it later on, he decided two things: Cornelia Oakum had had *something* in mind; and he didn't want anything more to do with that goddamned locket.

No, make it three things: he finally made up his mind that he was going to stop attending church regularly. It wasn't just that he might keep running into Anastasia there, but it was also the fact that he felt hog-tied to the organ music and such. Some folks just aren't *meant* for church, and Isaac figured that it was by-God about time he faced up to the fact that he was one of the soldiers in their camp.

## THE FATE OF THE VALISE FILLED WITH GOLD

Silas Potter was getting pretty old and took satisfaction from the thought that he had had what most folks would consider a successful life. He and his wife had four children, but then disaster struck when she was giving birth to their fifth. The boy was stillborn, and she died of childbirth fever.

Silas was distraught, the way it usually is, but being a physician saved him. He had been trained so close to the harness that he had to keep on pulling, even after his mare was no longer in the harness beside him. He couldn't keep on with his practice and still raise his children, so he hired an old woman named Felicia DeBow to take care of them and manage the house. Their maid stayed on. She was a girl named Rachel Hess. She'd been part of the household almost from the start, only she was somewhat slow-witted and couldn't have taken over managing the household as Felicia DeBow did.

Isaac had first gone to Silas in the winter of 1868 to see if he could relieve a painful muscular rheumatism that had settled in his neck. Being a doctor, the first thing Silas had done was give him a name for his misery, torticollis, or stiff neck.

"What the hell, Silas, I *know* I've got a stiff neck," Isaac had told him. "You don't have to tell me that, or give me a fancy name for it. A stiff neck is what I've *come* here for."

"I'm telling you it's a muscular rheumatism," Silas snapped. "Diagnosis comes first, then treatment."

The two of them had glared at each other for a moment, Silas taking in the grim-looking old pirate sitting on the other side of his desk.

"And what might the treatment be?" Isaac said.

"Quinine and iodide of potassium for a start. Mustard plasters as often as you can stand them. You got anybody in that big house of yours who can nurse you?"

"I've got a couple of maids and a housekeeper."

"They should be able to help you out, then."

"What are you talking about? I don't need anybody to help me fix a mustard plaster on the back of my neck."

Silas shrugged. "Suit yourself. Any way you want to do it is all right with me. Just so long as you get it done."

"I reckon I can get it done, all right."

So it was obvious from the start that the two men hadn't hit it off. Sometimes it happens like that; but what was strange this time was that within a year or so they had gotten to be close friends, and often in an evening he came over and visited with Isaac. Sometimes three or four others showed up and they had a game of poker, but often it was just the two of them, and they sat and told stories and talked about politics and how the world was going to hell until the stars had turned over in the sky and the lamps had burned low.

They wouldn't have become such good friends if they hadn't started off by snarling at each other. Once they got that out of their systems, they figured they could just sort of relax and say whatever they wanted. They figured there was no other way to go in their friendship than up, and they were right. They didn't have to pretend, so they didn't bother. And then before you knew it, almost without realizing it, they woke up to the realization that they were close friends. You could tell it by the way they insulted each other, only now the words didn't mean what they had at the beginning.

Their friendship ripened even further late one night after a lazy hour's talk, when without any warning, Isaac confessed one of his deepest secrets. He said, "Maybe you've heard the story about something that happened a year before I came to Brackenport."

"What story?" Silas asked him.

"The one about how I was approached by a couple of ruffians on a steamboat about ten miles downriver from here. I was on my way back east to join my family after leaving the mine fields in California."

"Yep, I've heard it, all right," Silas said.

"Well, there's something you haven't heard, because I haven't told anybody around here."

"What's that?"

"That part about me throwing the valise overboard is true. And it was filled with gold, all right. Not just hundreds of dollars worth of gold, but thousands. I'll tell you, that valise was *heavy* with gold!"

"Yep," Silas said. "That's what I heard. Everybody wondered about all those times you'd disappear and stay away for several hours in those days, then later on Loftus Gandy said he'd heard you were out dragging the channel for the valise. Along with several other scoundrels."

"Watch who you call a scoundrel, you scoundrel!"

"I'll call a scoundrel a scoundrel whenever I see one."

Isaac thought about that a moment, then nodded. "Well, maybe I did have a touch of the scoundrel in me back in those days."

"Yep, back before you read Nehemiah's diary and got religion."

"You leave my brother's diary out of this, you damned charlatan."

"Get on with the story."

"All right, I will. Even if you did tell me to. The reason for it was what they said, too."

"What who said? The reason for what?"

"Those ruffians. And the reason for me tossing that valise overboard. Those damned villains had knives in their hands and were coming at me and fixing to take it away, so I just tossed it. You should have seen the looks on their faces."

"Everybody knows about that," Silas said. "I thought you said you had something new to confess."

"Just hang on to your pants. Where'd you think that gold came from?"

"You struck it rich it, didn't you?"

"I sure did, but I didn't strike it rich in the ground."

"You mean to say that—?"

"Yep, I killed a man for it. One reason I shot him was for the gold, but there was a lot more to it. Everybody figured I'd killed the son of a bitch, and they were fixing to try me the next morning and string me up sure as hell, so I snuck out in the dead of night, leaving behind more than half of the loot. I'll tell you I was a different man in those days, Silas. A different man. Looking back, I can hardly believe how I was."

"Well, I'll be damned!" Silas muttered. "I'd heard about how you had to skedaddle and leave most of it behind, but the way I heard it, you'd been innocently accused."

"That's the way it was told, and I was content to leave that version undisturbed."

"By God, you *were* a black-hearted scoundrel then, weren't you?"

"I was and I was not."

"What's that supposed to mean?"

"You remember what Wilmot Chandler said when he was prosecuting Eugene Biddle?"

"I do."

"He said some of the truest and most undemocratic things I've ever heard. It's a wonder he got away with saying such things. It's a wonder he wasn't run out of town or maybe hanged for the things he said."

"You mean about how some folks are just naturally more killable than other folks?"

"I do. His argument was that in spite of what the law says, killing people isn't an absolute. That's the term he used. He said killing some folks is a lot more heinous a sin than killing others. He said that with some it's hardly a sin at all, but with others, like Nehemiah Dawes, it's about the worst there is and the killer deserved to be hanged."

"Which he was. If you think Biddle did it."

"Which he was," Isaac agreed. "But he claimed it worked both ways: he said the guilt attached to murdering somebody depends upon two things—who's murdered and who does the murdering. So hanging a killer depends upon who he is and who he killed."

"Yep, that's undemocratic, all right."

"Never mind that. Do you agree with it?"

"Nope. I wouldn't like to think that way."

"Of course you wouldn't, but what does *that* have to do with it? You don't like to think that people die of fevers and steamboat explosions either, do you?"

"I don't see the connection, Isaac. Get back to the subject."

"All right, I will. I didn't kill that feller in California just to get his gold. I killed him partly because he was the meanest son of a bitch I've ever set eyes on. I happened to know that he'd killed his partner to get all that gold he had, so I reckoned it wasn't any more of a sin for me to send him packing to hell than if I'd squashed a skeeter with my hand."

"So that's what you reckoned, was it? An eye for an eye and a tooth for a tooth. And taking justice and the judgment of God in your own hands."

"Yep. That's about the size of it."

"Well, I'll be damned."

"You probably will be."

"So you reckoned you were some kind of instrument of justice? Is that it?"

"It is and it isn't. That's part of it, all right. But the other part was the money. If there hadn't been two parts, I'm not sure I could have done it, not even as bad as I was then. I had my limits, after all."

Silas nodded. Then the two of them fell quiet for a while.

But finally Isaac said, "Don't feel sorry for me, Silas. I only killed one man; God knows how many you've sent to their grave."

## THE LOCKET, THE LOCKET

Isaac's fascination with the locket was such that there were times when he couldn't get it out of his mind. He asked everybody and anybody who might know about Cloverland and was finally able to piece together a pretty good sense of its history. He was almost sure that it had belonged to Lysander Crenshaw's wife, Lydia, who'd died several years back. Early on in his investigation, he'd suspected this, but had packed his suspicion deep down in his mind so that he wouldn't have to think about it. We all fool ourselves like that, only Isaac could do it better than most.

Now that he'd changed his mind about matching the locket, he began to think about it differently, and what he thought was that the poor woman's son should have it. He was her only survivor, and his name was Abel. He had returned home to inherit Cloverland after his pa had shot and killed himself back in the spring of fifty-seven. Like his pa, Abel Crenshaw was also a sot and ne-er-do-well, and in those days seemed intent upon letting the place go to ruin and decay. Captain Billy told him that folks said you wouldn't recognize that beautiful place any more. All that wealth and beauty turning into stubble and weeds and rot.

Maybe so. Nevertheless, Isaac told himself that whatever Abel did was none of his business; but returning the locket to him was. He told himself it had already caused enough trouble; in fact, it was almost like a curse. He told himself that he should have faced up to this fact long before now and returned the damned thing. He told himself that there are loops in a human life, where things leave and then come back, and such departures and returns should be respected and attended to, for they are much of what our days and years are made of.

He told himself he should write Abel a letter, so he sat down and did, as follows:

Abel Crenshaw
Cloverland
Kanawha Valley
West Virginia, U.S.A.

Sir:

I have in my possession a gold locket that I have reason to believe contains the likeness of your deceased mother, Lydia Crenshaw. I purchased this locket years ago, but have decided that I should not keep it any longer. Thinking you are the proper owner, I am convinced that you should have it and will be happy to give (not sell) it to you if it is indeed what I think it is. Please inform me of your interest in this matter. I await your reply.

Yours,
Isaac Dawes

Having mailed the letter, Isaac settled down to await an answer. He did more than wait, for he was always kept busy with the affairs of his various enterprises, but whenever he paused to take a breath, he wondered what kind of answer he would get.

But while he was waiting for a letter from Abel Crenshaw, he was surprised to get one from somebody unexpected, Anastasia Eckert, as follows:

Dear Isaac:

I'm sure you must be surprised to hear from me, but there is a reason I feel compelled to write to you. I fear that I was uncivil and ungracious when last we met, and I want to apologize. I don't know what possessed me at that time, but for some reason I "went too far" and what I had somewhat intended as banter suddenly became morbidly fascinating to me, and I soon found a certain feverish enjoyment in making you so obviously miserable. But you must believe me, Isaac—this was not my original intent, and I truly do beg your forgiveness.

Having said all that, I must be honest with you and make it clear that I see no future for the two of us together. My heart will forever belong to my dear dead Henry, and I must remain faithful to his memory as long as it beats.

Please realize that this is a most painful letter for me to write. In penning it, I have forced myself to dwell upon things that are far from pleasant. Alas, we are not as good and fine and noble as we should be! Perhaps I should not include others in such a broad generalization; but it is surely true of your

Penitent Friend,
Anastasia Eckert

Isaac studied this letter, and then studied it again. At first it made sense to him, and then it didn't. He went back to it late in the evening, and drank a small glass of whiskey as he studied it word for word.

He figured that now he knew how to take a sip and not keep on until he got the blind staggers, and he figured he could attend church without overdoing his religion. He didn't want to give up on the Bible entirely, because he was getting on in years and beginning to groan and ache and creak like an old rowboat. Rheumatism and gout both attacked him, and Silas couldn't do much for him. Isaac had also noticed having a problem remembering things, now and then.

Yes, it was time he settled some of his moral and spiritual accounts in life, just in case. So he sat down and wrote another letter to Abel Crenshaw. Isaac figured that maybe old Lysander's boy hadn't gotten the first letter, so he'd give him another chance.

But he didn't get an answer to this letter, either, and so he continued concentrating on his many business affairs, along with the gloomy dreams he'd been having lately, which he reckoned were part of becoming an old man and drawing near to the End, as eventually we must all do. So for a while he forgot all about returning the locket.

Then he remembered again, and wrote a third time, but he didn't get an answer to that letter, either, so he figured there was only one thing to do, which was to take the locket to Cloverland himself. After the second letter, he'd wondered if maybe Abel Crenshaw had died or moved away, so he asked Captain John Heckman about it. His steamboat, the *Liberty Eagle*, made regular trips up the Kanawha, and he should know. Which he did, and told him that the last he'd heard, old Abel

Crenshaw was still alive and kicking, only he'd gone eccentric and never poked his nose out of that big old house of his.

"Well, I guess he has to be pretty old by now," Isaac said.

"Yep, he sure is. He was an old man when he come back to Cloverland to claim his inheritance and that was many years ago now. He hadn't been nothing but a damn wastrel for years. Everybody knows it. They say he looked as old as his pa, and just as seedy. If you'd ever seen that old scoundrel, you'd know that was saying something. A life of dissipation will do that to a body."

"I reckon it will," Isaac said.

"Yep, 'the sins of the fathers,' like the Good Book says."

"There were a lot of stories about Lysander."

"And likely all of 'em true."

"They say he has a brother still living up in Lancaster."

"If he's alive, he is."

Captain Heckman paused and thought a moment. Then he cleared his throat and said, "From what they say, it sounds to me like the wrong son died. Only I guess the other one was weak in the head. I guess there wasn't no way for the father to win out. But then, given a sinner of his dimensions, why should there be?"

"You're talking about Lysander," Isaac said.

"Yep. He's still the one."

"But you're pretty sure Abel's still living there at Cloverland?"

"Sure, I'm sure. Why's it so important?"

"I've got to return something that belongs to him."

"If I was you, I'd send it by post."

"No, that won't work. I've tried to write to him, but I can't get an answer."

"That don't surprise me none. They say he don't even answer you if you ask him a question right to his face! Most of the time, he don't even talk. You could be right there a yelling at him and he'd look right through you. Crazy as hell. Men that go to Cloverland on business don't never go back."

"I guess I'm not surprised to hear it."

"I wouldn't trust that devil for a moment. Everybody knows there's something wrong with him."

"Well, I reckon I'll have to just take my chances."

"I'd take a pistol with you, if I was you."

"So it's like that, is it?"

"All I know is what I hear."

"Maybe I'll take a pistol, then."

"Well, the *Liberty Eagle* will be leaving day after tomorrow. You want to book passage?"

"I was thinking along those lines."

"Well, then, I'll just see to it personal, Mr. Dawes."

"I'd appreciate it," Isaac told him.

# CLOVERLAND

Isaac asked Loftus Gandy if he wanted him to come along. Loftus was famous for his curiosity about everything under the sun and a few things that weren't. They liked to say he could ask more questions in an hour than two lawyers and a spinster in a week. That had always been his way. Questioning was just natural with him. And he'd always been curious about the Crenshaw plantation, so Isaac figured he'd be willing to come and good to have along. It was more than just doing Loftus a favor, though; it was having a back-up in case all those horror stories were true and Abel Crenshaw was as deranged as everybody said he was and started to make trouble.

Folks surprise themselves by what they think and what they do. Self-knowledge will carry you only so far, and then you're in over your head. It was this way with Isaac. He had to reckon he was just a little uneasy about going to Cloverland where he'd have to face Abel Crenshaw. No matter that he was doing him a favor. Often lunatics don't understand such things. And no matter that he himself had once been a ruffian of the worst sort, and breathed enough fire to face anybody, anytime, with or without knives or loaded pistols.

No, Isaac had gotten soft and genteel through the years, what with being sure of his next meal and a comfortable place to sleep and the responsibilities of running his businesses and reading Nehemiah's diary and becoming an occasional churchgoer for so long. So he figured it was a smart idea to invite Loftus along. Loftus was smart and dependable and had good sense, even though he had a peculiar way of talking and sometimes you didn't know how to take something he said.

He figured that if trouble reared its head, Loftus would be as likely to talk their way out of it as anybody.

Not only that, Loftus acted like a man with grit, so if the talk didn't work, he had some nerve to back him up. Such men are not all that common. But there was also something else: when you get a man who likes to talk as much as Isaac did, he just naturally enjoys the company of anybody who'll listen. And if there was anybody in Brackenport who'd listen to you, it was Loftus Gandy.

They said that a few darkies still remained at Cloverland from the slave days, including Hosea's old ma, who'd come back there to live after being in Charleston all these years. But there was no longer an overseer or any discipline observed in getting out the crops. There was rot and decay all over. The roofs of most of the buildings were beginning to sag and leak and the weeds around the fence posts were so high you had trouble seeing the fence. There were still a few horses left, but they were a sorry sight because nobody ever bothered to curry or shoe the poor beasts. The trees in the peach orchards were shaggy with suckers, and if you took one glance at the tobacco crop, you'd see it was hardly worth the bother of hauling it to the curing barns.

So when Isaac and Loftus boarded the *Liberty Eagle*, and when they were about ten miles up the Kanawha, Isaac told Loftus to come out on the deck with him. He opened his valise and took out two .45 caliber revolvers with walnut grips. He gave one of them to Loftus. He sighted through the other one and said it was just in case they needed them. But first they should try them out, so they loaded them, and then Isaac took aim and let fire at a crooked branch floating in the current.

They could see the water dimple about three feet away, where the bullet hit.

Then they took turns, and each let fly five times at various targets, after which Isaac said, "I don't seem to be able to hit any damned thing. How about you?"

"Not too much."

"Have you hit anything you've aimed at?"

"Nope."

"Neither have I."

But they kept on loading and firing and for the most part missing, although one time Isaac claimed he'd hit a limb he was aiming at. Still, their aim wasn't very good, and that had to be a little discouraging.

"Part of it's because we're moving," Isaac said. They'd fired about fifteen shots and he was letting his barrel cool off.

"I imagine," Loftus said. But what he didn't say was that if they would have to use the pistols, it wasn't likely their target would be standing still so they could have an easy shot.

After another five or six rounds, the *Liberty Eagle* blew her whistle, which sounded loud enough to deafen folks clear to Charleston, and then they heard the paddle wheel shift in reverse, spitting water as the old steamboat eased around and finally, after considerable serious puffing, nosed into the soft mud bank.

Captain Heckman came up and said, "Boys, this here's Cloverland. Wait for the gangplank to drop. We'll drop her high enough so it hits the sod and you can disembark without having to step in the mud. After that, it's all up to you. That's the best we can do for you, boys. Except maybe for a prayer."

Isaac and Loftus said that was just fine, then waited and stepped off, carrying their carpetbags. The last they heard from the *Liberty Eagle* was Captain John Heckman once again cautioning them to be careful. Then the big sternwheeler whooshed and reversed its wheel and eased back into the channel, blowing its whistle loud enough to wake the dead and shake the leaves off the trees.

So much noise made them uneasy, but then Isaac pointed out that nobody who heard it would necessarily assume that somebody had landed, because steamboats were always blowing their whistles. They do it to claim the channel from another steamboat, or to signal a flatboat or rowboat to ske-daddle. Or sometimes they don't need an excuse, they'd just do it to make a loud noise, and let the world know who they are, because no two steamboat whistles sound exactly alike, and they are all proud of how they sound and how much noise they can make.

After the *Liberty Eagle* pulled away and rounded the bend upriver, things suddenly got very quiet. Silence and heat dropped upon them like a thick comforter dropped upon a bed, but it didn't seem dangerous. Everything seemed peaceful enough, just depressing. It was a warm and sunny day, with the June bugs chittering away in the thick dark green underbrush that bordered the dirt road leading up to the house. You could smell the dust and the sunlight in the air, and the whole world seemed half asleep. Isaac and Loftus walked about fifty yards up the road before either of them said anything.

It was Isaac who spoke first. "I don't see any signs of life anywhere," he said. "Do you?"

"Nope," Loftus told him. "It doesn't even look like anybody lives here."

"Quiet as a graveyard," Isaac muttered.

Then they stopped and looked all around, feeling the hot sunlight on their faces. Isaac was wearing a frock coat that was too hot for the weather, but he didn't complain, because it was enough to conceal his revolver when he kept it buttoned. Not only that, if you're a gentleman, you should dress like one. Also, they didn't want any fireworks if they could help it. "Talk solves a hell of a lot more problems than gunfire," he said, "and all we can hope is, Abel Crenshaw will give us the benefit of listening to what we have to say."

"You make him sound like a surefire hellion," Loftus said, after they'd started in walking again.

"More like a demon from hell, from what everybody says," Isaac told him. Then in a discouraged voice, he said, "And all the reports are unanimous."

They walked on, side by side, each of them in one of the ruts from the wagon wheels. *One rut apiece and the Unknown up ahead*, as Loftus would think of it later. He kind of liked the sound of that, and began to think of how it was a figure of speech that might apply to life itself.

But then he told himself that this was no time for literary indulgence. He told himself just to keep his eyes and ears open and his hands ready.

The dirt road was only about two hundred and fifty yards long, but it seemed a lot longer. It seemed more like a half mile. And about halfway there, Isaac stopped and said in a loud voice, "How's come we're walking so quiet, Loftus? We don't want folks to think we're sneaking up on them, do we?"

"Nope," Loftus said in a voice that was just as loud. Then he added, "Because that's sure not what we're doing, is it?"

"Nope, it sure isn't!" Isaac yelled back.

They'd made enough noise to flush grouse from a thicket, but it didn't have any effect out there in the open sunlight.

So they just kept on walking, past the first curing barn and on past a working shed on one side, and a blacksmith forge on the other. Two sparrows popped out of a chinaberry tree and flew off toward a crab apple tree beside the house. But beyond that, there was nothing. Not even a sound.

"Maybe nobody's here?" Isaac said, stopping again to look around.

But then they saw that there was somebody. A skinny old black man over six feet tall and dressed in tatters came walking around the second curing barn and started toward them.

"We're looking for Mr. Crenshaw!" Isaac called out.

"He in de house," the old man said. "He spectin you, is he?"

"No, he isn't," Isaac said.

The old man rubbed his jaw. "Well, den, I jest dunno."

"Don't know what?" Isaac asked.

"Dunno, if you gemmens should just walk on up dere if he ain *spectin* you."

"Go tell him we're here, then."

"No sah. Doan wanna do nuffin like dat! No sah."

"Well, how are we going to talk to him, then?"

"Ain no way I kin see."

"So do we just stand here, then?" Isaac said.

"Yassah. Dat or turn round and go back whence you come."

"Did he say 'whence'?" Loftus asked.

Isaac nodded. "That's what he said, all right."

"Folks doan come here no mo," the old darky said in a discouraged voice.

"I've got something that belongs to Mr. Crenshaw," Isaac told him. "And I want to give it to him."

"Doan know nothin bout dat," the old man said. He had drawn breath to say something else when there was a gunshot so loud and sudden and unexpected it was enough to suck out your breath and leave you panting. The old darky disappeared like a magician's assistant on stage, and the quiet clapped about their ears again.

"You might thank the Lord you can still jump," a voice said from a nearby shed. "That means you're alive and still able to turn around and go back down that road and not turn back. I've got a double barrel, here, and the second barrel's filled with buckshot. I might be able to get both of you with one blast. But even if I don't, I can sure as hell get one of you. Now git outta here and stay out."

All of this was said in a dull, slow voice, the way you'd tell the cook how you want your eggs for breakfast. That made it worse. If he'd yelled at them, it wouldn't have sounded so sinister. But for a man to talk like that after deafening them with a shot from an over-loaded gun was enough to turn their liver to milk. Especially when they couldn't even see him.

But then they could. He stepped out from behind a shed, carrying his shotgun waist high. He was a thick old specimen, as pale as a corpse, with loose skin hanging from his bones and a face so craggy you had to just guess there were two eyes in it somewhere. Only you'd have to guess they were glaring at you. The mouth was a jagged scrawl and looked like it hadn't ever grinned, much less smiled.

Isaac cleared his throat and said, "Are you Abel Crenshaw?"

"It's none of your goddamned business who I am," the man growled. "Now git the hell out of here!"

"We will," Isaac said in a reasonable voice, "but I want to leave something with you. I'll just drop it on the ground and you can pick it up. It's your mother's locket."

Saying that, Isaac took the locket out of his pocket and threw it about four feet in front of his boots. Then he turned around and said in a voice that sounded calm, but loud enough for the dangerous critter to hear, if he had a mind to: "Come on, Loftus. We'll leave now, just like the man said."

So the two of them started walking back down the wagon path toward the river, walking slow and with a certain hesitation, the way you do when you kind of hope you'll be called back. And they were not disappointed, as that is what happened. They'd taken no more than ten or twelve steps when they heard that hoarse voice call out to them: "Turn around and come on back here."

Isaac turned around and said, "No, if you don't want us, we'll be on our way. All I wanted to do was return the locket where it belongs."

"Come on back here. I've got somethin' t'ask you."

Isaac thought about that a moment, then nodded and walked back to him, with Loftus following; then Abel Crenshaw, for they assumed that's who it was, nodded toward the house, so the three of them walked up to the side door and went inside, where it was cool and dark. Abel Crenshaw led them into a big parlor and offered them chairs to sit in. Then he carefully poured brandy into three good-sized glasses.

Before lifting their glasses, Isaac and Loftus looked all around, sizing things up.

It wasn't only cool and dark inside, it was old and decrepit looking, although so far as they could see, clean and free of dust. The floors didn't seem to have enough rugs to swallow the noise, so just moving your chair caused a hollow sound, half scrape and half echo. The rooms had high ceilings, polished six-panel walnut doors, and were awash in shadows.

You might have thought that this was a place where old sins and old regrets had festered through the years, soaking into the hardwood banisters and moldings and broad pale slabs of pine flooring.

Isaac took a long drink and said, "Mr. Crenshaw, I wrote to you three times, but you didn't answer."

Even in the darkness, you could see Crenshaw frown as he considered how best to respond to that. But then he didn't respond at all—which is often the best way to do it. Instead, he just took a long drink and then smacked his lips and sighed.

Isaac picked up the beat and drank, too, only he didn't sigh. He was waiting for an answer. Loftus was watching both of them, but kind of holding back on his own drinking, which was a good thing, because both of the other men had already emptied their glasses, like they were in an almighty hurry.

Everything remained quiet for a little while, then Abel got up and poured more brandy for Isaac and himself. Then he motioned toward Loftus's glass, but Loftus shook his head no.

Finally, Isaac couldn't wait any longer. He said, "Why didn't you answer my letters?"

"There was a reason," Abel Crenshaw growled in a faraway voice.

"I don't doubt it. Only I can't help wondering what it was. I am aware that you don't owe me an explanation, but that doesn't keep me from wondering."

"Well, I don't suppose it does," Abel admitted. It was along about then that Loftus noticed that when Abel talked to you, he never looked at you. It wasn't just that he didn't quite look you in the eye—a lot of people don't do that—but he somehow managed to miss your head altogether. He seemed to be talking to somebody about two feet higher than you. Loftus found this all very curious, and a little distracting, which it was.

Abel lifted the locket at arm's length before his eyes and gazed at it for a moment, then said, "Yep, that's a picture of my ma, all right. She sure was a beautiful woman."

Isaac and Loftus both agreed that she was, which was not only the polite thing to say, but the truth.

Abel shook his head with the wonder of it. "And here I never thought I'd ever see her image again. And yet, there she is, once again smiling out at me. Not exactly smiling, but almost. *Kind* of smiling, you might say."

"I'd call it a smile," Isaac said in a judicious voice, and Loftus nodded.

Everybody was quiet for a moment, then Isaac said, "If you felt that way about it, Mr. Crenshaw, how's come you didn't answer my letters? I made it clear what I intended to do. All I wanted to do was return the locket to you. Nothing else."

Abel sighed. "I know what you said in those letters, only I figured it might be some kind of a trick."

"What kind of trick?" Isaac said.

Abel thought a moment and sighed again. He acted like a man who's been climbing up a steep hill and suddenly finds himself wondering why he'd bothered. "I guess it doesn't matter anymore."

"What doesn't?" Isaac said.

"That my pa was the one who had your brother killed."

Isaac tottered, like a man who's just been struck a terrible blow. Finally, he found his voice and said, "Would you mind going over that again?"

"Don't pretend you didn't know."

"Didn't know what?"

Abel took a drink, and put his glass down on a single-stem Duncan Phyfe table.

He stood up and walked over to a large plantation desk, piled high with papers, and rummaged around among them for a moment, then withdrew a sheaf of foolscap tied together with string. "It's all in here," he said.

"What is?" Isaac asked. "

"The Devil's diary, that's what."

Isaac turned to Loftus and said, "Loftus, do you know what Mr. Crenshaw is talking about?" You could tell that he was still trying to recover from the shock of what he'd just heard. Loftus shook his head no, but didn't say anything.

"Don't think I wasn't aware from the start. Don't think I didn't know how you were fixing to come here and put a bullet in my head. Just looking for an excuse, that's what you were doing!"

"Loftus," Isaac said, "I'm afraid that Mr. Crenshaw is laboring under a misconception."

Maybe he was, but he wasn't listening. He just looked about two feet above Isaac's head and continued talking: "This is my pa's diary, and it tells everything you'd want to know, and a few things you might not want to know. You can tell by the handwriting that it's the work of the Devil. But I guess you know all about that."

"Loftus," Isaac said, "Mr. Crenshaw seems to think we know all about what's written in those papers, but I've never set eyes on them, have you?"

"Nope," Loftus said.

But Abel still wasn't paying attention. He said, "It tells all about it. It tells how he paid to have your brother killed. It mentions him by name: Nehemiah Dawes. That was your brother, all right, and don't try to deny it."

Hearing his dead brother's name spoken by this dangerous lunatic was almost more than Isaac could stand, and it was no wonder he couldn't speak for a moment. Loftus heard him breathing in and out three times before he managed to make a noise. "Yep," he finally said. "He was my brother, all right. And it's always been a mystery who the son of a bitch was that killed him, only I didn't for one moment—"

"That son of a bitch was my pa," Abel Crenshaw said in a calm voice, nodding.

Isaac wiped his open hand all over his face, and then paused and did it again. Then, in a strangled voice he said, "Well, Nehemiah was rich and outspoken and had a lot of enemies in town, so I always figured it had to be somebody around Brackenport. Personally, I figured it had to be one of the Kittle brothers. I never did think it was Biddle. Biddle was the man who worked for my brother. He was convicted of his murder and went to the scaffold."

Isaac paused and took a drink of brandy, still shaking his head at the shock and magnitude of what he'd just heard. "You know, I never thought about how it could have been your pa and about how he might have paid to have Nehemiah killed for vengeance. The idea that—"

But he didn't get to finish his sentence, because Abel interrupted him, kind of singing his words, like a medieval chant. "Oh, my pa was vengeful, all right. Vengeful as hell. The son of a bitch." Then he raised his voice and yelled so loud that the word he shouted echoed from the walls and the ceiling, and up and down the stairway: "*Vengeful!*"

"That's the word," Isaac said.

"That son of a bitch!" Abel muttered.

"Who? My brother?"

"No, my pa."

Isaac nodded,

Abel took another deep breath, and then another deep drink of brandy. Finally, he licked his lips, pointed to his pa's diary and said, "It's all in there. There's more hatred and vengeance in that sheaf of papers than you'll find in the Devil's private library! My pa never forgave a wrong, and never forgot. Believe me, I know better than any living man what he was like. The only generous act he ever committed was killing himself, only he didn't do it soon enough."

When Abel looked at Isaac and Loftus, his eyes may have missed their mark by a foot or so, but when he looked at his pa's diary, they were right on target. "He never forgave anybody anything, and I'll never forget it, the son of a bitch!"

Loftus and Isaac thought about that, but didn't say anything.

Abel said, "What I'd like somebody to do is explain something to me: exactly why is it that our strongest terms of disapprobation for a man hinge upon the female?"

"What's that?" Isaac asked in a suspicious voice. He still hadn't quite recovered from the shock of recognition.

"When we hate a man, what are the worst two things we can call him? We call him a 'son of a bitch' or a 'bastard.' Now what I want to know is the reason for that."

"I don't get your drift," Isaac said.

"He's talking about the connection with women," Loftus said. Isaac was surprised, but nodded.

"Yes," Abel said, "that is right. Why should we have to bring in *women* for our most derogatory terms for a *man*? You'd think insulting men would be between men, but it isn't; it has to do with women, too. Only I never could figure out why!"

"Well, I for one," Isaac said, draining his glass, "have never thought about it."

Abel brought the bottle over and filled Isaac's glass again. And then he refilled Loftus's glass, although it hadn't been quite empty. "Bastard and son of a bitch," he said. "The two most common terms." He shook his head at the thought. "The two most vilifying terms in the language, and they have to bring in women. I'll tell you something, boys, it ain't right!"

Loftus took a good long look at the two of them and realized how drunk they were—which wasn't surprising, given the fact that they'd been drinking so fast. He was glad he'd managed to remain more or less sober and had a loaded pistol under his coat, in spite of how hot it was, because as everybody but a jackass knows, drink and firearms do not mix, and never have.

"My point is," Abel said, looking even higher on the wall above Isaac's head—at the part that almost reached the ceiling—"why should we bring women into it at all? Why don't we have words for a wicked and evil man that don't bring women into the picture?"

"I've never thought about it," Isaac said, repeating himself.

"Well, it so happens that I've got a word that's worse than either one," Abel said, by now looking clear up to the ceiling.

"What is it?" Isaac asked.

"Father," Abel said

"My pa wasn't like that," Loftus said. The other two men looked at him, surprised to hear from him, because he'd been so quiet that it was easy to forget he was sitting there in the room with them.

Abel took a deep breath. "My pa was the devil incarnate. He was a blasphemer, a sot, a gambler, and a fornicator. He slept with one of our poor slaves, and she gave birth to two boys, even while my poor mother was alive to witness his evil carnality. That's what it was, you know: carnality, pure and simple. Evil! So that's how it happened. Carnality is evil, and don't you ever forget it."

"I won't," Loftus said, surprised that he'd said it and wondering if he wasn't also beginning to feel the brandy.

"What happened?" Isaac said. "I don't quite follow you."

"How it was that I had two brothers with dark skin? *Half* brothers, that is?" Abel paused and took a drink, and then thought a moment. "I reckon you could say that since two halves make a whole, then two half brothers would make one whole brother."

Loftus thought that was so funny he almost laughed; but when he saw the look on Abel's face, he decided to remain quiet.

After another long and thoughtful pause, Abel went on: "But since my only real brother was only half there, I guess you could say that all I *ever* had was half brothers. My real brother was feeble-minded and drowned in the Kanawha back in eighteen fifty-seven."

"Ransom," Isaac said.

"That was his name, all right. Looks to me like you know all about us."

"Not by a long shot, but there's always gossip on the river."

"As for those two slaves—why, my pa was as much their pa as he was mine. And where did that leave *her*?" He pointed to the locket.

"My pa wasn't too bad," Isaac said.

Abel shook his head, "I was twelve years old when Hosea was born. He was a handsome little baby. You'd hardly ever guess that he was part African. But of course I knew what he was, and that made all the difference. I remember how it was."

Isaac swallowed a belch and said, "You remember how *what* was?"

"I remember everything. That's why I couldn't stay at home. That's why I never took over Cloverland until Pa died. I could not have abided to live under the same roof with that devil!"

Isaac said, "What is it you remember?"

"Growing up with two pale little pickaninnies running around in the yard. Pa had two of us outside and two of us inside. Two legitimate sons and two bastards. And all this time he was riding around on his little mare like a king, and everybody looked up to him and admired him and listened to everything he had to say like it was gospel! And my Ma . . ."

For some reason Isaac had suddenly gotten into a jovial mood. If you hadn't known he'd been drinking so much brandy, you might have thought his eyes were shining from excitement. He acted like a man who couldn't get enough of all the things Abel Crenshaw was saying. Loftus had never seen him like this, but then he'd never been around him when he was drunk.

"What about your Ma?" Isaac said.

Abel swallowed. "My ma never said a word. She was quiet and dignified and loved us the way they say everybody wants to be loved, but hardly anybody is. I heard somebody say once that nobody ever loved anybody the way everybody *wants* to be loved but whoever said that didn't know my ma."

"Except for you," Isaac said.

"Except for me *what*?" Abel said, almost looking Isaac in the face.

"You were loved that way. Isn't that what you just said?"

Abel thought a moment, then took another sip of his brandy and nodded. "It looks like I didn't turn out any better, though."

"Better than what?"

"Better than *him*," Abel said. "My *pa*! Do you know the only one of his four boys that might have turned out to be worth a good goddamn?"

"Who?" Loftus said.

Abel and Isaac were once again surprised by his interruption and turned to look at him, but Abel answered him nevertheless.

"Hosea. His other brother isn't worth a damn, and he's the one who isn't dead. Ransom wasn't worth anything, because he didn't have any brains. And I wasn't worth anything because I didn't have any character, and if you don't have character, you don't have *anything*!"

"Oh, I don't think it's quite that bad," Isaac said, getting up and walking over to help himself to more brandy.

Abel watched him, only about a foot off the mark, then fell silent a moment, after which he shook his head and muttered, "Oh, it's that bad, all right."

Isaac said, "Did you know that Hosea was the one who stole the locket? That's how I got it, after all. It was taken from his body. I think you should know that before you go overboard with praising him."

"I am well aware of the fact," Abel said. "It's in the Devil's notebook. It's all very clear. My pa couldn't forgive the poor bastard for doing what anybody would have done under the circumstances. Wouldn't you have taken it? But that's not it at all."

"What isn't?"

"It was my *pa* Hosea stole the locket from, not *her*. I don't think he would have stolen it from *her*. I don't think anybody could have done anything to hurt my ma, if they'd known her. Only one person, the devil she was married to. As for Ma, she was the kindest, gentlest, sweetest woman who ever set foot upon the earth, and there's not a day goes by but what I miss her and curse God for taking her from us."

Saying this, Abel picked up the locket and studied it. Then he sniffled a couple of times and before either Isaac or Loftus could figure out what was going on, he started in weeping, right there in front of them, sitting erect in the chair of a gentleman.

Loftus was embarrassed and hardly knew what to say, so he decided not to say anything. Isaac was probably embarrassed, too, only it was hard to tell.

When he finally got his feelings under control, Abel said, "Yes, this is an image of my ma, all right."

"I knew it was," Isaac said. "Right from the start. Didn't I, Loftus?"

But Loftus didn't answer. Abel sniffed again and said, "You know, I'd forgotten how beautiful she was."

"My mother was beautiful, too," Isaac said.

Loftus was going to say that his mother was, too, only he didn't want to be the last one to say it, so he kept quiet.

Abel said, "Is it any wonder I stayed away from home all those years? After she died, it was only him—Ransom, too, only Ransom didn't hardly count. There just wasn't enough of him *there!*"

"I understand how you must feel," Isaac said.

"Do you?" Abel asked, and Isaac nodded.

Still listening, Loftus remained silent.

Later, he figured it had been one of those times when he was listening too hard to say anything. Not to mention that he was getting a little bit dazed by the brandy, although obviously not as dazed as Isaac or Abel Crenshaw.

## NEARING THE END

Before long, Abel stopped talking and started humming. It sounded odd, and Isaac and Loftus hardly knew what to do. They figured the best thing was just to sit there and pretend that they either couldn't hear it or were enjoying it, but their pretence wasn't altogether successful, and at one point Isaac told Loftus in a low voice that he wondered what they'd gotten themselves into when they decided to visit Abel Crenshaw. Loftus was going to point out that he hadn't had any part in the decision; the decision had been all Isaac's. But he thought it over and decided, once again, not to say anything.

During this time when Abel was humming and gazing up at the ceiling, Loftus looked out into the hallway and saw a light-complexioned black woman walk by. She was wearing a long gray dress and had a red bandanna around her head. Her nose had been broken, and one eye was half-closed. Her face had been worked over, you could tell. But in spite of everything, there was something odd and fierce and strangely magnetic in her eyes that might have unsettled a man if he was in a certain mood.

But the instant Loftus got a glimpse of the woman, she was gone. Isaac was seated facing away from her, so he couldn't have seen her. And Abel hadn't seen her because he was too busy humming as he looked up at the ceiling. Just after she passed by the doorway, he lowered his gaze and pointed at his pa's diary and said, "I'll never have a moment's rest until I'm rid of that damned thing," he said.

"Why don't you just throw it away?" Isaac said.

"It doesn't happen like that," Abel told him, "It's too complicated for something as simple as that."

"Oh? And why is that?"

"Things like that take a hold of you and won't let go of you that easy."

Isaac nodded. "You know, I think I can see what you're getting at, because I had almost the same thing happen to me, only in the other direction. What I mean is, I came upon my brother's diary after he was dead, and I discovered that he was as good a man as you say your pa was evil. I learned things about him that I would never have learned in any other way. I figure that when people die and leave a diary, you learn things about them that you could have never understood while they were alive."

But Abel's thoughts were obviously far away. "I thought I hated him before, but I didn't know what hate was until he killed himself and I had to come home to claim Cloverland and . . . and there that damned thing was, just a waiting for me."

"The diary?" Isaac said.

Abel nodded. "The diary. And it will torment me as long as it exists. I may gather the courage to burn the damned thing, after all, only . . ."

"Only what?" Isaac asked.

But Abel still wasn't listening. At least, he wasn't listening to any voice that Isaac or Loftus could hear. Instead, he wiped his hands together fastidiously, as if he'd just washed them with soap and water, and then he stood up and said, "Brandy," and walked out of the room.

"Where's he going?" Loftus asked, and Isaac grunted and replied, "You tell me! I'd say he's as crazy as a jackass at a prayer meeting."

The two of them sat there for a while, thinking of that, and then Isaac got up and looked out the window. "I think he just walked around the shed out there."

Loftus said, "Do you suppose he's looking for brandy?"

"Who knows? From my observation so far, I'd say that just because he said the word doesn't mean a thing with Abel Crenshaw."

Loftus nodded, and then the two of them settled down in silence and waited a while longer.

"I'd kind of like to read that diary," Loftus said.

"Why don't you do him a favor then, and steal it?" Isaac said.

Loftus was quiet for a moment, then he said, "He'll be back before too long."

But it wasn't Abel Crenshaw who next entered the room, it was the high yeller woman with the broken nose and the half-closed eye. She looked at both of them for a moment, then said, "I think you gemmans would be smart to leave."

"You mean he's not coming back?" Isaac said.

"No, I mean he *is* coming back, only you'd better not be here when he does."

Isaac kind of grinned. "Oh? Why's that?"

"Didn't I hear him crying just now?"

Isaac nodded.

She shook her head. "It's bad when he cries. I wouldn't stay here a minute longer, if I was you."

"I'd still like to know why," Isaac said. "We've heard stories, of course, but he doesn't seem all that bad to me."

"You'd be smart to leave," the woman said. "I can't tell you no plainer than that."

"You must know something we don't know, or you wouldn't give us that advice."

The black woman thought a moment, then said, "I get feelings where I see things, and when I do, I pay attention to them like they was Scripture."

Isaac smiled. "Oh? You're what they call a prophetess?"

"You can call it anything you want. I just don't like the notion of having to clean blood off the floor."

"Is that what you see waiting for us?"

"In a way I do, and in a way I don't."

The way she said this took the smile off Isaac's face, but he managed to ask her what she meant by it.

"I cain't explain it," she said. "And I don't aim to try."

"All right, then: that blood you mentioned: is it his or ours?" Isaac said.

"Maybe everybody's," she said. "He's not right in the head. I guess you could figure that out though, couldn't you?"

"I could," Loftus said.

Isaac shook his head. "Well, I could, too." Then he turned to Loftus and said, "Maybe she's right."

"I think so," Loftus said, standing up.

Isaac stood up and said to the black woman, "Well, thanks for the warning."

"Never mind you thanking me," she said, "just leave this place while you can still walk."

Isaac nodded, and they were about to leave, when Loftus hesitated.

"What are you doing?" Isaac asked him.

"I think I'll just take your advice and relieve him of this," Loftus said, picking up the sheaf of papers that contained Lysander Crenshaw's diary.

Isaac grinned. "I'm sure he'll appreciate it."

"He won't never know the difference," the black woman said. "I think he's got it memorized, anyway."

So the two of them left and retraced their way down the wagon path to the Kanawha River, where they sat down to wait for the *Liberty Eagle* on her return trip.

They decided to keep a lookout toward the house, in case Abel Crenshaw took it into his mind to follow them. But he didn't, and some two hours later the *Liberty Eagle* splashed into view and they shouted and waved at it and it picked them up and took them downriver up to the Ohio, and then on to Brackenport.

## THE END

And that is pretty much the end of my story. Maybe you've already guessed my identity: Yes, I am Loftus Gandy, and the story belongs to me as the teller in ways it could not belong to any of the others who played a part in it. Telling my story is part of the story itself, because whatever I haven't personally experienced, I've had to make up the way I figure it must have happened.

Also in telling it I've had to step back and take stock of my life and contemplate what I've learned, or think I've learned. That requires self-knowledge, which is mighty hard to achieve, because no matter how far you step back, you'll never find a place to stand outside of what you are so that you can see yourself clearly. Trying to escape what you are is a little bit like trying to explain the mystery of time by saying it's whatever you can measure with a clock; nobody could say that isn't true, but it doesn't help.

Of course there are a few facts I can share with you: Years ago, I married Sophia Loomis, the beautiful daughter of Ezra Loomis, who owned some of the finest Arabians in southeastern Ohio. Sophia and I have raised three children, two girls and a boy, and now have five grandchildren. We live comfortably in an old Federal-style house only two miles upriver from Brackenport. My surviving sister lives some thirty miles away. My old Ma is still living, but she is poorly. Pa died eight years ago, long before he had a chance to read this account, assuming I'd have wanted to show it to him.

After studying law under Judge Stillman Bates, I hung out my shingle and practiced law until I was eventually elected Judge of the Common Pleas Court, where I served until my retirement last year. As a judge and lawyer I was privileged to experience humanity in its extremities of ignorance, viciousness, greed, stupidity, fear, vindictiveness, and spite. No doubt my association with the human species has been somewhat skewed to our shared disadvantage, but I can't think too highly of the motives and abilities of the general run of *homo sapiens.*

Still, I have not abandoned every shred of idealism. Blessed by a happy and generally healthy family, I have acquired some modest wealth, which enables us to live more comfortably than most people can hope for. And I have gathered together a small personal library of old books whose contents reveal the best of humanity as a lawyer's clients reveal the worst.

It is in my old books that I find solace, for there, in spite of the general cussedness and stupidity of the human species, I have come upon most of what I can understand of wisdom. Those books are filled with the words of people long dead, and it is in them that I find the balm of serenity and the honey of acquiescence. Those old authors lived and suffered, but in their language they attained to something like timelessness and some humble, mortal version of immortality.

In dramatic contrast to those lofty testaments, on my periodic visits to various of the great cities, I am appalled by what I see as the degradation of the teeming rabble. Everywhere there are people who have no hope of ever becoming rational and moral, and with no more capacity for becoming responsible parents than bagworms. I see increasing numbers of their dirty, angry, ignorant progeny wandering the streets and think that in a few years a good proportion of them will be going to prison or climbing the scaffold to the hangman's noose. And so it is that in every direction we witness the tragic betrayal of the great ideal of democracy as envisioned by Thomas Jefferson.

There hasn't been a hanging in Brackenport for almost ten years, now. Sometimes when I'm in a bad mood, I figure that's too long, considering the average measure of cussedness in the human critter; but then I remind myself that there's always tomorrow.

## ABOUT THE AUTHOR

Jack Matthews was born and raised in Columbus, Ohio. He attended Ohio State University, graduating with degrees in English Literature and Classical Greek. He published short stories while working a variety of jobs, and in 1959 began to teach at Urbana College.

Matthews has received many awards and prizes for his writing, including a Guggenheim Fellowship, an Ohio Arts Council Grant, and the Ohioana Career Award. His work has been translated into Spanish, German, French, Czech, Romanian, Japanese, and Farsi.

Matthews' work has been called "rowdy, boisterous, bold, and [flowing over] with comic energy." Of Matthews, Tim O'Brien wrote, he "is a master of prose conversation and deadpan charm. He is ironic, cool, and shrewd, and he writes a lucid prose."

Matthews continues to teach at Ohio University in Athens, Ohio, where he lives with his wife of sixty-three years.

## BOOKS FROM ETRUSCAN PRESS

*Coronology* | Claire Bateman
*The Burning House* | Paul Lisicky
*Nahoonkara* | Peter Grandbois
*First Fire, Then Birds* | H. L. Hix
*The Casanova Chronicles* | Myrna Stone
*Venison* | Thorpe Moeckel
*Incident Light* | H. L. Hix
*Peal* | Bruce Bond
*The Fugitive Self* | John Wheatcroft
*The Disappearance of Seth* | Kazim Ali
*Toucans in the Arctic* | Scott Coffel
*Synergos* | Roberto Manzano
*Lies Will Take You Somewhere* | Sheila Schwartz
*Legible Heavens* | H. L. Hix
*A Poetics of Hiroshima* | William Heyen
*Saint Joe's Passion* | J. D. Schraffenberger
*American Fugue* | Alexis Stamatis
*Drift Ice* | Jennifer Atkinson
*The Widening* | Carol Moldaw
*Parallel Lives* | Michael Lind
*God Bless: A Political/Poetic Discourse* | H. L. Hix
*Chromatic* | H. L. Hix (National Book Award finalist)
*The Confessions of Doc Williams & Other Poems* | William Heyen
*Art into Life* | Frederick R. Karl
*Shadows of Houses* | H. L. Hix
*The White Horse: A Colombian Journey* | Diane Thiel
*Wild and Whirling Words: A Poetic Conversation* | H. L. Hix
*Shoah Train* | William Heyen (National Book Award finalist)
*Crow Man* | Tom Bailey
*As Easy As Lying: Essays on Poetry* | H. L. Hix
*Cinder* | Bruce Bond
*Free Concert: New and Selected Poems* | Milton Kessler
*September 11, 2001: American Writers Respond* | William Heyen

Founded in 2001 with a generous grant from the Oristaglio Foundation, Etruscan Press is a nonprofit cooperative of poets and writers working to produce and promote books that nurture the dialogue among genres, achieve a distinctive voice, and reshape the literary and cultural histories of which we are a part.

Etruscan Press is proud of support received from:

The Bates-Manzano Fund

The Council of Literary Magazines and Presses

The National Endowment for the Arts

The New Mexico Community Foundation

The Nin & James Andrews Foundation

The Ohio Arts Council

The Ruth H. Beecher Foundation

The Stephen & Jeryl Oristaglio Foundation

The Raymond John Wean Foundation

Wilkes University

Youngstown State University

etruscan press

www.etruscanpress.org

Etruscan Press books may be ordered from

Consortium Book Sales and Distribution
800-283-3572
www.cbsd.com

Small Press Distribution
800-869-7553
www.spdbooks.com

Etruscan Press is a 501 (c) (3) nonprofit organization.
Contributions to Etruscan Press are tax deductible as allowed under
applicable law For more information, a prospectus, or to order one
of our titles, contact us at books@etruscanpress.org.